KV-191-097

The NINTH PASSAGE

A NOVEL

DALE O. CLONINGER

NEWMAN SPRINGS PUBLISHING
320 Broad Street
Red Bank, NJ 07701

First originally published by Newman Springs Publishing 2019

ISBN 978-1-64531-155-3 (Paperback)
ISBN 978-1-64531-157-7 (Hardcover)
ISBN 978-1-64531-156-0 (Digital)

Printed in the United States of America

*A*lthough inspired by actual events, *The Ninth Passage* is none-theless fiction. The thoughts, words, and conversations of the characters emanate solely from the author's imagination, and any resemblance to those of actual persons living or dead is purely coincidental. References to actual places serve only as a means of setting the historical context of the story. The Royal Palm Barbershop, the Palm Garden Restaurant, Louis Pappas's Restaurant, the hotel, and the churches did exist but for the most part, no more. The historical descriptions parallel the actual development of Florida's central west coast with little literary license taken. Laddie is authentic.

Dale O. Cloninger, 2019

No man is an island, entire of itself;
every man is a piece of the continent, a part of the main…
Any man's death diminishes me,
because I am involved in mankind…

—John Donne 1623
"Meditation 17," Devotions upon Emergent Occasions

Joy, thou spark from Heav'n immortal,
Daughter of Elysium!
Drunk with fire, toward Heaven advancing
Goddess, to thy shrine we come.
By thy magic is united
What stern custom parted wide.
All Mankind are brothers plighted
Where thy gentle wings abide.

—Friedrich Schiller, *Ode to Joy*, 1785

Prologue

*M*orning broke through the thin fog that crept onto the beach during the night. The sky, high and crystal blue, reached for the horizon where it met in a slightly arched line the azure-green water of the Gulf of Mexico. Calm after a night's respite from the stiff sea breezes of the day, the gulf would soon send its waves pounding the shore with ceaseless regularity until the quiet of the late night would arrest their action only to resume the following morning. The white sandy beach stretches north and south for over two miles and extends in some places more than a hundred yards from the shoreline. Despite the continued encroachment upon the white sand by parking lots, condos, and snack bars, nature's irrepressible forces continued to replenish the disappearing sand in a westward march rivaling that of developers.

People wander onto the beach in intermittent waves that match the rising tidal surges breaking on the beach's sandy shore. The sounds of the gathering throng increase by the square of their number. Children's screams and adult laughter mingle with the rumbling motorcycles racing along Gulf View Drive, the clatter of a Dempsy Dumpster turned upside down, its contents crashing into a sanitation department truck, and the shrill siren of a passing police car. The beach inexorably changes from white to blue, green, red, orange, yellow, and tan freckles of assorted sizes and shapes.

For more than an hour I watched and studied one of a seemingly limitless number of replays of that scene. I realized that there had been many such replications over my three score years, and yet it was as though I was seeing it for the first time. I shifted frequently in my deck chair trying to find a comfortable position that managed to elude me. My discomfort had little to do with the chair or my position in it. It stemmed from the realization that whereas, the sun, water, wind, and sand remained undisturbed by time, little else including myself, had escaped the dramatic march of the last half-century. The sights and sounds of my formative years no longer exist. The names and faces of those occupying the beach are no longer familiar. The sea of strangers that now engulfs Florida's beaches is the norm, but a generation ago strangers were quite conspicuous, exceptions rather than the rule. My thoughts turned inexorably to one of the more notable of those exceptions, a particular stranger who arrived in the midsummer of 1953 before the town underwent its metamorphosis from sleepy village to urban sprawl. He clearly distinguished himself from other migrants by the way he arrived—he walked and hitchhiked the fourteen hundred mile coastal stretch from Rhode Island to central Florida. His distinctive mode of long distance travel accompanied equally distinctive attitudes and values that stood in marked contrast to the stern customs of the established town residents. Though only thirteen years old, I readily recognized that he differed from any one I had ever known. More than forty years later I can still make that statement. Although his idiosyncrasy of walking wherever his interests led formed the most apparent feature of his persona, he later achieved notoriety for other more important reasons that touched the heart and soul of his adopted community. Alec Driver easily qualified as an unforgettable character to those who, through good judgment or fortunate circumstance, managed to avoid being swept up in the storm of emotions that swirled continually around him. For many others caught in the midst of the maelstrom, he became a persona non grata. I eluded the whirling winds but will be forever imbued by his admonitions and exhortations on music, education, and life. I am spared, however, the emotional and psychological pain that his personal touch all too often inflicted on others. For that reason, I have the luxury of considering him a unique and most unforgettable character.

Through the shadowy reaches of my mind I can still see him walking briskly along the road, his arms swinging in perfect cadence to his long loping strides, his hair disheveled by the wind of passing cars. He looked the same way that day a lifetime ago when he first walked into town. When I revisit the now barren grounds where his pointed instruction invoked both wrath and envy, memories of him reel through my mind like the slow motion replay of an old film. Only then do I realize the effect Alec Driver had on me and the many others who knew him even better than I. In another time or in another place the events that marked Alec's stay might have gone unnoticed by all but a few of those he directly affected. The strange combination of his personality, this place, and that moment in the history of this community produced a unique chemistry that is unlikely to reoccur. What Alec did after his arrival here had not happened before and to my knowledge has not happened since. Immediately after being discharged from the service following the Second World War, Alec planned to return to this part of Florida, an area he grew to love while stationed at one of the nearby military bases. His musical talents and the GI bill led him first to Princeton University where he remained for five years obtaining both a bachelor's and master's degree in music and a professional teaching certificate. As a child learning to play the piano he amazed his teacher with the facility he displayed in reading music. Alec often remarked in later years that the bars, notes, and symbols of a good musical score made more sense to him than the words of some novels. His talent lay in the ability to understand the message and the feeling the composer attempted to convey. His finger dexterity and voice never developed sufficiently to pursue a professional career in piano or singing. After high school he won small parts in Providence's local musical theater. Those roles paid little forcing him to rely on the family furniture business for income. World War II brought a merciful halt to both endeavors. Alec learned how to organize people and coordinate activities while serving as a supply sergeant and leader of a part-time volunteer choir during the war. The inspiration of one day directing a high school choir seemed a natural extension of his talents, abilities, and training. Following his discharge in 1945, Alec entered and breezed through Princeton's program with such ease that a mentor described him as one of the best pupils he had the privilege to teach. The one undeniable fact of the nine-year Florida passage in Alec's life is that his mastery of music and his ability to instill this mastery in his choirs never went unrecognized despite the misgivings some had of his attitudes and personal relationships. Alec's highly organized mind enabled him to develop a well-defined plan to accomplish his goal of settling in Florida to pursue a career in music education. Anticipating that a position might not be available the year he completed his studies, he applied a year before receiving his teaching certificate reasoning that if an opening were available he would accept it and apply for a temporary certificate. The interim certificate would allow sufficient time to satisfy the requirements of a permanent one. If an opening were not available the first year, he would simply complete the requirement's first and reapply the following year, a course he ultimately followed. Alec's affection for Florida was contagious. Taken by Alec's zeal, his sister, Denise, a young bride to an equally young physician, persuaded her new husband that their fortune might also lie in this part of Florida. The young, pragmatic doctor became interested when he discovered the physician-citizen ratio was considerably less than in the medically laden-northeast. Denise and Mark Hooker formed the advance party for Alec's sojourn south one year later. The rest of his family, a mother and two brothers, never caught the fever that infected Alec and then Denise. They remained in Rhode Island content with their own familiar surroundings. It was, therefore, not some accident of nature, some fateful, random event that brought Alec Driver, age thirty-seven, to Florida, but the deliberate actions of a man whose determination and abilities could take him wherever he wished. How different the lives of Tracy Ashbury and many others would have been had Alec chosen to go elsewhere. The thought of Tracy brings a smile to my face. Beautiful, charming, and gracious, she turned seventeen the year Alec came to town and was, by consensus, the prettiest girl in the senior high with an intellect that easily matched her beauty. Talented musically and popular with her classmates and teachers, she participated in as many activities as her time permitted. By the time she graduated her peers elected her cheerleader twice, May Queen, and homecoming princess—honors that would have satisfied most girls her age. Tracy also served as director of the senior class play and member of the student council. Why she was not voted homecoming queen is a question that only those who cast the ballots could ever answer. At the time, tradition dictated that only the football team voted and hallway gossip had it that Tracy had spurned the sexual overtures of the team's captain. Had there been an award for Miss Everything, Tracy Ashbury would have headed the list.

Tracy exuded a maturity and self-confidence well beyond her seventeen years. Many who knew her attributed most of her aplomb to her intelligent and inventive father, but those who knew her best gave equal credit to her concerned dedicated mother who nurtured Tracy's self-esteem from birth. Tracy never suffered from a lack of love, concern, or attention. Most of all, daughter and parents shared a mutual respect for each other.

Until the early sixties, the local high school served all the towns and villages in the central portion of the county. Tracy lived in one of the smaller towns that lay only a short distance north of the high school campus. The town, like several others in the county, enjoyed a reputation for its citrus products including concentrate, pulp, and rind, along with orange and grapefruit juices. Its orange groves survived the developer's bulldozers longer than any other community's in the county.

Tracy's father, dubbed "Einstein" by the high school boys because his long gray hair and mustache gave him an uncanny resemblance to the famous scientist, earned notoriety as an imminent scientist and inventor. The adolescent epithet served as a compliment, for Lloyd Ashbury's scientific skills and abilities had earned him the reputation of a genius. He held patents on most of the equipment used in the processing of elemental phosphorous from phosphate ore. Many people felt his intellectual abilities had fallen to Tracy.

On the other hand, Tracy's mother, Nancy, was of pioneer stock: friends describe her as a strong-willed determined woman blessed with a good heart. Her neatness and attractiveness contrasted with her husband's disarray. She couldn't match Lloyd's intellectual capabilities, but she supplied her family with a limitless source of moral support. While Lloyd's mind kept constantly occupied with forces, momentum, torque, and vectors, Nancy filled her time with schedules, meals, church, and Tracy, their only child. She never minded this division of labor because it gave her virtually complete control over the daily lives of her family. The fruits of her husband's inventions enabled her to hire a part-time housekeeper and cook to relieve her of the drudgery of housework. Their house, on the choicest waterfront lot, was one of the finest in town. She spent her time in many civic and religious activities, her avocations. While her husband's talents helped the town to develop economically, her talents, and those of many like her, encouraged the town's cultural development.

Lloyd adored Tracy from birth. As she grew older, Lloyd grew increasingly confident that she had inherited an intellect that allowed her to judge competently the decisions she faced. Her mother, also quite confident of Tracy's intellectual skills, feared, as most parents do, that her life experiences were too limited for Tracy always to know the correct course to take. Nancy felt her responsibilities as a mother included guidance and direction for her child.

During Tracy's first seventeen years, few occasions occurred when her views differed markedly from those of her parents. Tracy enjoyed a great deal of freedom with few restrictions on where she went, the time she spent away from home, and the people she met. Traffic, crowds, or crime did not warrant restrictions Tracy felt unreasonable. She enjoyed an enviable life with the independence and peace of mind that the slow-paced, stable communities provided.

Tracy is like so many of my early childhood friends and acquaintances—I cannot recall a time when I did not know her. She's four years older and consequently we were never close friends. I remember when our paths crossed once at the home of Denny Norms, a classmate and close friend who lived two blocks from the high school. Denny's older sister, Mattie, also four years older, co-captained the cheerleader squad with Tracy. I recall being struck both by Tracy's looks and personality. She had a way of making everyone feel she liked them. I think of that meeting because of the warm feeling I had when I left that evening, a young twelve-year-old smitten by the prettiest girl he had ever seen.

Although one could hardly call it a coincidence that Tracy and I met Alec Driver at the same time, it does seem remarkable even though the town and the surrounding communities were small. We both met him under identical circumstances, a realization that most assuredly contributes to the reasons why I think of them now. I knew them both, but entered their lives only superficially, and the relationships did not reflect the depth to which each of them entered my life. The events that touched me deeply at that stage of my life were ones that I could not have foretold as an adolescent, for they were not just of what I did or experienced but also what I observed. Although I became a part of those experiences and they are now a part of me, I felt little affected by them at the time although there has not been a time when I have been unaffected by Tracy.

I feel somewhat chagrined that the lives and events of those childhood years affect me as they do, but I realize that what I witnessed became a part of me, a large part of me. The sight of an open wound and large amounts of blood causes me to break out in a cold sweat. One New Year's Day, at the age of six, a loud crash and hysterical screaming drew me to a scene I shall never forget. A car, driven by a man returning from an all-night drinking binge, ran a red light, swerved into the side of the corner store at the exact time a sixteen-year-old girl and her friend emerged from the side entrance. One of the girls, dragged by the careening car along the side of the building, lay in agony. Her right leg, severed between knee and thigh by the force of the car, bled profusely until an adult fashioned a tourniquet. She remained conscious throughout the long ordeal, pleading for a drink of water that no one dared give. I witnessed her plight and saw her recover to walk again with an artificial limb. I did not have to experience the injury, thank God, to be profoundly affected by it. I am who I am because of what I have seen, heard, or read as well as what I have experienced, felt, and touched.

I have often pondered what drew Alec back to this part of Florida. I keep returning to the simple answer that Alec, like so many of his fellow servicemen who spent a portion of their war years in this Gulf Coast haven, sought the natural quiet and beauty of the landscape with its semitropical climate so vastly different from what he and his fellow ex-servicemen knew in their northeastern and Midwestern home towns.

The land lay mostly undeveloped in the early fifties, except for the large expanses of neat rows of orange, grapefruit, and tangerine trees that dotted the gently rolling landscape, juxtaposed against the clean, grassy, and shaded dairy farms. During balmy spring evenings after the stiff sea breezes subsided, the numerous groves emitted the smell of orange blossoms that permeated the air for miles around. The sweet fragrance lured us from our houses to sit outdoors and enjoy nature's fragrance. That pleasure has vanished forever. It seems ironic that the collective return of the servicemen and those that followed them ultimately destroyed much of the natural quiet and beauty they found so alluring.

Some of the qualities that made our lives enjoyable then still exist today: the bright, cloudless days; the mild winter temperatures; and the stark, white, sandy beaches with the clear, blue-green water of the Gulf of Mexico lapping at their shores. Fortunately, these marvels of nature have successfully eluded the touch of the developer. At the age of eight on a particularly pleasant Sunday afternoon, my father took me in a borrowed boat to a spot in Clearwater Bay and handed me an empty cup and told me to dip it into the water and drink its contents. I steadfastly refused until he adamantly insisted. Surprised, I found the water cool and fresh, not salty and warm like the water just a few yards away. He then asked if I then understood how the town had gotten its name. That conclusion had already occurred to me. The pleasure of drinking cool, fresh bay water has since vanished.

Life here during the forties and early fifties was small town and slow-paced. However, the usually placid community did experience, on notable occasions, surges of excitement. During the war years, some of the numerous vacant beaches served as bombing and strafing targets for the Army Air Force crews stationed at the three nearby training bases. I can still hear and feel the drone of B-17s flying night practice bombing missions over the deserted islands. Our house miles away on the main land shuddered from the concussions of the detonating bombs. From my bed I could hear the windows rattle and feel the room shake. The vibrations continued until late in the evening when I finally achieved some measure of rest. The sudden silence penetrated the night. Resort hotels, such as the Belleview Biltmore, served as temporary military quarters because the hastily constructed military barracks could not hold the hundred thousand men assigned to the bases. The bases and men played an important role in the development of this part of Florida. Two of the three bases reverted to civilian use immediately following the war. To the hundreds of thousands of men who trained here, this part of America was a paradise found. Some, like Jack Eckerd and Jim Walter, returned after the war to seek their fortune, while others migrated here after retirement. The impact of the air bases continued to transform our lives for many years after they ceased their military use. Born just after Hitler invaded Poland, I can remember spending many post-war Sunday afternoons riding through the countryside and along the bay shore. From the back seat of my father's black, two-door Ford coupe I watched as large dairy farms, numerous citrus groves, and flat-bottomed fishing boats docked along the shores of the bay glided passed my window. The groves, laid out in flawless grids, made the trees, no matter the angle, always fall into perfectly straight lines that seemed endless. The spaces between the rows, well-groomed and clear of any other growing thing, provided scant room for tractor and trailer at harvest time.

During the war, we lived in a two-bedroom, wood frame house my father and grandfather built. We had a single, basic black telephone and shared a party line with three other people in the neighborhood. Our number had four digits, a sequence I managed to master before the age of three. The poles that carried the lines to houses on our street contained open wire with crossbars dotted with glass insulators. Milk and eggs were delivered daily to our front door, dry cleaners picked up and delivered our laundry on a set weekly schedule, and spray trucks regularly spewed DDT for the millions of omnipresent mosquitoes. The odor of the spray penetrated every nook in our house. Air conditioning existed only at the ice plant. The doctor who coaxed me from my mother's womb made house calls and drove a car with running boards. Our mail came twice a day and the post office was open on Saturdays until noon. Money, which my father allowed me to hold on the way to the bank, included United States Treasury Notes, silver dollars, and half dollars. A penny would garner two pieces of candy. Banks opened at nine and closed at two and never on Saturdays.

Our house, located on the edge of town ten blocks from the town's center, sat on Cleveland Street, the main east-west thoroughfare that connected the beach with Tampa Bay, a distance of ten miles. Because of the location of our house, grocery stores were not within walking distance. Price and availability of needed items caused my mother to alternate grocery shopping among the A&P, B&B, Piggly Wiggly, and Margaret Ann stores. Like most of the community we bought fresh meat each day as there were few home freezers, only ice boxes. For the same reason we bought fish caught that day. The fish merchants wrapped each sale in the town's newspaper—a never-ending source of snide comments about the daily's usefulness. The fish merchants as well as the newspaper are no more.

Long before I took my first breath and throughout most of my childhood, relationships among friends and acquaintances were the result of people's religious lives. Churches occupied the center of cultural, social, and recreational lives. Parties, picnics, ball teams, charity drives, and political campaigns mostly emanated from or through the town's various churches, synagogues, and cathedrals. The framework of the respective religions formed people's perceptions of others. Religion constituted the basis for determining judgments of right and wrong. Everyone knew, everyone understood, for such was the nature of our town. It was a time when people either knew each other well or not at all. Almost everyone, including myself, was known as someone's aunt, uncle, niece, nephew, cousin, child, or grandchild. It seems I was always introduced as Reid's son, Harvil's nephew, or Sam and Minnie's grandson even when none of these relatives were present at the time. Conversely, strangers were noticed and their movements watched with some suspicion until they either left or embraced the community's entrenched norms, customs, and values. The best route into the hearts of the established residents was to marry one of them and thereby become somebody's aunt, uncle, niece, nephew, or cousin. I recall how my mother assimilated into the small town culture. In 1939, while vacationing in Florida with friends, she met my father and three months later married him. She thereby became, instead of a Yankee from Illinois, a member of an already established southern pioneer family.

My father's family migrated from Tennessee during the early years of the Depression after selling their farm to the Tennessee Valley Authority. The fertile soil became a munitions plant that operates to this day. My grandfather built houses during lean farming years in the Tennessee valley and farmed during lean building years. The sale of the farm allowed my grandfather to retire from farming at the age of fifty—not because the sum received for his farm was large, but because my grandparents required little money even though their youngest son was still in elementary school when they moved. By the fifties their twenty-year residence in the community qualified them for acceptance. A newspaper article described my Uncle Harvil, on the occasion of his retirement fifty years after moving here with the rest of the family, as a scion of pioneers.

My family assimilated quickly into a community that consisted of first, second, and in a few cases third generation pioneers. Born on the first anniversary of my parent's marriage, I became part of an elite group of residents—a native. Forty years later, native and family ties lost their importance as the incessant massive waves of northeastern and midwestern migration engulfed the peninsula.

During my adolescent and later teenage years, I experienced a long line of unusual Sunday school teachers. Being Baptist, my Sunday school classes were segregated by gender. At age twelve, near the onset of puberty, the gender of Sunday school teachers changed to match that of their students. Until that time, I knew only female Sunday school teachers. No one bothered to explain why the sudden change in gender of teachers. Baptists never spoke of such things. One of the line of male teachers was a veteran of the Army Air Force, a pilot who had ferried bombers during the war to one or the other of the three nearby bases. He told anecdotes of the war, a never-ending source of attention for fourteen- and fifteen-year-olds, particularly compared to Baptist Sunday school lessons. He confided that on occasion he and fellow crewmembers fanned one of the plane's four propellers and revved its engine so high that it would burn out, requiring the installation of a replacement. He and his crew (as well as other crews he revealed) would spend the ten days necessary to replace the engine sunning on the beaches during the day and cavorting with the opposite gender at night. He and many fellow servicemen recognized the area's allure, foresaw its growth, and swore to return to share in its future fortunes.

Thus, Alec Driver stepped into a setting that perhaps could be called provincial and parochial by those not inclined to be charitable or sympathetic to the community's mores as well as those who now possess the privilege of hindsight. It was a setting that Alec Driver was either unaware of or never fully understood.

*****

Julie, my wife of half a lifetime, sits beside me in the only other deck chair on the hotel balcony passing the time by flipping the pages of the latest issue of *Architectural Digest* with the constancy of a metronome. She makes an occasional comment that I chose to answer with a grunt or other equally unintelligible sound. I have little doubt that she is painfully aware that my thoughts had drifted backward in time. Her insight results from not only our more than a quarter century of marriage, but my prolonged silence, body language, and intermittent furrowed brow along with the circumstance that brought us back to Florida constitutes the most telling evidence. After a twenty-year absence we returned to the town where I first drew breath and lived for most of my first thirty-three years, a place that she had grown to know during the first few years of our marriage, but one that she does not know as I do. A newcomer then, she saw the community only after its metamorphosis of the 1950s. We met in college introduced by a mutual friend, a scholarship football player and childhood friend of Julie. Intelligent, determined, and attractive, she, in a weak moment, finally succumbed to my persistent entreaties to get married at a time well in advance of what she considered prudent. We returned to Florida to attend my fortieth high school class reunion and decided to spend our last day quietly enjoying the beach before returning to Houston.

After visiting with classmates and childhood friends and encountering the many changes that the town continued to experience, I lapsed into the melancholy of remembering the way things used to be. My age and the growing presence of "male-patterned baldness" could spur a midlife crisis, behavior that no one has so far accused me of exhibiting. I suppose my professional training as an economist instilled in me a scientific and rational approach to most aspects of life, a characteristic that has not always enamored me to close friends and family. The memories of my childhood experiences that occupy my mind are thoughts and feelings that somehow escaped this professorial mental regimen. The nostalgia of a pleasant and carefree youth is too strong for me to dismiss as mere sentiment.

I long for the time when the beach did not resemble its current likeness—a mass of strangers each not knowing who the others are, the sounds of humans and their machines, the stench of garbage, all are in ugly contrast to the beach I knew. I continue to shift in my chair.

"Dean, let's take our shoes off and walk along the beach for a while," Julie said, finally breaking what had developed into a prolonged silence.

"Sounds good," I answered with an audible sigh after taking a moment to return from my thoughts. "Let's walk to the north end of the beach where there'll be fewer people and less noise. We can sit behind one of the dunes amongst the sea oats and relax in relative quiet."

I rose from my chair and stretched to relieve the kinks and aches accumulated by the contortions my body suffered during its hour-long confinement. I packed our beach bag for the two-mile trek from our hotel.

"By the way, in the confusion of the reunion last night I forgot to ask, how did your old schools look when you drove around yesterday while I shopped?" Julie asked as we loaded ourselves down with various beach paraphernalia.

"They're gone. Only a few bare areas remain where the grass and weeds have not grown through the old parking lot and volleyball courts. Several of the massive live oak trees that dotted the lawns remain, but they're old, sparse, and dying," I answered with a notable sigh.

"What happened to the schools?"

"One of the nearby residents said that they had become the frequent target of vandals and arsonists. The school board razed the massive old structures—they hadn't been used for years. The entire block where they stood now rests in the hands of a private developer, so even the faint skeletal outlines of the old foundations may soon be gone."

"I'm sorry. I know you would have liked to have seen them and, of course, your name that you etched over one of the doorways. Your etching may have been permanent, but the buildings obviously were not."

"I'm afraid you're right on that one. It's sad. I felt like I was standing on my own grave. That experience started me thinking about those days and the people I knew."

"I thought as much. Anyone I know?" she asked coyly.

"I'm not sure. Do you remember me talking about Alec Driver and Tracy Ashbury?"

"Alec Driver?" she asked, managing to sound a little disappointed I had omitted her name. "Oh, yes. Wasn't he one of your teachers, the choir teacher?"

"Yes. I had him in the eighth and twelfth grades."

"What was so special about him? Was he a good teacher? And who is Tracy Ashbury?" Julie's tone indicating that her curiosity grew with each succeeding question.

"Surely I've told you the story of Tracy and Alec," I answered, somewhat surprised that she didn't recognize Tracy's name. "I remember you telling me something about Alec some time ago. I can't recall you ever mentioning a Tracy Ashbury. However, you've sufficiently aroused my curiosity, especially because you have been so reticent this morning. I'd like to know just what it is about this person that has occupied your mind so," she stated as we swung open the lobby doors and confronted a blinding morning sun. The sunlight reflecting off the bleached white sand caused us to squint and our eyes to water.

"Are you part of the story?" Julie pursued with a bit of agitation in her voice. She removed her sunglasses from the beach bag and whipped them on with one quick even stroke.

"Yes and no," I replied, fumbling with my glasses. "I knew them both, of course, and shared in some of the things that happened, but I was only a witness to other events. Later, Alec talked openly about the early years he spent in Florida to any and all who would listen. I've heard some of the stories so many times I feel a part of them."

"Well, get on with the story," Julie urged as she adjusted her straw hat.

The thought of retelling the story of Alec and Tracy offered a measure of satisfaction, even a sense of relief, for the opportunity it presented to relieve me of the melancholy so heavy on my mind.

"Okay, but where shall I start?" I asked rhetorically.

"Try the beginning, or better yet, try Tracy Ashbury," she offered sarcastically.

"No," I countered. "Instead, I think I'll start with the first time I saw Alec."

Chapter 1

August 1953

*L*addie saw him before we did. His ears perked up, his head rose, and then off he sprang as a tiger bent for prey. Denny, Jimmy, and I were busy planting a tree I had rooted in the tradition of my grandfather, and at first we took little notice of Laddie's abrupt departure from our midst. Engrossed by our work, we didn't sense the stranger walking briskly and stealthily along the sidewalk toward us.

It seems a strange coincidence that the three thirteen-year-olds were seriously and quietly engaged planting a tree rather than playing ball in the park, exploring the nearby woods or fishing in the bay just a few yards away. Normally, we did all of those things but not at that particular moment. I had spent weeks rooting the cutting in a jar of water and deemed it ready to grow on its own. I had made a few previous attempts to grow one thing or another. Watermelon, cantaloupe, and various vegetables had all been planted and half-heartedly tended from time to time. I never did understand why something I dearly loved like watermelon would grow so profusely with lush vines reaching in all directions but never manage to yield a single melon while radishes, carrots, or other equally undesirable vegetables yielded harvests by the bucket.

Jimmy lived at the end of a short street cut off by the Atlantic Coast Line railroad tracks less than 100 feet from the side door of his house. The other end of the street, a scant fifty yards away, intersected Stevenson Drive directly in line with my bedroom window. Jimmy was the closest boy to my age for a radius of several blocks. Consequently, we spent a great deal of time after school, weekends, and summer vacations doing what most adolescent males do in a small town surrounded by vast areas of undeveloped land and large expanses of water. At age six, Jimmy migrated to Florida with sister and parents from the northern industrial section of Ohio. At the young age of thirty, his father assumed charge of a modest size marina owned by a wealthy businessman from Maine. Visiting the marina, its dry docks and repair sheds was always an adventure. Occasionally we would get a ride in one of the large yachts moored or being repaired at the facility. For many summers, Jimmy's dad allowed us to ply the bay waters with a twelve-foot wooden boat fitted with an inboard one cylinder Briggs and Stratton engine. The engine starter consisted of a flywheel propelled by a jerking motion on a short rope wrapped around a slotted hub. On numerous occasions, it took many pulls to fire up an engine that literally went put-put when it ran. Its resemblance to a gasoline lawnmower engine was not coincidental. Steering was by a wood lever attached to the starboard gunnel: forward to port, back to starboard. Speed, incapable of exceeding six knots, was controlled by a throttle attached to the engine that set at amidships. While the craft's draft was shallow, its propeller was not. We managed to get stuck numerous times in the shallow waters that surrounded the mud flats at low tide. Occasionally, for some reason not understood by us, the engine would give out requiring a rescue by Jimmy's father in a larger boat. Our delayed return would send him scurrying about Clearwater Bay. Usually we weren't very far from my house or his marina.

Jimmy and I were constant companions during the long days of summer. Daylight saving's time, instituted as an energy-saving measure during WWII, had long since been abandoned in favor of God's time. Jimmy served as surrogate master for Laddie, caring for him in my occasional absences that ranged from overnight stays to two-week vacations. Denny, also a transplant from Pennsylvania at the tender age of four, lived at some distance but spent many days playing in and around our waterfront property.

Most summer days found us bareback and barefoot building tree huts in one or more of the many large live oaks that filled the slowly diminishing woods surrounding our neighborhood, digging tunnels in the abandoned sand pit behind Jimmy's house, catching fiddler crabs under the nearby railroad trestle, or simply hanging out at the corner store eating anything crunchy or chocolate and drinking anything carbonated. Television existed only in Jacksonville and Miami, much too distant for middle-class families in a small central Florida town to justify the expense of a set that produced a minuscule picture with snowy images and garbled sound. The scheduled opening of a station in St. Petersburg promised to end the poor reception and ultimately many adolescent outdoor activities. Air conditioning existed only in a very few places, certainly not in people's homes. Aside from eating and sleeping and not always then, our recreational activities including card and board games took place outdoors. Maybe coincidence dictated our presence and activity that day, but then maybe not. Whatever the cause, our concentration was interrupted by loud barks and the sound of an angry voice shouting, "Get back! Get away from me!"

I remember looking up and seeing a rather strange-looking man whom I didn't recognize. His right arm raised and both fists clenched, he yelled again at Laddie, "Get back! Get away from me!"

I called to Laddie, "Laddie, get back. Laddie, come here!"

Laddie took only a begrudging step back and resumed his barking. The fur on the back of his neck and shoulders stood straight up. He remained within inches of the man with teeth snarling and barking incessantly. I knew then the man was a stranger for Laddie's reputation was known far and wide as a vociferous but nonviolent defender of our property. The man obviously truly feared Laddie.

"Boys," called the man, "come get your dog!"

Without rising, I called Laddie several more times, and he began to back off slowly. The man lowered his arm and continued his way his fists still clenched. Laddie continued to bark as he escorted the stranger passed our house and property.

"You boys need to keep your dog under control," the stranger admonished as he briskly walked passed, arms swinging in long arcs.

"Ah, mister, he ain't gonna hurt nobody," I replied defensively and then added in a more subdued tone, "much." We snickered.

The stranger didn't hear my last remark as his increased pace quickly took him beyond earshot.

"Who's that?" I asked in a manner that let Jimmy and Denny know that I had not liked what I saw and heard from the man.

"I don't know," replied Denny.

"He looked like Ichabod Crane," Jimmy said with a grin.

We giggled. The description contained an element of truth. The man, slight of build and average in height, had a sharp pointed nose, an angular jaw, and wore horned-rim glasses. His features that evoked images of Ichabod Crane were a conspicuous Adam's apple that bobbed up and down as he spoke and knobby knees apparent below his khaki walking shorts. His legs, lean and muscular from thigh to calf, clearly indicated that they had taken him either very far or very fast. The timidity and defensiveness he exhibited when confronted by Laddie seemed uncharacteristic considering the strength evident in his legs. Maybe he was just startled and embarrassed.

This particular stranger wasn't the first person intimidated by Laddie. A mixed breed between collie and German shepherd, Laddie's shoulders stood knee high to a man. His nose, short and stout, contrasted sharply with the long and pointed snouts of collies. His tail, covered with jet-black fur, contained only the faintest hint of red and white that covered the rest of his body. He weighed over eighty pounds and possessed the capability, if he so chose, to knock down the largest of men. Fortunately, this capability had never been tested.

Full of adventure and curiosity, Laddie wasn't the type of dog who settled for the slow-paced and quiet life around the house. He often wandered off in search of excitement frequently, but not always, in the form of female companionship I later discovered. At first, his absences lasted a few minutes, hardly enough to even notice. Later the trips would extend to hours and eventually to days. Where he would go and what he would do remained a mystery to me for years. I speculated that Laddie treated the entire town as his home and ventured out on occasion to check on it. I later learned there was more than just an element of truth in my speculation. Eventually Laddie would drag himself back home dog tired. Exhausted, he would drink from his water dish while lying with the pan between his front paws.

After a good long drink that often emptied the dish he would roll over on the spot and sleep for as much as a half day at a time, rising only long enough to eat the food I brought to him and then lie back down to nap again.

Laddie, a strong, aggressive dog not only to strangers but to animals as well, would stalk and chase with the stealth and tenacity of a wolf any living prey that dared to draw near. Once while walking Laddie soon after his arrival, I watched him engaged five cocker spaniels at a time while on the end of a six-foot leash. The cocker spaniels retreated licking their many wounds. Without the constraint of a leash, single dogs would find little mercy when tangling with Laddie.

The only fear Laddie ever expressed was that of a loud, sharp noise such as the report of a gun (the sight of which caused him to react by frantic, persistent barks and raised fur on his back) and loud claps of thunder when lightning struck close to our house. The initial flash and consequent loud report caused Laddie to bolt from his favorite lair in the garage on the top step next to the kitchen screen door where the smells of the evening meal were the strongest. The second clap of thunder brought him back with equal speed. He trembled against the screen door so much that it thumped in a nervous cadence. Mother was the first to suggest that Laddie associated the loud clap of thunder with the report of a gun.

The experience with thunder was frequently replayed for the rest of Laddie's life as this region of Florida is noted for its numerous afternoon summer thunderstorms. There are as many as three or four on some days and few days when there are none. The slice of central Florida extending from St. Petersburg and Clearwater on the Gulf of Mexico through Tampa and Orlando and ending near Cocoa Beach on the Atlantic coast is known as Thunder Alley so numerous are its thunderstorms. Meteorological studies reveal that this area is among the highest in the world in the frequency of recorded electrical storms.

The warm, moist southeasterly sea breeze blowing off the Atlantic across the Florida peninsula during the mornings and early afternoons of late spring, the entire summer, and into early fall combines with the heat that rises from the land and forms the huge cumulonimbus thunderheads from which these storms spring. The nocturnal storms can be dazzling. On one particular Fourth of July, the fireworks show on the downtown waterfront took a back seat to the brilliant and awesome display of electrical energy that took place in the southern sky. Lightning bolts repeatedly zigzagged across the sky ending at some unfortunate place on the ground too far distant for the consequent thunder to travel. The flashes separated only by nanoseconds crisscrossed each other, or so it seemed. Flashes appeared then faded and immediately reappeared in the same spot with the same configuration. The show was electrifying. Perhaps God was saying that his was the best show in town. Laddie never got used to it.

*****

"A funny-looking man walked by the house today," I remember remarking at dinner while poking at the peas on my plate with my fork.

"I noticed someone when I heard Laddie barking. I wonder who it was?" Mother asked politely.

"He looked like Ichabod Crane." I giggled.

Her curiosity piqued she turned to my father and asked, "Do you know who that might have been Reid?"

Finishing his mouthful of food, Pop wiped his face with his napkin and answered, "I believe that was Alec Driver, I just caught a glimpse of him out the window when I heard Laddie fussing so."

"Who's Alec Driver?" Mother asked a bit miffed that Pop knew some gossip that she didn't.

"He's the new choir director at the high school and junior high." Pop looked in my direction as he answered knowing that I had signed up for choir next year. Band was out of the question, for I had spent the last two years laboring with that most wicked instrument of torture, the clarinet, and still had not recovered from the experience.

Still sounding miffed at having missed out on this bit of news, Mother asked, "How do you know that?"

"He visited our choir practice Thursday night," Pop answered, adding, "he said he was going to direct the choir at the Presbyterian Church on an interim basis and wanted to get acquainted with some of the other church choir directors."

"I do wish you would do as I've asked you for over two years and give up being choir director. It takes away every Thursday night and every Sunday morning and evening. I would like for us to do something special on a weekend occasionally," Mother complained.

"Didn't I tell you? You don't have to worry; the new minister wants to bring in his own minister of music."

"Minister of music, now that's a fancy title for choir director," she stated almost defensively. Then returning to her real concern of the moment she asked, "Did he say where he is from?"

"Who?" Pop asked quizzically.

"This man, Alec what's-his-name—" Mother scolded.

"Driver. I didn't know who you meant; we were just talking about the new minister of music—"

"Reid, just answer the question," Mother admonished with some exasperation.

"I think he said New Jersey, or was it New York? I can't remember. He said he was from one and went to school in the other. I didn't pay much attention."

Details on someone else's life, or even his own, were rarely of lasting interest to Pop. The present consumed most of his thoughts. Preoccupied with the day-to-day operations of his insurance business and his duties with the church choir, he seldom allowed his thoughts to become cluttered with what he regarded as trivia.

Businessman, choir director, father, and husband were as much as Pop felt he could do. His personality, perfectly tailored for the independence of self-employment, demanded that he answer to no one save his customers and not always then. He enjoyed the distinction of being the first and for many years, the only business owner in town with a "No Smoking" sign on the front door. The mayor looking for a vote or a derelict looking for a handout, all received the same treatment. No one entered with a lighted cigarette, cigar, or pipe. Fellow Chamber of Commerce members marveled at how his business prospered despite his rigid adherence to his no smoking policy. In some ways Pop was ahead of his times.

Pop once worked for a woman and still shuddered at the experience. He blamed their conflicts on her gender, but he knew he simply disliked working for anyone else. The problem ceased when he decided to buy her out, a decision that brought him a great deal of satisfaction.

As a youth he dreamed of a different kind of life, a life of music. Voice lessons were as much a part of his education as his academic studies. He seized every opportunity to sing in recitals, choirs, musicals, and operettas. A recording was made of one of his performances. He envisioned a career in the musical theater.

A boyhood dream turned into an adult nightmare when voice teachers and medical doctors revealed that something as ordinary as his sinuses would prevent him from achieving his aspirations. Had he been born thirty years later, the miracles of antihistamines might have allowed him to pursue what he had to abandon. On advice from physicians he moved to Florida from Tennessee twenty years earlier in a vain attempt to escape the source of the incessant drainage in his throat that prevented voice clarity. He found no relief in Florida and thus resigned himself to seek other endeavors and dabble as an amateur in local musical presentations.

His interest in music and his dependable attendance (he didn't miss a Sunday morning or evening service in more than ten years except for rare vacations—he was never sick) at the Baptist church led the former pastor to ask him to develop a suitable choir, something that had long suffered from neglect. His tenure was only to be as long as it took to find someone who could devote more time and energy than a man with a family and a business to manage. The search lasted ten years.

Pop found some solace in directing the church choir, for it allowed him to be close to the music he loved on a regular and continual basis. Having no other hobbies, the choir offered him an escape from his usual business and family regime. It wasn't what he had dreamed, but with his business and the choir he spent his time in a way that he found at least partially satisfying.

Inwardly he resented the new minister's decision to hire a minister of music. He had always made weak protestations about having to shoulder the responsibility of the choir and paid lip service to Mother about ridding himself of those duties, but secretly he found contentment with things as they were. The promised arrival of the minister of music represented a godsend to Mother, but to Pop it was what he secretly dreaded.

Call it pride or ego, Pop would never admit to his inward resentment. The message would soon become clear, however. Upon the arrival of the minister of music, Pop graciously suggested that he not rejoin the choir immediately to allow the new director time to establish himself without the fear of divided loyalties. This professional courtesy turned into a ten-year sabbatical.

Pop represented the stable foundation upon which churches and communities rested. Imagination and initiative would have to be borne by others, for all those like Pop are stalwarts of stability, dependability, persistence, and most of all great patience. These people provide the endurance necessary to complete what others envision.

"Reid, stop being so coy and just tell me about this man. What was he doing around here on foot?" Pop had not satisfied Mother's curiosity.

"He must have been on his way to his sister's," he replied between bites. He was having some difficulty answering Mother's questions and downing his favorite meal of meat loaf, green peas, and creamed corn.

"His sister's?" came a surprised response. Mother thought she knew nearly everything about her neighbors and wondered how she had missed this tidbit of information. "Who's his sister?" she continued, trying unsuccessfully to restrain her inquisitiveness.

"Denise Hooker," Pop answered.

At the mention of the Hooker's name, I giggled, and Mother admonished me saying, "Dean, I don't want to hear any more of that—I know what you're thinking. Finish your peas and stop playing with them."

"Martha, leave the boy alone. It's not his fault that the only OB-Gynecologist partnership in town is named Hooker and John. These men must have known the connotation before they became partners. Don't go blaming the boy for snickering whenever their names are mentioned."

"I just thought," she rebutted, "that Dean should respect them as professionals and disregard the distasteful play on their names. It's childish of him, his friends, and you too for that matter."

Changing the subject she asked, "I wonder why he was walking. Why didn't he just drive to the Hooker's?"

Again I giggled but stopped abruptly when Mother gave me one of her famous (or infamous) stern looks.

"For one thing he doesn't have a car," Pop replied.

"He doesn't have a car?" she repeated. "How does he get around?"

"He walks. He said he never has owned an automobile and doesn't have any intention of buying one. He rides a bike and catches rides when he can."

"May I be excused?" I interrupted, eager to get back outside and finish the game of Indian ball with Jimmy.

"No, dear," Mother answered with an admonishment, "we're going to the Hardmans' tonight. You need to get your bath now before we leave."

"Oh, nuts," came my disgruntled answer. Spending an evening with the Hardmans didn't constitute my idea of entertainment nor did an early bath. But then my parents did not visit them out of any concern for my recreation. The Hardmans were childless. Consequently, I had no one to play with except Sandy, a spoiled yellow, fat cat that could have easily been the model for Garfield. Sandy had a way of either ignoring you with an aloofness of indifference or making your stay uncomfortable by annoying habits such as pulling the threads in your socks until holes began to appear. On occasion whenever the mood suited him, Sandy would make my stay enjoyable by being playful and cuddly. I never could tell what would make Sandy be one personality or another.

Ray Hardman was Pop's best friend. They had grown up at the same time in Chattanooga, Tennessee, without knowing each other. They also shared one other common element—Ray's wife, Gail, and my Aunt Bee (Uncle Clyde's wife) are sisters.

Picking up the conversation, Mother commented to Pop, "I didn't think any bachelor this day and age went without a car."

"Maybe he dates in a taxi and pays the driver to park in some deserted place and makes out in the back seat," Pop said with a laugh.

Mother, being the daughter of a Christian minister, did not appreciate the humor. Ignoring his last comment Mother added, "It just seems a bit strange. I suppose that means every time he visits Denise Hooker, Laddie will fuss at him the way he does at most strangers. I do wish that dog wasn't quite so protective. People who don't know Laddie are afraid to get out of their cars until I come out and put him in the garage. Isn't there something you and Dean can do?"

By this time Pop had started to help Mother clear away the dinner dishes. He and I both knew that she wouldn't take one step out of her house until everything was washed, dried, and returned to its place.

Mother's fastidiousness knew no bounds. For as long as I can remember she spent countless hours on every detail about her house. If Shakespeare is right and cleanliness is next to godliness, our house was a virtual sanctuary. Venetian blinds and floors would be meticulously scrubbed weekly. Sinks, tub, counter tops rarely kept watermarks long enough to dry thoroughly. Repeated ardent efforts finally overcame Mother's objections to having a dog. She simply did not want the dirt, fur, and mess that usually accompany the acquisition of an animal. She relented only after extracting sworn oaths from Pop and me that Laddie would never be permitted in her house. That pledge suffered only rare and brief breaks when she and Pop left me home alone for short periods of time.

Mother, the eldest child of a Midwestern hellfire and brimstone Christian minister, met Pop while visiting friends in Clearwater. They married just three months after their first meeting and only one year after she graduated from high school in Broken Bow, Oklahoma.

Their marriage came so fast that Mother corresponded frequently with an old beau while he served overseas in the US Army during WWII. She still keeps his letters wrapped with a blue ribbon tucked away in a storage chest. Pop did not seem to mind. His ten-year advantage in age kept him out of the war. Maybe a tinge of guilt kept his objections at bay. I do wonder if Mother's correspondence had anything to do with the fact that Pop insisted all our mail be delivered to his office and not our house. That insistence lasted until sometime after I left for college.

Despite fleeing a house dominated by a strict, unforgiving father, Mother maintained more than a fair amount of strictness in her own household. Rigid schedules, meals, baths, bedtime, and prayers were the standing orders around our house. Misbehavior brought swift and sharp reaction. Nonetheless, I managed to get into more than my share of trouble especially during my junior high years. Fortunately, some obviously divine force kept my transgressions from my mother.

Pop responded to Mother's entreaty tangentially, "You're probably right. It's fortunate most people know Laddie and he knows them. It's only strangers that have a problem. If I know Laddie, he will not forget Driver. As you say, he yelled too much at Laddie and the boys for Laddie to forget. Yes, their paths will probably cross many times and not very quietly I'm afraid."

Pop's assessment proved correct in terms of tone and frequency of contact between Alec and Laddie. Our street lay on the direct route to the Hooker's house from Alec's temporary apartment. There wasn't a witnessed time when Laddie failed to charge out and bark in a loud and prolonged manner at the passing choral director.

As much as Laddie disliked other animals coming onto what he considered his property, he disliked two other similar intrusions into his domain. The first was any stranger walking passed. In most instances, repeated trips past our house would calm Laddie's concern to the point that he would sometimes just bark at them from wherever he lay in the yard without bothering to get up. If he liked whoever it was or if they were openly friendly, he would bark mostly for effect, rise, and slowly trot over to the person with his tail in a half wag. Friends of the family were greeted by a bark, a lick to the hands and, on occasion, with a set of soiled paw prints on their shirts or blouses.

Laddie also expressed a distaste for loud vehicles of one sort of another. Any vehicle that could ply by our property quietly would be left alone whether Laddie saw it or not. On the other hand, if it made a loud noise it would get an equally paced and equivalently loud escort from property line to property line. Bicycles were an exception. For whatever reason, Laddie always barked at bicycles. Others driving by in quiet automobiles were ignored. Laddie had his rules.

On the short drive to the Hardmans' house that evening, Pop finished telling Mother what he knew about Alec.

"There is something else about Alec Driver that might interest you," he said to her.

"And what might that be?" Mother's curiosity piqued again.

"Not only does he walk around town, but that's how he got here from Providence or Princeton, whichever."

"He walked all the way?" Mother asked skeptically.

"A lot of it. He hitchhiked the rest."

"But what about his things, his bags, his—"

Interrupting, Pop said, "He probably had them sent ahead. He said all he brought with him was a backpack, which is the same luggage he uses when he travels. He said he has seen most of Europe and hopes to tour Russia, Mexico, South America, and Africa in future years."

"All of this on foot?" Mother still sounded skeptical.

"Obviously he takes a ship or flies abroad, but the rest, he insists, is by foot, bike, or a bummed ride. He said now that he's seen the world at war, he wants to see the world at peace—all on foot."

"Well, that's certainly different. I wonder why he wants to do that?"

At this statement I chimed in from the back seat, "Maybe he likes being different."

Chapter 2

*A*s had been the tradition for as long as anyone could remember, the new school year began the Tuesday following Labor Day. Alec Driver settled into an upstairs garage apartment a few blocks from the high school and just around the corner from my grandparents' house. He would not have minded walking more than a few blocks to work each day, but the possibility of arriving at his destination soaking wet drove him to set up housekeeping in a somewhat less appealing apartment than what he might have otherwise chosen. The downtown area with its attendant cafeterias, diners, restaurants, two theaters, library, and the Presbyterian Church, where Alec would spend every Thursday evening and Sunday morning for the foreseeable future, also lay within a few-minute walk. The house and garage were wood frame construction and more than thirty years old. Similar houses, occupied by mostly elderly residents long past retirement age, lined the streets of the neighborhood. Interspersed among the most senior of citizens were younger working age families and a smattering of lower income families that rented rooms or apartments at extremely low rates. Within a half mile in different directions lay the black section or "colored town" as we called it where the income level was even lower, a country-club section where the houses were less than half the age and twice the price of those in Alec's new neighborhood, the senior and junior high schools, and the downtown area. Each section contrasted strikingly with the others, but in a community of ten thousand residents no part of town lay very far from another.

The neighborhood covered an area four blocks wide and eight blocks long, from the Seaboard Airline Railroad tracks on the west to

Greenwood Avenue on the east. Greenwood Avenue separated Alec's neighborhood from the country club section. It also served as the main street into and out of colored town, a town within a town. Our house lay two miles north of town and an easy walk along the Atlantic Coast Line tracks. A less direct route circumvented colored town along Garden Avenue to the west or alternatively Betty Lane on the east.

Other than the railroad tracks there were no routes through colored town, only dead ends that stopped at Stevenson Creek. No bridges crossed the creek thereby entrapping colored town's residents within railroad tracks and marshland created by the Gulf's tide that backed up the creek for three miles. The school bus I rode to junior high school traveled Betty Lane, a narrow road that split the marshlands and formed the eastern boundary to colored town. If I attended the schools nearest my house, I would have attended the colored schools.

Colored town was either a self-contained enclave or ghetto depending on one's point of view. I cannot recall how often as children we asked why Negro children did not attend the same schools as white children. The answer remained the same: they had their own schools, churches, library, restaurants, gas stations, grocery, and liquor stores. They also had their own sections of the hospital, railroad stations, and jail. From kindergarten to high school, I lived in a white only world, no black, no brown, no yellow, no red. On Sundays, we sang that Jesus loves all the children of the world, but the song obviously did not apply to the Baptist church, the school district, the hospital, the parks, and the beach.

Alec's apartment and the adjoining house closely resembled the rest along the street. Most were one-story, only an occasional two-story house interspersed. A few like Alec's had garage apartments and fewer still had the apartments on top of the garage. His sister, Denise, recommended that he rent one of the latter because, as she explained, the sixty plus inches of rain each year made the older houses very damp and mildew prone. The one drawback to second floor garage apartments was the placement of the staircases on the outside of the garages. The unprotected location rendered them hazardous to navigate when wet, a nearly daily condition during the summer months in this region of Florida.

Alec's apartment contained a living room with a dining area at one end open to a small kitchen. The bedroom was barely able to hold the double bed, a chest of drawers, and a night table that had been crammed into it. It did have an adjoining bath with a tub so old and dirty that Alec wished for a shower instead. A patchwork of various wallpapers covered the entire apartment. The montage gave Alec the impression that someone had decorated the apartment who either possessed a strange sense of taste or who took advantage of a remnant sale at McCroy's Dime Store. Oh well, he thought, the tub could be cleaned and the walls painted. After all, Denise and John had offered to lend him a helping hand. It's the apartment that needed the helping hand, he mused. Besides, the apartment offered one very important redeeming feature—it was cheap. In addition, the landlady expressed a willingness to rent by the month; a desirable feature because he knew a new senior high school was under construction five miles to the east. Before its completion he would find more suitable housing near the new campus.

This section of town, being older, did offer something that Alec appreciated: trees. Massive live oaks surrounded the houses and formed a canopy over the narrow street. The dense shade created by the numerous trees made the grass beneath them thin and sparse. The trees provided a much-needed cooling effect that helped make living in a semitropical environment tolerable.

With only a little more than a week before classes started Alec, having only seen the school buildings from the outside, decided a closer examination of the plant and its facilities was in order. Built during the twenties in the midst of Florida's first boom and in a neighborhood of inexpensive wood frame houses and grapefruit trees, the senior and junior high schools stood back to back. Architecturally similar to many public buildings constructed during the same period, the two-story brick buildings possessed elaborate sculpted concrete arches over the doorways. Both buildings formed the shape of the letter T with the fronts represented by the top crosspiece of the letter. The windows consisted of heavy wood frames of four panels to a frame and three frames to a window. The heavy frames and the dark brick gave the buildings the effect of a city jail or state prison. The metal bars covering the machine and wood shop windows made the image even more convincing as did the combination fire, police station, and city jail just a few blocks away constructed in the same style and materials.

The senior high faced east and the junior high faced west, which under ordinary circumstances would make them very hot during the late spring and early fall. Fortunately, both front lawns, like the yards in Alec's neighborhood, contained numerous massive live oak trees. The deep shade and the exuberance of the junior high youth completely obliterated any semblance of grass that once graced the front lawn of that building. The senior high building with its somewhat more mature students still managed to enjoy some resemblance of a lawn.

As he approached the campus, Alec decided to enter the senior high first hoping to meet the principal and get directions to the choir room. As he entered the side doorway, he noticed that the floors consisted of tongue-and-groove oak planks. As he walked, the sound of his hard leather heels striking the floor echoed loudly down the long, dark, empty corridors. The ceilings seem unusually high, he thought. After what seemed many steps, he reached the door of the principal's office. He stopped, reached into his pocket, and withdrew a torn slip of paper on which he had written the name of the principal. He double-checked the name to make sure he did not embarrass himself by blurting out the junior high principal's name. He met the junior high principal during an interview at the district office while visiting his sister the previous spring. The senior high principal had been out of town on school business. Alec's academic credentials, coupled with the right kind of recommendation from an influential faculty member at Princeton, whose programs in music and arts enjoyed a long and enviable reputation, ensured Alec's appointment. He opened the door a crack and peered in lest he had found the private entrance. He found not one office but a large open work area where the school's administrative staff worked. A large wooden counter separated him from the only person he saw in the room—an elderly looking gentleman with white hair and wire rim glasses. He wore a white shirt with a navy blue and yellow polka dot bow tie and seersucker slacks. A navy sports jacket lay over a nearby chair.

"Excuse me," began Alec, "could you tell me where I might find Mr. Furst?"

"You might find him right here. I've been known to answer to that name," the gentleman answered with a twinkle in his eye and a broad smile on his lips.

"Oh, good, I'm Alec Driver. I apologize for not recognizing you. I expected—"

"A younger man perhaps?" interjected John Furst with a bit of a grin.

"No. Well, yes. But I didn't mean—" Alec stammered.

"That's all right," came the reply, "two more years and they put me out to pasture. Actually my retirement is due this year, but the board graciously extended my term two years so that I might spend my last year in the new school. You're our new music teacher, we're happy to have you," he answered, extending his hand.

John Furst's tenure spanned forty years of which more than half were served as principal of the high school. His four children attended the school while he served as a teacher of history and social studies. His last five years in office saw his ten grandchildren graduate from the same school. He looked his part, a loving grandfather, an understanding principal, and dedicated educator. A student could be in serious trouble, but John's face, demeanor, and tone never reflected the possible consequences. He had a way of putting people he engaged at ease no matter what the circumstances. No one could remember John ever saying anything in a threatening manner.

Clasping John's hand firmly in his, Alec responded, "Thank you. I look forward to working with you. I just dropped by to take a peek at the choir room and get a feel for the place before setting up shop next week," Alec explained.

"I'm afraid you might be a little disappointed with what we have to offer you in the way of facilities this year, but next year everything will be brand-new."

"I suppose I can live with most anything for a year," Alec stated, trying to sound optimistic. Glancing out the door and down the hallway he continued, "Just point me in the right direction, I'm sure everything will be fine."

"Actually…" John Furst paused, searching for the best way to soften the coming blow, "you have not a room but a whole building to yourself," he said with some satisfaction.

"Oh?" came an inquisitive reply.

"Yes, we ran out of space in the main buildings, so last year we renovated one of the remaining houses on the property to be the choir room. The entire interior of the house was gutted except for the baths and a couple of closets. Window and floor fans have been installed. You will have to make do for the time being. But don't worry, you won't be lonely, the band room is right next door in the old Salvation Army building."

*****

The following Monday, a week before Labor Day, Alec reported for work. The day began with orientation for new teachers of which there were a larger number than usual. Introduction of new faculty took place at the general faculty meeting that followed the orientation session. The faculty meeting adjourned to the auditorium stage where citrus punch, coffee, tea, and assorted home-baked pastries filled two large tables set up for the occasion. Alec made a point to meet the band director and arrange a meeting later that afternoon to choose an appropriate schedule for their respective classes, a necessity because of the proximity of their practice rooms.

After the reception, Alec settled into his 1920s wood frame house turned choir room. A wave of hot humid air struck him as he opened the back door and entered the room. He turned on the lights and noticed two large floor fans at the front and two window fans in the rear. He switched on the window fans and opened the front door creating a draft from the door through the room and out the rear windows. He shed his sports jacket, and in a few minutes the room, while not cool, became tolerable.

The front of the room faced the south side of the house. The ceiling, Alec guessed, was ten feet high. He preferred the taller ceilings in the main buildings, but quickly realized he must make do for one school year. Raised platforms of three tiers constructed in a large arch consumed nearly all the open floor space of the room. Support posts, necessitated by the gutting of most of the house's original interior walls, disturbed the openness of the room. Making lemonade out of a lemon, Alec decided the posts could be used to mark the places for each section of the various choirs. He tried to imagine what the room would be like when crammed with fifty or sixty young bodies. *The heat, what about the heat?* he thought. The room felt fairly comfortable now, but he worried about the extra heat that the young bodies would generate. Classes would have to be in the morning, he decided, preferably first thing in the morning before the sun moved from behind the live oaks on the building's east side. Afternoon classes were definitely out.

He settled in at his desk in the front corner of the room to complete the tax and insurance forms provided during orientation. He decided to skip lunch and spent the time getting familiar with the choir's audio equipment while waiting on the band director. During the interim he turned on the floor fans.

The remainder of the week he spent committing to paper all the plans he made while walking and hitchhiking from New Jersey that July. It had been an ideal opportunity to plan, for the thoughts occupied his mind during the long, hot stretches through the Carolinas, Georgia, and Florida.

He hoped that out of a senior high choir of sixty, he could find a dozen students who possessed both good voice quality and a proclivity for music. *That would be enough*, he thought, *to start*. He planned to select that group very early and work with them one or two afternoons a week after school to form the nucleus of a good choral group. Through training and practice, he hoped to add another dozen by the time of the traditional spring concert. He had no illusions of building a quality choir of sixty in his first year that would take four or five years to develop. He intended to identify and encourage talented voices in the junior high choir to continue to take choir until they graduated. *In four years*, he thought, *I should have a choir consisting, in the main, of trained and dedicated students. It will be this choir that will be capable of achieving the level of excellence I intend. But,* he mused, *that will require patience, perseverance, and the willingness to practice, practice, practice, three very demanding qualities that hopefully can be found in a sufficient number of students to form a decent choir.*

After a week of planning and organizing his coming classes, Alec welcomed the respite of the Labor Day weekend. He finished the last of his scheduled housekeeping chores just before noon on Saturday. Just enough time, he thought, to bathe, walk to town, get an overdue haircut, have lunch, and take in the matinee performance of Gary Cooper's new movie, *High Noon*. The haircut would also provide an opportunity to learn more about Clearwater, as barbershops in small towns are notorious as a rich source of local gossip.

Charley Bennett operated one of the town's three barbershops for as long as most people could remember. His shop, The Royal Palm, along with Pop's insurance agency, the Western Auto, the citrus store, Mal's News Stand, and the Post Office occupied the north side of the one-hundred-yard strip of Cleveland Street between the Atlantic Coast Line and Seaboard Airline Railroad tracks. A native of north Florida, Charley moved to town thirty years earlier as a newly licensed barber seeking a community with fewer established barbershops than existed in his own hometown. He apprenticed with his hometown barber and decided early in his apprenticeship that he wanted a shop of his own. Charley quickly melded into his adopted community mainly because of his easygoing, slow-talking, and unabashed personality. He became a steadfast and loyal citizen of the community and devoted member of the First Baptist Church. Thirty years later, Charley knew everybody.

Rather than ask someone the location of the nearest barbershop, Alec decided to walk toward town and stop at the first shop he saw. He spotted the familiar lighted barber pole of Charley's shop from the Post Office a half block away. He entered the propped open door and felt the draft created by the oversized fan in the back window. The shop was busy, all three manned chairs were occupied and four men were waiting their turn. Alec turned and started to leave when a deep voice from the rear called out, "Have a seat, it won't be long."

Alec sat down and thumbed through a copy of *Look* magazine stacked with a multitude of others on the adjacent table. As each chair emptied, the barber said the name of the next man waiting. Alec listened as one barber or another called out in turn the names Tom, Doug, Boyd, and Ray. When Alec's turn came, the barber who had stopped him from leaving said, "Next."

As Alec sat back in the barber chair, the barber spread the apron over his lap and fastened it around his neck, asking in the process, "Stranger in town?"

"Yes and no. I was stationed here briefly during the war," Alec answered, a bit self-conscious that his newness had been noticed.

"Visiting, passing through, or moving in?" Charley's comments were always terse until he got to know the man in his chair or until a subject he had some interest in arose. As with most barbers, Charley had an opinion on everything.

"Moving in, or moved in actually. I'm staying in Mrs. Smith's garage apartment on Vine Street," Alec responded, trying to give him some identity.

"Annie Smith? Fine woman, as true a Christian as there ever was. What's your trade?" Charley asked as he began to trim Alec's hair.

"I'm the new choir director at the junior and senior highs."

"You must be taking Wally Goss's place. Good man did a fine job with the choirs. He's a hard man to beat."

"I'm sure you're right. I haven't met him yet, but I'm sure I will soon. He is my district supervisor," Alec explained

"By the way," Charley said, stepping from in back of Alec's chair and extending his hand to Alec, "my name is Charley Bennett. I'm the owner of this shop."

"Glad to meet you. I'm Alec Driver," answered Alec, grabbing Charley's hand and taking note of Charley's firm grip.

Hearing the two men exchange greetings, the man in the first chair called out, "Hey, Charley, who's that you got down there?"

"New choir director. He's gonna work with Herb Dudley at the high school," came Charley's reply.

Charley took a close look at Alec's hair, studied it for a moment, and asked, "You want just a trim?"

"Yes, that will be fine," Alec replied.

In contrast to most of Charley's regular customers Alec's age, Alec wore his hair long on all sides and the top of his head. He combed it straight back giving him a streamlined look. It was the sort of look one would get with long hair while riding a motorcycle at high speed without a helmet. A light hair cream kept it in place.

"Say," came the voice in the first chair, "what do you think Herb will do if the Bombers win the first game tonight?"

Charley replied, "He won't go past midnight. Gerald Overcash will have to pitch. They'll just have to win without Herb."

"You think he'll do that in the finals of the World Tournament?"

"What do you think?" Charley replied.

"Yep, even in the finals of the World Tournament," came the reply.

For the remainder of time spent in the barber chair, Alec sat quietly, mostly listening to the conversation about the town's fast pitch softball team that he knew nothing about when he entered, but a great deal of before he left.

With only an occasional question of his own, he learned that the Clearwater Bombers (originally the Blackburn Bombers named for a local lumber yard, the team's first sponsor, and the men and planes stationed in the area during the war) enjoyed a national reputation in fast pitch softball circles over the past four years. The town and team took pride that every member of the team was a native of Clearwater or one of its surrounding towns. The Bombers gained notoriety during the 1949 season when they were runners-up in the World Tournament (so named since teams from Canada were included).

The team's uniqueness lay not only in having all native sons as players, but that its sponsor was a town of less than ten thousand population rather than a corporate sponsor like the other teams. The native son make-up and the small town backing took back seats to the outstanding individual performance of one particular team member.

As the story unfolded, in a disjointed manner as each man in the shop contributed to it, Alec, who played baseball in high school, listened attentively. In 1949 the Bombers had lost an early game in the double elimination tournament but fought their way to the finals as enormous underdogs via the loser's bracket on the incredible strength of one man's arm. Herbert Dudley, the team's best pitcher, and after the tournament one of the best in the sport, pitched Saturday, the opening day of the tournament played in Little Rock, Arkansas. He pitched again on Monday, Tuesday, and then again on Wednesday against one of the best teams in the country, Phillips 66 of Oklahoma. Herb pitched a game that would end up in sports' folklore alongside the football game between Georgia Tech, under John Heisman, and Cumberland University in which Tech won 222–0. The Bombers won in twenty-one innings, 1-0 with Herb Dudley pitching the entire game striking out an unbelievable fifty-five batters and walking only one. With only fifteen minutes rest, Herb returned to the mound and pitched another seven-inning game in which the Bombers won 4-0. The next night they lost in the finals to Toronto to finish second. The following year the Bombers won their first world championship.

After thirty minutes (evenly divided into cutting and talking time), Charley finished Alec's hair. Alec asked, "How much do I owe you?"

"Four bits," Charley replied.

Alec withdrew a liberty half-dollar from his pocket, handed it to Charley, and asked, "What was it you said about Herb Dudley quitting after midnight? I don't understand."

"Today is Saturday. After midnight, it's Sunday. Herb won't pitch on Sundays or do anything else for that matter except go to church and rest. He and half the team are members of the First Baptist Church."

"But why?" Alec started to ask.

"Doesn't believe in it, he feels the commandment means what it says, 'Remember the Sabbath and keep it holy.'"

"But couldn't that hurt the team's chance of winning? What will the team do? What about the town's people, what will they think?" Alec countered, still unconvinced.

"Yep, it could cost them the championship. People here won't mind. Herb has never made his feelings secret. People respect him for it," Charley explained.

"Incredible," Alec almost whispered. He thanked Charley and headed across the street to Brown Brothers Dairy for lunch.

The more Alec mulled over the barbershop conversation, the more incredulous it seemed that a man so talented and important to a team would jeopardize the team's success because of a religious conviction. Then he remembered, as a boy of nine, hearing his parents speak about a runner from Scotland refusing to participate in an Olympic event because he would have to run a preliminary heat on Sunday. As Alec recalled, even royalty could not dissuade the runner.

He vowed to check the local papers for the results, but that may have to wait until Monday because the second game might not finish until after the Sunday edition's deadline. In any event, the conversation roused his curiosity about the outcome of the tournament.

The following morning, the paper only reported the results of the first game that the Bombers had won. The second game started too late for the Sunday edition. That afternoon as scheduled, Denise and Mark arrived, children in tow, to begin the refurbishing and cleaning that Alec's garage apartment so desperately needed. Alec asked almost immediately if they had heard what happened in the second Bomber game. Mark answered, "Yes, the Bombers lost and finished second."

Alec then asked, "What about Herb Dudley? Did he pitch?"

"Until the stroke of midnight, after that he wouldn't go on the field," Mark replied.

Alec responded, "I don't believe it. Won't the manager or team hold it against him?" he asked to determine if Charley Bennett's assessment was correct.

"Not likely," Mark replied, adding, "as for the manager, he and Herb are in the same Sunday school class."

"I've got to meet this man," Alec said.

"Don't worry," Denise replied, "you will next week. He's the baseball coach at the high school."

Chapter 3

*T*uesday after Labor Day, Alec rose early after a fitful sleep. Uncertain whether his insomnia was due to nervousness about his first day of classes or simply the result of the lingering odor of drying paint, he quickly showered, shaved, and dressed. After downing orange juice and a stale doughnut left over from Sunday's work party, he briskly walked the short distance to the house-turned-choir-room, arriving with ample time to compose himself for his first period senior high class. His first class went smoothly and more quickly than he anticipated. He had a one-period break before the junior high class met, but as much as he was prepared for the senior choir he was ill-prepared for the lack of maturity and discipline the younger students displayed.

What a motley crew, Alec thought as our third period class ended. He praised the wisdom that led to scheduling the senior high choir first followed by a break before the junior high choir met. Even experienced teachers found it difficult to face eighth graders at the start of the day. Time is required to brace oneself accordingly. He felt confident that he could handle the older students as choir served as an elective at that level. Presumably they preferred singing to painting, drawing, cooking, wood working, or engaging in any other alternative. The lower grades had only three alternatives: band, choir, or art. How good this forced choice of the fine arts must have sounded at some school curriculum meeting. The reality, as we knew and Alec soon discovered, was that many students didn't take the imposed choice graciously and as a result discipline suffered. During one his many sermons on deportment, Alec bemoaned the attitudes that frequently led parents to downplay musical training in deference to the traditional subjects of math, English, and the sciences. If Jane's or

Johnny's deportment in choir was disruptive, there was little need to express the same concern as with other subjects, he often lamented.

Adding to these attitude problems, Alec also faced unusual logistical difficulties involving both band and choir. These classes met in large groups with a mixture of grades while the other elective classes were small and met with students in the same grade.

Another reason existed for scheduling both choirs during the morning hours; the young throats would not yet be hoarse from talking, yelling, screaming, and countless other untold adolescent abuses. From a tactical standpoint Mr. Stanovich, the band director, scheduled the respective bands during the last periods of the day to facilitate after school practice for the marching band. The scheduling had a side benefit in that the two instructors would not have to compete with the sounds the other's class would generate. Less than six feet separated the two buildings and the lack of air conditioning meant that during warm weather all windows in both buildings would be open permitting uninhibited sound transmission.

Alec did not relish being relegated to an exterior building even if Mr. Stanovich suffered the same fate next door. Mr. Stanovich, a recent transplant himself, offered Alec numerous helpful hints on how a novice teacher could survive his first school year in a new district. The imposed exile left him feeling ostracized. His experience in the military taught him that personal relationships developed quickly and easily with casual and frequent contact with his peers. He felt more comfortable meeting people in a natural, relaxed manner than in the formal situation that would result from physical separation. He feared conversations would be deliberate rather than spontaneous, artificial rather than natural, and stilted rather than relaxed.

He resigned himself to making the best of it, for things would not be any better next year. The plans for the new senior high that the principal displayed during orientation revealed that the band and choir rooms would again be adjacent. At least, the new facilities will be air-conditioned and sound-proofed. They will also share the same building with the gym, at the far end of the campus, next to the football stadium.

"Remember, class," he reminded us as we crushed our way out the narrow front door, "walk down the sidewalk to the corner and up the street to the north entrance of the main building. You're not to enter the building through the front door and are *not* to cut across the softball field."

These instructions met with a chorus of boos that undoubtedly sounded flat to Alec's musically trained ear. The route he proscribed was the longest path to the main junior high building, but that was what Mr. Furst, the principal, had specified. Unlike Mr. Furst, we were unconcerned with the dirt our feet would track on the newly varnished hard wood floors or with the loud noise the traffic would generate as we trouped passed the administrative offices. Our concern centered on the shortest distance between choir and the next class.

After the last student bolted through the front door, Alec settled into the swivel chair at his desk. The renovations had rotated the house's orientation. The front and back of the original house became the east and west sides of the choir room. The house's back-turned-side door stood slightly behind and to the right of Alec's desk. Only the sound of the window fans penetrated the quiet of the empty room. Engrossed in the papers before him, he didn't hear anyone enter the room yet he sensed the presence of someone even before he heard a voice.

"Mr. Driver." The voice spoke with such a distinctive tone that Alec immediately recognized it as a soprano.

"Yes," Alec automatically responded as he turned in the direction of the voice.

"I'm sorry," the voice went on, "I wasn't able to be here first period. I had to help new students find their classes."

His eyes riveted to hers, Alec scarcely heard a word the voice uttered. Dark and penetrating, her eyes appeared to sparkle as she spoke. Her long, straight hair ended with a flip as it graced her shoulders. She wore a green print sundress so appropriate to the still dog days of summer in central Florida. Her skin was olive, darker than what he expected of southern belles, and without a single noticeable blemish to spoil its clear, smooth complexion. She stopped speaking waiting for a response from Alec. The sudden silence brought him out of his stupor.

"That's no problem, we were just getting organized today," he said with a broad smile.

Her name, what's her name? he thought. He couldn't remember whether she said it or not.

"Let me make sure you're on my roll and if I marked you absent, I'll change it."

"It's Tracy Ashbury, with a *u*," she offered.

Looking up and answering, he asked, "Like the village in England?"

"Yes, but how did you know?" came her surprised reply.

"I've been through there. It's a beautiful country village." Catching his thoughts, he fumbled through his papers until finding his roll. "Yes, here you are right at the top of the list. It's nice of you to drop by and explain why you were absent; most students wouldn't be so thoughtful."

He hoped she would pick up on his last statement, for he found himself in no hurry to end the conversation.

"I have another reason for seeing you after class. I understand you're going to be the choir director at the Presbyterian Church."

"For the foreseeable future at least, are you interested in join-ing?" he asked, hoping not to sound too anxious.

"That's what I wanted to ask you," she answered.

"You certainly don't need my permission, I mean, I would…ah, the choir would welcome you," he stumbled, hating himself for it.

"Teenagers usually aren't allowed in the adult choir. There's a youth choir but not many kids join. I'd rather be in the older choir," she explained.

"You just show up Thursday night and I'll handle the rest," he replied, making no attempt to control the broad smile on his face.

"Thanks. That's great. Oh, I've got to run. I'm already late for my next class. Thanks again. See you tomorrow," she called back over her shoulder as she left the room.

Alec thought he noticed a definite lilt to her voice as he watched her scurry off in a half run, her hair bouncing as she moved. It was the first time he noticed the matching green ribbon through her hair. She left through the building's back door not following the circuitous route laid out for the junior high students. The senior high students were permitted a more direct route from their building because of its location at the other end of the block. The five-minute break between classes proved insufficient for the longer route.

The exchange lasted at most three minutes, an interval he would never forget. She created an impression highly disproportionate to the short time she spent with him and many times more powerful than that left by any other woman he had ever met. It wasn't that he lacked experience with women, but all the others (including a former wife) he found dull and lifeless. He didn't know much about Tracy Ashbury yet, but he could already tell that she was vibrant and full of life. For the first time that day, he looked forward to the next day's first period class.

As the last days of summer turned into autumn, Alec became deeply immersed in developing his choirs with an intensity he hadn't anticipated a few weeks earlier. His love and devotion to music accompanied by the challenge of organizing new choirs proved to be both engrossing and time-consuming. Mere academic interest quickly transformed into excitement by the overriding allure he felt for the enchanting young lady whose presence graced two of his three choirs. He never considered himself a very religious man, but the godsend that had provided frequent opportunities to be near Tracy was causing him to believe that some higher authority was guiding these events.

In the school choir, Alec's fondest dreams could not have envisioned the fortuitous occurrences that took place in the first days of the new school year. Tracy's voice, though not of professional potential, was more than sufficient to qualify as lead soprano in both choirs. Her talent, charm, and avid interest in the senior high choir made her an obvious choice, by Alec and classmates alike, as one of the choir's officers. With school Monday through Friday, church choir on Thursday night, and Sunday morning, Saturday was the only day of the week that Alec would not ordinarily see her.

Occasionally, as the opportunity presented itself, Alec watched Tracy and the other cheerleaders practice after school. He stationed himself in a position not in clear view of the squad and then for only a few minutes at a time not wishing to call attention to him. He was amused by and grateful for what had become known as "the short flap." The story swept the school at the beginning of the year. It seemed that the new girls' PE coach hadn't paid any attention to the change in style of girls' PE shorts when she placed the order for the girls' PE classes. Previously, the girls' shorts were quite modest, even a longer length than the boys' and cut rather full to the point of being baggy. The manufacturer changed the standard short according to changing national trends that had not yet reached rural Florida. The new shorts more closely matched the girls' contours and were significantly shorter than the older models. They were now shorter than the boys' shorts. Needless to say, significantly more of the girls' forms and legs were exposed in the process, too much so for the new PE teacher. The teacher's dilemma was compounded by the fact that she was a rather stout woman whose new shorts made her look, for the lack of a better term, conspicuous. She opted for a more modest pair of bright red Bermuda shorts. Given her size, she still looked conspicuous. When she discovered her error, she tried to return the shorts for the more modest style, but the distributor balked and school had already started. She had no choice but to distribute the two hundred pairs she ordered. Not a single girl complained, nor did any of the boys for that matter. Tracy, with her athletic legs and dark complexion, looked stunning in her white shorts. The school never returned to the longer short length.

Besides Tracy's physical and sexual features, Alec soon discovered that she had other equally attractive qualities. She shared many of his musical interests. She played the piano as well as she sang and possessed an impressive collection of recordings from classical to popular although she was partial to stage musicals like Rogers and Hammerstein's *South Pacific* and *Oklahoma*. Whenever the opportunity arose, he sought her advice on possible choir programs for school and public performances. She enlisted him to help in the production of the senior class play, Gilbert and Sullivan's *H. M. S. Pinafore*. How incredible, Alec thought, how many interests they shared and how fortuitous that they could spend so much time together pursuing them.

Alec's choral duties rarely occupied him so much as to miss school athletic events. His interest in athletics stemmed from his high school and college days when he ran varsity cross-country. He loved the sport that knew no season, required very little in the form of a uniform or equipment, and did not need, but allowed, a partner. He enjoyed being outdoors and feeling the exhilaration of running. In recent years, running had given way to extensive walking, a pleasure that provided him a great sense of contentment.

He willingly agreed to assist Mr. Stanovich in transporting the band and its equipment from the school to the stadium for the Friday night home football games. That gave him a ride to and from the stadium on home game nights and, if he chose, to the out of town games.

Alec also felt a sense of duty to support the high school's various extracurricular activities. Certainly choir was one of those activities, and he believed that each should do its best to support the other, although he didn't entertain any illusions about the football team showing up for choir concerts. This attitude wasn't simply a *quid pro quo*; it was a matter of pride and loyalty to the city and the school that bore its name. He planned to be a regular at most of the school's activities and to volunteer as chaperon at many of the post-game dances.

Alec had another incentive to attend the school's games, pep rallies, and dances—Tracy was always there. Alec's new allegiances would have been reason enough to assume his obligations, but as he soon discovered, they also provided him an opportunity to observe Tracy away from school and his influence. In this quiet manner he became familiar with her interests, friends, and behavior. He quickly became a student of Tracy Ashbury with a *u*, and the more he learned the more captivated he became. She rapidly changed from a subject to a major. Indeed, she became a curriculum in herself.

Tracy dated Buster Forbes, the starting fullback and team captain, regularly but not steadily. She also dated, on occasion, other boys when she thought Buster became too possessive. She enjoyed dating Buster as long as their relationship remained casual. Her vacillation stemmed mostly from her inability to find a boy she liked enough to go steady. She supported Buster in athletics, however, and cheered especially hard on plays in which his number was called. Buster simply could not match her maturity and intellect.

Alec bided his time patiently, keeping his public actions toward Tracy at what he considered a respectable level. He made certain that the frequency of their contact alone wasn't sufficient to cause any eyebrows to rise. He was equally careful to cast meetings within his official school capacity fully aware that the frequency combined with any emotional display could create criticism where none was warranted, at least not yet, he thought. As far as he knew the feelings he had were entirely one-sided. Tracy, while always seeming relaxed, unrestrained, and comfortable around Alec, gave him no overt sign of any similar feelings toward him.

Patience and caution slowly gave way to the growing emotion and virtually complete captivation for Tracy that dominated most of his conscious thoughts. Somehow, some way, he must express how he felt, however subtly, to her. At the same time, he wanted desperately to determine Tracy's feelings, if any, toward him. He had little interest in pursuing unrequited love or nursing a bruised ego for that matter. Describing his own feelings as anything other than love simply didn't do justice to the depth of emotion he felt for her. The opportunity to suggest his feelings and simultaneously test Tracy's presented itself in an entirely unexpected way.

After choir practice on Thursday nights, Alec walked the mile and half back to his apartment, stopping for coffee or a late night snack at the Owl Diner—an all-night diner formed by the merging of two symmetrical halves shipped from the Midwest on flat bed rail cars—just half a block from the church on Park Street. On the first Thursday in November, choir practice ended later than usual because the choir began preparations for special music Alec scheduled for the Sunday before Thanksgiving Day. He planned an overture of juxtaposed nationalistic and religious hymns that required smooth transitions, without pauses, between songs, a difficult technique, he discovered, for some older choir members.

As usual, Alec waited until everyone in the choir left before turning off the lights and locking the east door. The door opened onto Ft. Harrison Avenue but faced east straight down Park Street. The skies had been clear when Alec left for rehearsal that night. By the time practice ended three hours later, the first cold front of the season had already moved through the city. The temperature dropped almost thirty degrees, and a slow but penetrating drizzle had begun. Clad only in a short sleeve sport shirt and cotton slacks, he shivered as he stepped out into the night.

He looked up and muttered, "Where in hell did this come from?" forgetting for the moment where he was.

He dashed the half block to the diner for refuge, thinking maybe tonight he would take a cab home. As he sprinted passed the parked cars along the curb, he heard a clearly recognizable voice call from a lowered window of a parked car.

"Mr. Driver."

Lingering after practice to talk with one of the other choir members, Tracy had just entered her car that was parked on the diner's side of the street. Combing her damp, windswept hair, she saw Alec, so inadequately clad, leave the church. Immediately recognizing his plight, she waited until he approached her car before she rolled down the window and called.

Alec stopped, turned, and said with welcome relief, "Hi, Tracy. Great weather, I wonder where it went?" It must appear silly, he thought, for a grown man to be standing in a bone chilling rain with such a broad smile on his face. He made no attempt, however, to hide his pleasure.

"Would you like a ride home?" she offered.

Alec hesitated for an instant, looking up and down the street and seeing no one, he answered, "Well…" He looked again at the empty taxi stand just a half a block away. "You've talked me into it," he answered as his smile broadened. "How about a cup of coffee or hot chocolate at the diner first, my treat?" Uncertain where the nerve came from to ask her for coffee, he delighted in the fact that he managed to muster up the courage.

Not wanting to prolong Alec's exposure to the weather Tracy quickly answered, "Okay."

He opened the door for her to get out, and together they quickly walked the short distance to the diner.

Once inside they found a booth and seated themselves. Alec excused himself for a quick trip to the men's room where he dried his face and arms with paper towels and combed his hair back into its usual neat streamline place. Returning to their booth he glanced around and noticed that the weather had reduced the usual small number of other diner patrons to four. To his relief he recognized only the cook and waitress. The waitress sauntered over to their booth and made the inane remark about the weather being nice for ducks that Alec had deliberately avoided in his greeting to Tracy. Each made a pretense at laughing. Upon learning that the cook had baked a fresh apple pie, they each ordered a piece. After a few exchanges about how rehearsal went that night, Alec turned the conversation to a more personal note.

"It's really nice of you to offer to drive me home. I thought I would have to get a cab at the stand down the street."

"That's okay. I'm happy to do it. The weather has really turned miserable," she responded.

"Will your parents be worried if you don't get home on time? After all practice lasted later than usual and taking me home will get you back even later," he said, hoping to gain some insight about her relationship with her parents.

"They'll probably already be in bed and even asleep when I get home. With all the activities I'm in, I get home very late some nights. Besides, they're very understanding and trust my judgment more than some parents would." Tracy toyed with her water glass as she spoke.

"You're very fortunate to have such understanding parents," he offered. Without fully realizing it, Alec began to toy with his water glass.

As they were talking, the owner, who talked with Alec on most his previous visits to the diner, walked out of the kitchen carrying two pieces of hot apple pie. As he placed them on the table he looked at Tracy and then at Alec.

"I admire both your taste in company and pie," he said with a wink that Alec hoped Tracy didn't see.

"Yes," Alec quickly responded, "this young lady has graciously offered to drive me home after choir practice. I thought the least I could do is buy her a cup of coffee—your delicious pie was a pleasant surprise."

"Yeah, sure," was his only reply as he walked away glancing back over his shoulder and smiling.

"I'm sorry about that. I hope I haven't embarrassed you," Alec offered nervously, watching for any sign of disapproval.

"I'm not embarrassed. I think it's cute." She grinned.

"I guess being twen…er, a good deal older than you makes me fear that you might feel uncomfortable," he said in a low voice, still looking for any sign of disapproval from Tracy.

"You're not that old, and besides, I think age differences aren't that important. There're a number of girls I know that do, though. Ruth Ann is dating a senior at the university, and some of the other girls think that's just awful. I think it's fine."

"Then you wouldn't let a large difference in age prevent you from seeing someone older?" he ventured.

"Not at all if I liked him," she responded.

"Then if someone older were to ask you out, you would consider it?" he realized he was pushing for a definitive answer that came more forthrightly than he expected.

"Why, Mr. Driver?" Tracy responded, looking straight into Alec's eyes. "Are you asking me for a date?"

Chapter 4

Sleep didn't come easily to Alec that night despite the lulling sounds of the steady, gentle rain falling on the roof and against the windows of his garage apartment. Adrenaline, stimulated by a crazed mixture of anger, excitement, depression, and elation, caused every nerve in his body to be at full alert. Sleep, for the moment, was definitely out of the question. He had successfully broken the ice without dashing his hopes of seeing Tracy more often outside the milieu of choir and class. He felt chagrined at his lack of poise and sophistication at a time when he felt he needed them most. Twenty years his junior, a mere seventeen years of age, Tracy exhibited more maturity than he. He found the role of the nervous schoolboy not knowing what to say or how to say it depressing. He knew only that he had to say something. *Surely*, he thought, *I could have acquitted myself better than to stammer something to the effect that I would enjoy having coffee with Tracy after choir on Thursday nights.*

"Shit!" he unexpectedly shouted aloud in such a volume that he startled himself.

"Why," he continued aloud while pacing to and fro at the foot of the bed dressed only in his shorts and a pajama top, "did she have to ask if I were asking her for a date? Why did I not ask her outright so that she would not have had to ask? Why didn't I respond to her question, 'Hell yes, I'm asking you to go out with me?' I'm a coward that's why. I was afraid she would say no and that's depressing. I've got to get my act together."

Alec finally managed to wrestle himself into bed where he spent most of the night staring at the ceiling. The flood of adrenaline created by the surge of emotions he experienced was not the sole reason for his insomnia. A twinge of guilt gnawed at his conscience. He kept thinking of the difference in their ages. He decided that the twenty years difference didn't matter; it was her age that mattered. What business did he have pursuing the affections of a seventeen-year-old? He hadn't even told her of his recent divorce. What would she say to that revelation? he wondered. He had to tell her, but how, when? Then a thought so chilling that it matched the sudden change in the weather occurred to him. What happens if he asks her out and she says yes? What would her parents say, what would the principal say, and what would the minister say? *For that matter, what would I say?* he thought. In spite of his misgivings he decided it was a risk well worth taking.

Sometime later after some fitful attempts to fall asleep, he suddenly bolted upright in bed and yelled into the quiet of the cold, dark night, "I've got it!"

It had just dawned on him that the Roger Wagner Chorale would be appearing at a concert in Tampa as part of a current southern tour the first weekend in December. What a wonderful opportunity to ask her out, he thought. Who could seriously object to the school music teacher offering to escort one of his best pupils to such a concert—never mind the fact that this particular student is the prettiest member of the choir. The plan is ingenious, he mused. He decided to ask her the next Thursday night over coffee after choir. He lay back down, took a deep sigh, rolled over on his side, and fell asleep; it was three o'clock in the morning.

As he prepared to leave for school a few hours later, the excitement of the night before caused his hands to shake as he shaved. Next Thursday night seemed so far away, he wasn't sure that his nervous system could take the stress of that prolonged wait. Somehow he would have to find the patience, for there was simply not a better opportunity to ask her in a casual but deliberate and measured manner.

"Casual? I'm going to be a nervous wreck, maybe even a nervous ramblin' 'reck." He smiled to himself and began to whistle the famous fight song as he walked the short three blocks to school.

An eventful week made Alec's nervous wait go by quickly. The school choirs practiced special music for the Thanksgiving school assembly. Homecoming fever struck as the traditional homecoming game against Largo High was on the Wednesday night before Thanksgiving Day—a strange time, he thought. Everyone expected Tracy to be elected to the homecoming court and was the odds on favorite to be queen. With the parade, the bonfire, the game, and the dance, Tracy's social calendar overflowed that weekend. It would be her weekend; the weekend two weeks hence occupied Alec's present thoughts.

Preoccupied with the speech he planned to give to Tracy that night, Alec muddled through the day. He reminded the church choir that evening that they would not practice on Thanksgiving night. He planned for the congregation to join them in singing familiar hymns on the following Sunday. He could have scheduled practice for another night, but the truth was that he didn't wish to schedule anything that would conflict with the homecoming activities the next week. He planned to attend them all, admiring and adoring Tracy Ashbury and her extraordinary beauty even if it had to be, at least for now, from afar.

Tracy waited patiently and quietly while Alec tidied the choir room and closed and locked the church after practice. He turned the key in the aging lock until there was an audible click as the bolt sealed the door. He turned, smiled, and said, "The weather is certainly better tonight than last week. I just hope it stays this way for homecoming next week."

"It had better," she replied, "my mother has invested a small fortune in my gown and…my hair, I will look simply dreadful if it gets wet."

"Oh no, you won't," he rebutted.

Tracy looked a bit puzzled at his remark, and he quickly added, "What I mean is," he paused, "that there is scarcely anything that the weather could do to make you look dreadful." He smiled as he took her arm and guided her across Fort Harrison Avenue. Traffic on the town's rolled-up streets did not create any concern for safety. Alec simply took advantage of the opportunity to touch Tracy.

"Why thank you," she replied and smiled back.

They walked silently for a few moments until the message of what Tracy had said finally registered in Alec's mind. He stopped, turned her by her arm toward him, and said, "Wait a minute, gown, hair, does that mean you, you're on the—"

"Homecoming court? Yes, Miss Meeks told us officially today. Buster told me last Friday. Joanna White is queen."

"That's great! I mean about you being named to the court. As for me, you are a queen. Congratulations." He felt his grin go from ear to ear.

"Thank you," she replied with a smaller but equally pleased smile.

Alec opened the door of the diner for Tracy, and once inside he instinctively led her to the same booth where they sat the week before. The owners, seeing them enter and seat themselves, strolled over and in his own inimitable manner said, "Encore performance, eh?"

Responding, Alec offered, "Yes, this just may become a habit." He smiled and glanced at Tracy.

"Well, what'll you have, the usual?" The owner asked.

"The usual?" Alec responded with a laugh. "We haven't been coming in that often…yet." Looking at Tracy, he said, "More pie and coffee?"

"Just coffee please," she answered.

"Make that two," Alec added.

Without wasting any time and before losing his mustered courage, Alec cleared his throat, looked straight into Tracy's eyes, and said, "Tracy, I didn't answer your question last week candidly. Let me start over. Yes, I would like to ask you for a date." Not allowing her enough time to respond he continued, "If you recall I mentioned in class yesterday that the Roger Wagner Chorale will be giving a concert in Tampa in two weeks. I'd like very much if you would accompany me."

Tracy had a premonition that Alec would soon ask her for a date, so she was not unprepared for his question. Her suspicions were based on Alec's attentiveness, the tone in his voice, the way he would look at her while they talked, and the increased frequency of his touch, always courteous and caring, but ever more frequent. She did nothing to discourage what she saw coming. She didn't want to. Had the same overtures come from any other man she knew, she would have been repulsed and incensed. In Alec she found a combination of qualities sorely lacking in any other male she knew outside her own father: masculinity, sensitivity, maturity, confidence, personality, intelligence, scholarship, and creativity. The comparison with her father ended at Alec's masculinity and physical features. Tracy had watched Alec workout with members of the track team on numerous occasions. Dressed only in brief running shorts and track shoes, he looked lean and powerful as he matched stride for stride with the fastest members of the team. The definition in his muscular legs, evident when he walked or ran, she found sensual and engrossing. As if these qualities weren't enough to draw her interest, she also found in Alec a man who not only shared her interest in music and theater but also was an authority on them. Behavior that would have offended her if committed by other men, she welcomed when committed by Alec. Inwardly she felt flattered by the attentions of an older man whom she admired and respected. She had already decided what her answer would be when he finally got around to asking her out. She hesitated for a moment, not wanting to respond too quickly lest he suspect that she had rehearsed her reply. What she had not yet considered were the consequences of her reply. She glanced down at her hands then back at Alec. Even though her reply took only a few seconds, it seemed like an eternity to Alec. By the time she finally answered, Alec's heart raced so fast he thought he might have a heart attack.

"Yes," came her quiet reply, "yes, I would like that very much."

"Great!" came a very loud, sharp response from Alec, causing everyone in the diner to stop talking, turn and look in their direction. Alec clasped his hand over his mouth, looked around into the dozen stares in his direction, put his head down on the table, and laughed, Tracy laughing with him.

After several abortive attempts to regain his composure he said, "Now to particulars—"

"I know," Tracy interrupted, "you want me to drive or should I plan on wearing sneakers?" she teased.

Alec burst out laughing so loud that everyone again turned and looked at him.

"No, no," he finally managed to utter, "I can borrow my sister's Plymouth. I really can drive, you know."

The waitress brought the coffee and said as she set them down, "You two certainly seem to be having such a good time." She gave Alec a disapproving glance and walked away.

Turning more serious Alec said, "Tracy, I'd like very much to take you to dinner before the concert, but this first time," he paused, "maybe it would be best to skip dinner and perhaps stop for coffee somewhere after the concert."

"That's fine. What time should I be ready?" she asked.

"The concert starts at eight. It will take almost an hour to get there...let's say six thirty, okay?"

"Okay."

Tracy finished her coffee and Alec his all the while chatting about this and that of school life and the concert's program. As they were getting up to leave, Tracy asked, "Would you like me to give you a ride home?"

"Yes, please."

Alec placed a tip on the table and paid the bill at the register near the door. They slowly walked her hand in his, to her car parked across the street from the diner. They exchanged comments and started laughing.

Later, as he prepared for bed, Alec reflected on the evening's events and realized that he still didn't conduct himself in quite the manner he envisioned before the evening began. The more he thought of it, the more he was a bit chagrined that he didn't act with any more maturity than the week before. But then, he thought, all's well that ends well and the evening ended with the accomplishment of what he sought—a date with Tracy. The main difference between this week and last is that he would not lose any sleep tonight. He threw back the covers, fell into bed, and drew up the double wedding ring quilt his sister had provided for color and warmth, rolled on his favorite side for sleeping, reached for the lamp on the stand next to his bed, and switched off the light. Ten seconds later, he turned the light back on, removed his glasses from his head, placed them on the table, and again switched off the light.

Despite his busy schedule, the following days didn't pass quickly enough to suit him. Both choirs presented their special Thanksgiving music not completely to Alec's satisfaction but well enough to elicit comments like, "Best music program ever," "Great job," and "I would have never believed our choir would sound so good." He wondered what they sounded like before.

Much to his consternation, Alec missed the homecoming parade and bonfire due to an unexpected parent-teacher conference. He did, however, manage to arrive early for the game as the band performed that night before the game rather than at halftime. The latter would be devoted exclusively to introducing the homecoming court and crowning the queen. Busy helping the band director, he was unable to spot Tracy before halftime. After the teams left the field he watched as the court walked onto the field with their escorts most of whom were stand-ins for players preparing for the second half of a game in which they trailed. The weather had again turned cool and the chill of the evening forced the court to abandon plans to wear evening gowns and substitute woolen suits. For an instant Alec didn't recognize Tracy; he looked again at each member of the court and only then did he find her.

"She's cut her hair!" he exclaimed aloud.

He didn't realize he made the statement audible until a lady standing next to him turned and looked at him quizzically and asked, "Who? Who are you talking about?"

He turned and gave the lady a blank stare until he realized what he had done, and then returning his attention to Tracy, he muttered, "Oh, just a student in my class."

Tracy's long, dark hair no longer graced her shoulders. Her shorter hair with a flip just below her ears gave her the look of Merle Oberon and maturity well beyond the rest of the girls on the court.

The jacket to her burgundy suit buttoned to the neck with only the narrow white collar of her blouse showing above the jacket collar. The shoulders were slightly padded and the sleeves tapered to where the turned-up cuffs of her blouse covered the cuffs of her jacket. Her straight skirt ended just below her knees. Her high heeled shoes, clutch purse, and the ribbon in her hair perfectly matched her suit. Alec could not detect a single object out of place. He found her incredibly beautiful.

Alec missed the longer hair but was struck with the added maturity that Tracy now radiated. There existed no doubt that she was simply the most beautiful young lady he had ever seen. He knew she had talent, intelligence, personality, and charm, but what had captivated his heart tonight was her unblemished, innocent beauty. He knew then there would never be another woman in his life. Indeed, there never was another woman in his life. He said in a low, audible whisper, "Tracy Ashbury, I love you."

*****

The evening of the concert finally arrived. Alec bought a double-breasted navy blue blazer and contrasting gray slacks especially for the occasion. He maintained his military habit of keeping a spit shine on his black patent leather shoes but gave them an extra polishing anyway. He walked to his sister's house after school to pick up her car and complained to her about the "damn Collins's dog" down the street that always scared him to death when he passed our house. She said he was stubborn for not going a little out of his way and avoiding the confrontation as she had previously suggested.

As he adjusted his tie in the dresser mirror, he retraced his mental checklist to make certain he hadn't left anything undone. It suddenly occurred to him that Tracy had never mentioned having to clear this evening's engagement with her parents. In matter of fact, she had been rather reticent about her parents. He shrugged his shoulders and thought it must be okay. When she lingered after class to confirm the time when Alec would arrive, she had not mentioned any problem, leaving him to assume she had notified her parents. It also occurred to him that he hadn't told his sister or anyone else, for that matter, that he was escorting someone to the concert. He wondered whether the omission was significant. No, he decided, no one had asked.

The drive to Tracy's house was short, but Alec left well in advance lest he get lost as the skies turned dark around six. He found her house with little difficulty. He circled the block slowly three times and would have made it a fourth but feared the neighbors would think he was a thief, or worse, a lost tourist. He pulled into the drive from a side street because the street, or what there was of it, in front of the house was narrow and unpaved. He got out of the car, took a deep breath, walked briskly to the front door, and rang the bell.

His eyes became as big as his horned rimmed glasses when the door opened a moment later. In the dim light of the lantern beside the door he saw the figure of a man with a slightly receding hairline. His remaining hair was light gray and radiated from his head like a star burst. He had a matching color mustache and big, bushy, gray eyebrows. He wore a faded blue V-neck sweater and baggy pants. Alec stood, mouth agape, as a voice said, "You must be Mr. Driver. Please come in, Tracy has told us so much about you. She admires your mastery of music."

He opened the door, stood aside for Alec to enter, extended his hand, and continued, "Tracy will be down in a minute. I'm Lloyd Ashbury, Tracy's father."

Alec clasped his hand in a firm handshake that was returned. It was either the handshake or the mention of Tracy's name that caused Alec to recover from his initial surprise, and he managed to utter, "Please, please call me Alec. I'm very pleased to meet you, Mr. Ashbury."

"Let's make a deal. You call me Lloyd and I'll call you Alec, okay?"

"It's a deal, Lloyd."

Alec wasn't quite sure, but he believed he was going to like this man no matter how eccentric he looked. Still recovering from the shock of Lloyd's appearance, Alec did a double take when a becoming and sophisticated-looking woman who appeared no older than he entered the room.

"Dear," Lloyd began, "this is Alec Driver. Alec, I'd like you to meet my wife, Nancy."

Alec barely listened to Lloyd's introduction. Instead, Nancy consumed his full attention. She wore a tailored skirt and blouse with heels, hose, and meticulously and tastefully applied makeup.

Her short, dark hair, contrary to Lloyd's disheveled appearance, was perfectly arranged with not a strand out of place. The resemblance between mother and daughter was remarkable. Alec, who looked a great deal like his own father, expected Tracy to resemble her mother, but a replica he never expected. Only a time warp separated mother's appearance from daughter's. Tracy may have inherited her father's mind, he thought, but she definitely inherited her mother's looks.

Nancy and Alec exchanged pleasantries, with Alec again insisting that Nancy call him by his first name. Nancy, however, did not return the request. They invited him into the living room to sit while he waited for Tracy. Alec sat in the armchair while Nancy sat on the sofa with Lloyd choosing to sit on the sofa's arm next to her. Not wishing to stare at Nancy, Alec mentioned that their house reminded him of many similar ones built along the New England shore. There was a definite nautical flavor about the house. Despite circling the house three times, he had failed to notice its proximity to the water until he glanced out the large picture window behind Nancy onto a moonlit expanse of Clearwater Bay. The sun had set almost an hour earlier and the moon in full glow cast its soft radiance on the ripples of the bay waters that danced gracefully into the Ashbury living room.

"What a magnificent view and a lovely home you have, Mrs. Ashbury," he remarked with genuine sincerity.

"Thank you," she replied adding, "but we can't take credit for the house. It was built by an industrialist from New England at the turn of the century as a winter residence. It's rather astute of you to recognize its style." Nancy sat with hands folded primly in her lap.

Determined to return her compliment Alec added, "Well you've certainly kept it in excellent condition. It doesn't appear a fraction of its age. I love two-story houses. I wish more homes in Florida had a second story."

"Actually," Lloyd broke in, "it has three stories, Nancy has placed my study in the third-story garret either to keep my mess out of sight or to discourage me from using it too often, or perhaps both!"

"Lloyd is a scientist, Mr. Driver, and whereas his thoughts are highly organized, I'm afraid his desk and papers are not."

"A neat desk is just a sign that you have nothing better to do," Lloyd shot back jokingly.

Alec fidgeted a bit in his chair thinking of how neat he always kept his workspace and not knowing quite how to respond to these comments. Saved by the appearance of Tracy at the foot of the staircase, he rose as she walked into the room wearing a tailored long sleeve white blouse with a contrasting maroon straight skirt and matching shoes. She carried a jacket over her arm and a purse in her other hand; each matched her skirt as did the ribbon in her hair that Alec now realized was her trademark. For a brief moment, mother and daughter stood next to each other, each a generational replica of the other.

Despite their resemblance, it was the younger that made the adrenaline flow in Alec's veins. Unlike his introduction to Lloyd, Alec detected a cold aloofness about Nancy that decried her physical attractiveness. For some inexplicable reason, she seemed determined to establish an arm's length relationship between them. The feeling was barely noticeable at the time but later, in retrospect, it proved to be prophetic.

Not wishing to appear enamored before her parents, Alec remarked in an as innocuous manner as he could manage. "How nice you look, Tracy," he said, trying unsuccessfully to suppress a broad smile and a facial expression registering sheer delight.

"Thank you," she politely responded, adding, "I love your blazer." She almost added, "Isn't it new?" but thought that might appear ungracious.

Glancing at his watch, Alec stated, "Well, we better be going."

"Yes," Nancy interjected, "the others are probably waiting."

"Others?" Alec queried.

"The other students that are going with you," Nancy answered with a note of surprise in her voice that he should ask.

"Mother, Mr. Driver has just asked me to accompany him to the concert, there are no others."

"Why, Tracy…" she paused, "when you said Mr. Driver was taking you, I just assumed that it was with a group of students, not alone." Her voice became sharper as she spoke.

"Mrs. Ashbury, may I explain," Alec offered. "I did announce to all my classes the time and place of tonight's concert and encouraged all who could to attend. Knowing Tracy's love for music and her talent, I asked if she would be my guest. I'm very pleased that she accepted."

"I do not question the value of the concert, Mr. Driver, I only question the propriety of a high school teacher…dating one of his students, no matter how innocent the occasion." Nancy nervously pressed out the wrinkles in her skirt as she spoke.

"Mr. Driver, I'm sorry," Tracy interjected. Turning to her mother she said quietly but deliberately, "Mother, I told you and Daddy who I was going with and where I was going almost two weeks ago, you are embarrassing me!"

"Please, Tracy, don't feel embarrassed on my account," Alec said reassuringly. "I want your mother to feel comfortable about tonight."

"That's the problem, Mr. Driver, I am not comfortable. I am distressed that a man of your age and position would…" Not knowing exactly how to say what she felt needed to be said, Nancy sought help. "Lloyd, don't you have something to say?"

Lloyd Ashbury quietly took in the entire discourse, watching, listening, and thinking about the situation at hand. He watched Nancy's eyes and could see the wheels turning in her head. In contrast, the looks on Tracy and Alec's faces were anxious and fearful.

"Let's see," he began, "what do we have here? We have two nicely dressed, groomed, and anxious people who have planned to attend together a concert by a nationally renowned musical group. We also have, on the other hand, a mother concerned for the reputation of her daughter. In addition, we have a teacher who has a reputation of his own to protect." Pausing a moment to reflect on these statements as he would any scientific problem, he repeatedly ran his hand down his jaw and tugged gently at his chin. Having reached a conclusion, he continued, "I think we should allow them to leave before it is too late and request that Alec return Tracy home at an hour that neither risks daughter's reputation nor mother's wrath. Shall we say midnight with the stipulation that if she is thirty minutes late no one will be unduly concerned?"

"Thank you, Daddy." Tracy kissed Lloyd somewhere midst the disheveled gray hair.

Alec shook his hand and reassured Lloyd he would comply with his request. He said good night to both parents as he assisted Tracy with her jacket. All the while Nancy remained silent, eyes darting back and forth between Alec and Tracy, seemingly resigned but unconvinced. No one believed for an instant that the subject was closed.

The drive across Courtney Campbell Causeway that connects both sides of Tampa Bay is restful and is surrounded by small white caps. Due to the high phosphorous content of the water the caps often glow in the moonlight of a cool crisp early December evening. The cloudless sky that night displayed countless stars, their clusters and configurations distinct and brilliant. Had the moon been anything less than full many more would have been able to reveal their heavenly presence.

The night was right for romance, but reassurance was what Alec offered Tracy. He told her that her mother's comments and concerns were appropriate and didn't disturb him other than to double his efforts to gain her confidence, for if they were ever to see each other again her mother's anxieties would have to be addressed. Tracy agreed, then asked, "Are we going to see each other again?"

This young lady certainly has a way of getting right to the heart of an issue, Alec thought.

"Tracy," he began, "it has to be obvious to you how I feel. Tonight isn't just another teacher taking a pupil on a school field trip, as your mother so clearly saw. As far as I'm concerned I want very much to see you again but will only do so if I'm convinced that is also what you want. I understand your mother's concern. Among other things, she doesn't want you placed in the awkward position of having to fend off the unwanted attentions of an older man, especially when that man is also one of your teachers. Whatever your mother thinks of me, the last thing I want is your attentions because of any pressure or obligation you may feel however slight."

"I don't do anything I don't want to," she replied, dividing her attention between Alec and the moonlit bay waters.

They drove for several minutes in silence each lost in their own thoughts about what had transpired and what would become of the remainder of the evening.

Tracy had been deliberately vague when she told her parents about the concert. She did not say specifically that she and Alec would be going alone, or for that matter that they were not. She never once used the word *date*. She hoped to get through the evening without the subject coming up. She fully intended to tell her parents but only after the fact when she was sure that the outcome of the evening would dampen any fears or reservations they might express beforehand. She felt uncomfortable about being vague with her parents, for the three of them had always discussed their concerns openly and frankly. Tracy didn't fear so much that her parents would prohibit her from going with Alec only that they would question her judgment. She felt she would not be prepared to answer their challenges completely until after her first real date. Inwardly she knew her own reservations wouldn't be answered until such time. She could only address her parents' concerns once all of hers were answered.

Alec decided to change the subject, at least for the time being, but he fully intended to discuss it further with her at a more appropriate time. *After all*, he thought, *this is our first date and come tomorrow she may decide not to see me again.* Any further discussion at this time, he concluded, would be premature.

The rest of the evening went according to schedule with subjects of conversation turning to lighter and more casual topics. At intermission they were encircled by a contingent of Tracy's choir mates who had seen them from the students' balcony seats.

They chatted about the program and how glad they were they came. Alec found something disturbing about the manner in which they said how glad they were. He noticed the knowing glances that were exchanged among the girls and felt uncomfortable by what was obviously adolescent titter.

On the return trip after the concert, they stopped briefly for a late dessert. They didn't linger long, for Alec was determined to meet the twelve o'clock deadline and not encroach upon the half hour grace period set by Lloyd Ashbury. Unless, Alec felt, he had Lloyd's confidence he could forget any future engagements with Tracy no matter how she might feel. Nancy made it clear that if it were up to her, there wouldn't have been any contact that evening.

They arrived back at Tracy's house exactly at the Cinderella hour. Alec escorted her to the door, stopped, clasped her hands in his, and said, "I can't tell you how much I enjoyed being with you tonight. I'm sorry for any misunderstanding I may have caused between you and your parents. I know the three of you are very close, and I want to do nothing to alter that relationship."

"Thank you for asking me, I had a lovely time. I want to confess that I didn't know how I would feel with you as my…well, date and accepted partly to find out, I feel very good about it. Don't worry about my parents. Our family is very close, we'll be able to survive this test, especially now that I know how I feel."

He wanted to lean over and kiss her immediately, but resisted the temptation hoping there would be other opportunities later. Instead, Tracy rose to her toes and kissed Alec on the mouth. Startled, Alec instinctively grabbed her by the arms and returned her kiss.

"Good night," he whispered.

Tracy responded, "Thank you for asking me," she said as she entered the house and closed the door.

*****

The sound of the telephone ringing brought Alec out of a deep sleep. The morning sun flooded the bedroom through the two easterly windows whose draperies he had not bothered drawing before retiring. *What time is it?* he thought as it rang again. He grabbed his glasses off the nightstand, placed them on his head in a cockeyed position, and looked across the room at his alarm clock that he had failed to set. It was almost eleven. *Wow*, he thought, *I haven't slept this late since high school.* The telephone rang again. He bounced out of bed, rambled into the kitchen where the instrument sat on the counter, and picked up the receiver just as it rang again.

"Hello," he managed to say, trying to sound like he had been up for hours.

It was Tracy. She asked if he could come to dinner Sunday evening at her home. He responded, "Sure, but wait. What about your parents?" sounding a bit confused.

"They suggested I ask you," she replied. "We have dinner at six."

"I'll be there," he replied assertively.

She said she was late for her piano lesson and would see him in the morning at church.

"Yes, okay," he said and quickly added, "and thank you."

As he replaced the receiver he sensed there was more to the invitation than just dinner. Exactly what, he wasn't sure. He felt certain he would soon find out.

Chapter 5

Tracy awakened extraordinarily early for a Saturday morning. Awake a full hour before her alarm sounded, she lay in bed pondering the events of the prior evening. She wasn't sorry for being vague to her parents before her date with Alec. Even in hindsight she believed she made the right decision. Postponing the inevitable confrontation until she felt certain of her own feelings only made sense, she thought. Upon reflection, the confrontation with her parents the evening before ended quickly and with the desired result. So far things were going her way, a momentum she wanted to sustain. Determined to confront her parents for the first time in her life, if the situation came to that and she knew that it would, she resolved to use all the decisiveness and conviction that she could muster. There existed no doubt in her mind that after she and Alec left for the concert the night before, her parents spent the evening discussing Alec's intentions and her likely response. They undoubtedly arrived at a common position that would prove contrary to her own. Primed and ready to do battle, she bounced out of bed, threw her robe on over her T-shirt in which she preferred sleeping, and marched without hesitation downstairs to the kitchen where she knew her mother would be.

As Tracy entered the kitchen, Nancy glanced up from her scouring the iron skillet she inherited from some distant aunt, smiled, and said, "Good morning, dear."

"Good morning, Mother. Where's Daddy?"

"I believe he's in the garage tinkering with something, the lawn mower, I believe. Did you have a pleasant evening?"

"Yes, I did. The Chorale performed wonderfully. Ruth Ann and a bunch of the girls were there also." She guessed that her mother was being coy about the subject of Alec, so she decided to take matters into her own hands and force the issue. She added, "I think they were surprised to see that I came with Mr. Driver." That should do it, she thought.

"Probably not half as surprised as I was," Nancy retorted, casting another quick glance at Tracy.

"Mother, I've decided that if Mr. Driver asks me out again I'll say yes and if you and Daddy feel I should do any different I would like to know now so that we can discuss it and avoid any future embarrassment like last night," she stated, almost running out of breath.

To this point in the conversation, mother and daughter spoke with each avoiding eye contact with the other. Nancy concentrated on cleaning kitchen implements and Tracy on some imaginary object outside the kitchen window. After returning the skillet to its place in one of the many solid oak cabinets that lined the kitchen walls and wiping the dampness from her hands with her apron, Nancy ended the visual evasiveness. She looked straight at Tracy and responded, "Your father and I did discuss the situation last night at length after you left. We're most curious to learn what it is about Mr. Driver that attracts you to him. I, that is, we still feel that it's most improper for a man of his position and his age to seek your…your attentions. If it were not for your apparent recognition of his interest in you and your willingness to permit him to pursue those interests, we would absolutely forbid any future contact outside of class."

During Nancy's discourse, Lloyd entered the kitchen through the back door that led to the detached garage. Tracy said good morning to her father and wasn't sure exactly what her mother said, but she got the impression that her parents weren't going to come down hard and absolutely forbid her to see Alec again.

"Lloyd, I'm glad you came in. Tracy's about to say what she finds so attractive in Mr. Driver, aren't you, Tracy?"

"I don't know that I'm particularly attracted to—" she hesitated, not knowing how to refer to Alec when her father interjected, "Alec. Go ahead and say it. If you ever intend to see him again, you're going to have to get used to saying his name. It would sound a little silly to keep calling your date Mister, wouldn't it?"

"Yes, it would," she answered while buttering the whole wheat toast she fixed. She continued, "While I think that he's rather good-looking and very athletic, I'm not sure that it's his looks that I find the most appealing, at least not yet. He's different from anyone else I've ever met, aside from Daddy, in an intriguing sort of way. Yes, that's it. I've never met anyone quite like him. He's so much more mature than all the guys I know that they seem pale by comparison, but he can also let down, relax, and be a real cutup."

"But, Tracy," her mother broke in as she placed a large bowl of mixed citrus and other fruits in the center of the kitchen table, "the man is more my age than yours. I almost feel that he should be calling on me, not my daughter."

"Now that would be something to see," Lloyd chuckled. "Miss Priss and Mr. Man-About-Town, what a combination."

Nancy cast Lloyd a cold, disapproving stare but said nothing in return.

"Mother, at this stage I don't know his age and don't care. I'm not in love with the man. I admire his approach to life, his love of the arts, his intellect, his mastery of music, and his steadfast willingness to say exactly what he thinks."

"But, dear, it sounds like you are describing your father," her mother commented.

"I bet that's the part your mother objects to the most," Lloyd teased.

"Lloyd, please be more serious. We're talking about Tracy's interest in Alec…ah, Mr. Driver," Nancy pleaded as she sat down at the table. At this slip, Lloyd and Tracy looked at each other. Lloyd winked and Tracy smiled. Tracy, seeking to reassure her mother, said, "Alec and I may not want to see each other that much anyway. All I ask is your approval when and if he asks and I agree to see him again. The main purpose is to see if we have enough in common to continue dating. At least at this point, it's nothing more serious than that."

"Speak only for yourself. At this point, you can't be certain what his intentions are," Nancy cautioned as she served herself a portion of the fruit she had prepared. Continuing her lecture on romantic etiquette she said, "Despite what false reservations you may think I have, you must realize ours is a small community where most find it improper for a young lady to be courted by a man much older than she and who just happens to be one of her teachers. The three of us can sit down and discuss what we think and arrive at a mutually agreeable decision, but the entire community cannot. I wouldn't be surprised if the school board didn't have some policy that prevented such relationships, as the two of you appear to want to establish. And if they don't, they certainly should!" Nancy quickly added.

"Mother, we don't have much of any relationship yet. I don't even know if Alec feels the same today as he did last night," Tracy rebutted.

"We can't just sit and wait to see what happens. By then it may be too late to do anything about it. I can just imagine what people will think," Nancy implored.

"Is what other people think really that important?" Tracy pleaded.

"Yes, because it happens to be what we think also," Nancy retorted. "Neither they nor we want to see you get hurt. Besides, we have to live in this town," adding parenthetically, "and I'll be damned if any Johnny-come-lately is going to make me afraid to walk down the street for fear of what some people might think or say."

Lowering her voice, Nancy added, "Many of these people are our friends and would want to protect you from what they may perceive as a potentially dangerous situation. It's not that they would be malicious, only protective."

"Also remember, Tracy," Lloyd offered, "you're just seventeen. Ethics aside, the law says you're a minor and will remain so until you're twenty-one. Two adults can go places and do things together and no one will object. A minor going the same places and doing the same things with an adult of the opposite sex can lead many to wonder. There're more people involved than just you and Alec, as your mother said, the school board may not want to be placed in the position of sanctioning social meetings between a student and a teacher of the opposite sex for no other reason than the precedent that it may set."

"Is the only answer to simply forbid all meetings for fear what may happen in a few cases?" Tracy asked, hoping she knew the answer her father would return.

"No, it isn't the only answer. What you don't seem to realize is that once last night's events and any future repeats get around, and believe me they will, your mother and I will have to fend off all manner of questions and critical comments, something we don't relish doing. I don't worry for myself, I can handle it. It's your mother that concerns me. She doesn't like being put on the defensive."

"Daddy, I guess I didn't consider what I would be putting you and Mother through. I knew that I'd have to do some explaining to my friends, but I can handle that. It just didn't seem that it would be anyone else's business or that they would really care."

"That's what concerns me the most, you should have. Even at seventeen, you should have been aware of the repercussions that could come as a result of your seeing Alec. But that's water under the bridge. What we have to consider now is what we're going to do about the future. The alternatives, however, cannot be decided just by three of us."

"Why don't I invite Alec over for dinner next Sunday?" Tracy chimed in.

"I think he belongs somewhere in this conversation," Lloyd responded.

"That would be tantamount to sanctioning their courtship," Nancy countered.

"After the discourse last night and a week to think about it, the invitation may worry him a little," countered Lloyd. "Besides, as I see it we have three options: absolutely forbid any social contact outside of class, ignore the situation and hope it goes away, or address it head on."

"Putting it that way I suppose we have little alternative," Nancy signed.

Without any hesitation, Tracy answered, "I'm going to call Alec."

*****

The following week with Tracy in school, Nancy wandered into Lloyd's study garret on the third floor of their house. Lloyd, busy at his drafting table on the latest of his inventions, hardly looked up when Nancy entered the room. He had been expecting her visit now that Tracy had left for school.

"Lloyd," she began, "I'm not comfortable with our 'decision' to invite Alec to dinner. It signals an approval that I'm not willing to give."

"It never hurts to discuss a problem," Lloyd answered without looking up from his drawing.

"I don't know any other parents in this town that would even be having this discussion," Nancy quickly interjected.

"But then we're not like any other parents in this town," Lloyd rebutted as he continued his drawing.

"Lloyd, I can't believe you are so dispassionate about your own daughter."

"You know full well that I have Tracy's best interest at heart," Lloyd responded, looking up at Nancy for the first time.

"All I see is Tracy's welfare put in jeopardy if we allow this... this—"

"This what? Are you concerned for her virtue?"

"No, I'm concerned about propriety and the message we are sending. Between us and the people in this community, Tracy has developed a sound moral character. I do not worry about her actions, it's that man's that concern me. I don't trust him."

"Look, Alec has reputation of his own to protect. If he steps too far out of line, he'll never work in this state again. With family, Tracy, and career here, I don't think he wants that. He knows that to continue to see Tracy he has to stay on our good side." Lloyd had stopped drawing during this discourse.

"I just want to tell him to *get lost*!"

"That attitude may very well create unacceptable risk," Lloyd suggested.

"I'm not following you."

"Remember the elder Collins forbade their youngest son to see the Douglas girl, and what happened? They ran off to Georgia and got married and didn't tell anyone until after they graduated from high school. Don't you see that if you try to prohibit youngsters from something they really want to do, they end up sneaking around and doing it anyway?" Lloyd resumed his drawing.

"Does that mean that we just throw caution to the wind?"

"Of course not, we make them adhere to a strict set of rules. If they break those rules, then we come down hard. Knowing that, I believe they will bend over backward to abide by the conditions we set."

"And you think that is less risky?" Nancy countered, sounding not yet convinced.

"If I know Tracy, she will insist the rules be honored to the letter. If Alec thinks otherwise, then I believe she will take care of the problem on her own. That's the best deterrent of all. Besides, what's not to trust? He certainly has been above board. He didn't shy away from showing up on our doorstep and denied nothing. The fact is that I kinda like the guy. You can't beat his credentials...and don't forget that I'm almost eleven years older than you."

"That's different!" Nancy huffed as she left the room.

*****

On the next Sunday evening, Alec approached the Ashbury home with some trepidation, uncertain how Lloyd and Nancy would receive him and, most importantly, the stance they would take regarding any future contacts he may have with Tracy. Without some sanction by her parents, any relationship with Tracy would be impossible, at least in the foreseeable future. Tracy met him at the door, all smiles, and ushered him into the library that housed an impressive collection of books along with a grand piano, a large oak secretary, and matching glass-covered bookcases filled with the family's finer volumes. He sat down at one end of the English sofa with Tracy seating herself at a close but discreet distance from him. Alec began the conversation by relating his uncertainty as to appropriate dress for the evening. He told her that he finally settled on compromise attire—one that he developed a habit of wearing in Florida—a sports coat, dress slacks, and a polo shirt buttoned to the collar. Trying to make him feel comfortable, Tracy remarked that the way her father usually dressed Alec could have worn anything and felt right at home.

Nancy entered the room a few minutes after Alec arrived to announce that dinner would be ready when Lloyd finished smoking the mullet. Alec soon discovered that mullet was a native fish that required a net to catch because it fed only on plant life. Local fishermen would drag nets behind their boats forming a large circle around a school of mullet clearly visible by the ripples it formed on the water's surface. This method usually required two men, a long length of weighted net, a flat-bottomed boat, and small motor. A less efficient method would have a single fisherman wading into waist-deep water to cast a circular net eight to ten feet in diameter. If the fishermen were lucky, they would not only land the desired mullet but an occasional fish of a different species or perhaps a crab or two. The latter enjoyed a poor reputation among fishermen for the damage they did to the nets that required laborious mending by hand.

Nancy excused herself to return to the kitchen to finish the remainder of the evening's dinner. Within minutes Lloyd entered amid the strong odor of smoked mullet emanating from the large iron skillet he carried in a gloved hand and pronounced his part of the evening meal ready.

Alec smiled to himself at seeing Lloyd. Whereas Nancy had dressed impeccably with not so much as a single hair out of place, makeup done to perfection, wearing a tailored blouse and straight woolen skirt with hose and heels, Lloyd wore a faded pair of denims, a dress shirt frayed at the collar, a wool sweater pushed up to his elbows, and a well-worn pair of sneakers. Just seeing Lloyd made Alec feel more comfortable.

Alec was pleased with how smoothly the evening seemed to be progressing. Nancy suggested that he sit across from Tracy while she and Lloyd would sit at opposite ends of a rather large wooden early American dining table. Things were going too well, it must be the calm before the storm, he thought. Had Alec lived in Florida longer, he would have learned that the calm came in the middle not before the storm. After a blessing delivered by Lloyd, he noticed a thick, white substance making the rounds along with the mullet, green beans, and dinner rolls. At first he thought it was mashed potatoes and thought it an unusual vegetable to serve with smoked fish. As the dish reached him he realized it was not mashed potatoes. Not wanting to be too venturesome nor offend his hosts, he politely served himself a small portion.

"Oh, do have more grits, Alec," Lloyd urged.

Grits! Alec thought. He recalled his mother's warning about the southern corn dish when she learned he was moving south. She suggested he try it at a restaurant first lest he offend some hostess should he wait to try it in her presence. *Surely*, he thought, *this is a torture test administered by a disapproving mother—she intends to poison me.*

"Oh, this is plenty for me, Lloyd, I'm not a very hearty eater," offered Alec.

"The trick, Mr. Driver, is to eat grits with plenty of butter while they're still very hot. They complement most grilled or fried fish," explained Nancy.

It was Tracy who came to his rescue.

"Mother, Alec is from New Jersey and probably has never tasted grits or even mullet before, I think we should let him just sample them tonight."

I'm getting to like this young lady more and more, Alec thought.

"This is a bit of an adventure for me," Alec uttered as he tried his first mouthful of the butter, grits, and mullet combination.

"Not bad," he managed to mutter as he swallowed hard, reached for his glass of water, and thought, *Ugh, dear Lord, please help me survive this meal.*

Survive he did in heroic fashion, having finished the portion he served himself along with the rest of the meal. He welcomed the dessert of orange sherbet although he half expected pecan pie.

As they finished the sherbet, Nancy asked Tracy to begin clearing the table. Alec offered to help, but Nancy stated that she and Lloyd would like to talk with him. Lloyd suggested they retire to the living room. As they got up and followed Lloyd, Alec thought, this is it, the living room must be the grilling room, recalling his encounter with Nancy two nights earlier.

Nancy and Lloyd sat next to each other on the sofa after insisting Alec sit in the more comfortable easy chair with ottoman. *Where are the straps?* he thought, giving the chair arms a quick glance.

"As you may have surmised, Mr. Driver, we had an ulterior motive for inviting you to dinner tonight," Nancy began with Alec giving an affirmative nod. "We wish to discuss with you the...the situation with Tracy, you and Tracy that is, without the pressure of an impending engage...ah, appointment," she corrected.

It was unlike Nancy to stumble or search for words. Resolute and principled, she rarely hesitated in saying what she meant. She possessed a confidence lacking in some women totally dependent upon their husbands for support. Undoubtedly she had the capability of providing for herself if she chose, for she never failed to accomplish any task she assumed. Nancy enjoyed the comfort of being born, raised, and married without the necessity of having to leave her native community. She met Lloyd twenty years earlier following her own graduation from high school at age eighteen. Lloyd, already an accomplished inventor and patent holder at age twenty-eight, was spending a summer assisting the local phosphorus processor install equipment he had designed. He met Nancy at a church social his host insisted he attend. He spent a long, hot summer at Nancy's doorstep. His usual work regimen of ten- or twelve-hour days reduced to the mandatory eight by their strong desire to spend as much time together as possible. Her father often chased Lloyd out of their house after midnight. At summer's end, Lloyd accepted his host's offer to stay with his firm and design equipment and processing phosphate ore. His decision was heavily biased by his desire to marry Nancy and her desire to remain in Florida.

Nancy, a product of a strong, close family, proved a perfect complement to Lloyd. She either inherited or acquired a keen sense of awareness of events and people from her father, a successful banker whose grandparents emigrated from Sicily. Raised in the Presbyterian tradition of her Scottish mother, Nancy adopted a dedicated sense of morality and charity. Like a banker, she learned to judge people by their character as much as their pocketbook, by what they did rather than what they said. Lloyd trusted everybody. Details were something Lloyd reserved for his inventions. When it came to people and relations, details of a person's life or business were less important than the goodwill of a handshake or a friendly pat on the back. Nancy guided Lloyd through the social graces of church, community, and family. She relied heavily on Lloyd's reason in those instances where she felt she either lacked the knowledge or experience to judge adequately the consequences of her decisions. Lloyd felt comfortable with Nancy handling his nonprofessional affairs, for he knew that she would respect his counsel when he chose to offer it just as she had two nights earlier.

Nancy's speech was halting, not because she lacked the resoluteness to confront a stranger among their midst, but because she realized she was not confronting a stranger, she was confronting her daughter. The experience was novel; her speech betrayed her uncertainty and discomfort as well as the resentment she felt toward Alec for placing her in that position. The only reason she did not scream for Alec to get out of her house and out of her life was Tracy and, of course, Lloyd. She simply feared that sending Alec away would create a schism between parents and daughter. Physical separation did not worry her. It was an emotional separation that bothered her most. Then, in a moralistic sense of fair play, she felt obligated to give Alec sufficient rope with which to hang himself. Why, she thought, should she take the responsibility totally upon herself when circumstance and Alec's own behavior could do it? Lloyd and Tracy seemed determined to give Alec a chance despite what seemed to her overwhelming reasons why they shouldn't. Nancy reluctantly decided to take the path of least resistance, something she knew Lloyd appreciated.

"I understand and want to thank you and Lloyd for caring enough to invite me and provide an opportunity to talk with you," Alec offered.

"It's Tracy's best interests that concern us," Nancy quickly replied, "but before we go too far I believe it best to make certain that Lloyd and I are not being too presumptuous. For that reason, we wanted to speak with you out of Tracy's presence, at least for a while. She has informed us that you expressed an interest in seeing her again socially."

"With your permission, of course," Alec responded.

To this point in the discussion, both Nancy and Alec spoke in relaxed but deliberate tones. Lloyd always seemed relaxed. He sat next to Nancy with one arm extended around Nancy's shoulders resting on top of the back cushion. His other arm rested on one of the sofa's arms. Nancy was the first to lean forward and pick up the pace of the conversion.

"Surely, Mr. Driver, you must know how we feel about this situation. This is not New Jersey or even Rhode Island. This community is quite close in many respects, and the people frown very seriously at older, authority figures trying to take advantage of young people particularly of the opposite sex. Admittedly, Tracy is very mature for her age, but nonetheless she's still a child and you are, after all, old enough to be her father!" Nancy exclaimed almost out of breath.

"Yes, Mrs. Ashbury, perhaps I am, but there is one very important difference," Alec countered as he too leaned forward in his chair.

"And what might that be?" she asked, sounding miffed.

Looking her straight in the eye, Alec answered with all the sincere determination he could muster, "I am not her father."

Nancy huffed and fell back against the sofa.

Lloyd broke the icy silence with a deep prolonged chuckle. He turned to his wife and said, "You asked for that one, Nancy." Turning his attention back to Alec, he continued, "Without prolonging this ordeal too long, Alec, Nancy and I have agreed not to forbid you to see Tracy provided that you agree to do so within certain parameters."

"I'm willing to consider your wishes, of course," Alec pledged. Alec returned to his more relaxed position in the armchair. Lloyd had captured his complete attention.

Having regained her composure, Nancy began offering their terms and conditions, "We feel quite strongly that your meetings, outside of choir, with Tracy should be limited to no more than once per week, that they not unduly interfere with dates she may have with boys her own age, that extreme caution be exercised in where you take her, that she maintain the same curfew as with her other dates, that you refrain from any undue attentions at school, and that you respect Tracy's wishes when she chooses to terminate your social contacts."

Alec was more than willing, for the time being at least, to abide by their wishes—so relieved he was not to be prohibited from seeing her again. He feared Nancy would have forbidden any future contact and surmised that Lloyd's influence had been important in changing her position.

Lloyd must have sensed the bewilderment in Alec's mind and offered an explanation. "Nancy was dead set against Tracy ever seeing you again," he began. "Upon reflection, however, she and I realized that both you and Tracy seemed determined to see each other. We decided to allow a limited amount of dating for two reasons: first, we have never been placed in a position and would, therefore, feel uncomfortable having to forbid Tracy from doing anything she was intent on doing; second, we would rather the two of you see each other openly on a limited basis than be forced into clandestine rendezvous. The only thing we ask in return is your word that the terms we have outlined are honored in spirit as well as letter."

"You have it," Alec replied, extending his hand to Lloyd. Turning to Nancy, he continued, "I won't do anything to make you regret this decision, Mrs. Ashbury."

"I want to believe that, Mr. Driver," she replied.

Tracy came in the room from the kitchen wondering aloud if the conversation had reached a point where she could join it. Her mother advised her that they had just finished discussing with Alec the same topics they discussed with her earlier over the past two days. Alec told Tracy that he agreed to her parents' terms and conditions should Tracy decide to see him again.

The remainder of the evening found Tracy and Alec retiring to the family room where she played her recent piano recital piece, Rachmaninoff's "Concerto No. 2," after which Alec joined her at the piano where they broke into a series of the season's carols.

Nancy and Lloyd retreated to the kitchen to finish the cleaning Tracy started. Against the backdrop of music from the nearby family room, Nancy confessed to Lloyd, "Lloyd, I'm not at all certain that we've made the right decision, but I feel that it was the only one we could make under the circumstances. I have a feeling that even though we have settled the matter, at least temporarily amongst ourselves, we haven't heard the last of it."

"You may be right. We'll just have to face each situation as it develops. Let's not worry about it anymore this evening."

Bidding Alec good night in advance, they finished their tasks and retired to their bedroom on the second floor. Alec again thanked them for their understanding and pledged his commitment to honor their wishes.

Alec left the Ashbury's home that evening with mixed feelings: excited that an agreement had been reached with Nancy and Lloyd but acutely aware of their lingering misgivings that, he hoped, would soon dissipate as he gained their trust. It was Tracy's attitude that bothered him the most—not because she exhibited any change of heart but because she had displayed little emotion all evening. It was obvious to him that the battle for her heart had only begun.

One step at a time, he thought, *one step at a time*. After less than four months he had met the most beautiful and charming girl he had ever seen, attracted her attention and hopefully her interest, and, under very unusual circumstances, won limited visiting privileges from her parents. *Now*, he thought, *all my energies can be devoted to the goals of earning her respect, admiration, and, most of all, her love. No easy task for an ordinary man twenty years her senior but then*, he thought, *I'm no ordinary man.*

His thoughts were broken as he entered the drive to his sister's house. She had given him a set of keys, so there was no need to bother her tonight. From all appearances, the whole family had already gone to bed as the hour was late. He parked her car in the drive, locked it, and started the two-mile walk back to his apartment that, as usual, took him past our house and, of course, Laddie. He braced himself for the expected charge as he neared our house not a block from his sister's. Any minute now, if only it wasn't so dark, he thought. With teeth and fists clenched, he quickened his pace as he approached our house. Step after step he took and still no sound until finally he realized he was beyond our yard. "Huh?" he grunted aloud, the dog must have wandered off—what a stroke of luck. *I wonder where he went,* he thought.

Chapter 6

O n the first day of school that fall, I immediately realized that the funny-looking stranger with short pants who evinced so much fear of Laddie was, just as Pop said, my music teacher. It took a while for Alec to place Laddie with me and me with my father. Even after Alec put the three of us together, he still treated me with the same impartiality (some might characterize Alec's attitude to most students as complete indifference—I was too young to appreciate the difference) he exhibited to every other student in our junior high choir. This treatment surprised me, as much as any thirteen-year old would be, for I knew the rapport that existed between Alec and Pop. That rapport obviously didn't extend to me.

Choir proved to be an easy early morning adjustment to school, for it demanded little mental acuity—meaning I felt that I didn't have to pay too close attention. Such was not the case for many of my friends who had greater difficulty than I mastering the musical symbols, terms, and concepts that I already knew as a result of two horrible years playing the clarinet. I also had little difficulty reading music or matching voice to notes despite never fully understanding why music contained different keys—a note was a note, I thought. My awareness of musical concepts had never been astute. It's still too embarrassing to admit the age when I finally realized the words to the church hymns run from bar to bar and not consecutively down the page like a text.

I also never understood why Alec spent so much time on what he called fundamentals: stretching, posture, breathing, vocal scales every day for twenty minutes. Nor did I understand why it was necessary to learn unfamiliar songs like "Kentucky Babe" when I would have much preferred Frankie Lane's latest hits, "Do Not Forsake Me" and "I Believe." In a word, I quickly became bored with choir, and Alec's breaks from his normal serious approach to teaching music didn't help. At first, I welcomed the diversion provided by slides of his many walking tours of the world. After several sessions of slide lectures of one country after another and the numerous souvenirs that Alec passed around, I recognized the similarity between these sessions and the travelogues that I utterly despised, shown between double features at the movie theaters. I often wondered how it was that a man who purportedly walked everywhere could manage to carry so many rolls of film, cameras, and souvenirs.

As the Christmas season approached that year, I groaned when Alec announced his plans to travel to Mexico over the Christmas break. I could see the days spent viewing the latest round of slides, souvenirs, and anecdotes that Alec would so proudly and willingly share after the New Year. My boredom was communicable, for it wasn't long before some of my friends, perhaps taking their cue from me, exhibited the same symptoms. To relieve the tedium of class and rehearsals we improvised new words, in typical adolescent style, to the Christmas songs we rehearsed. For example, the second verse of "We Wish You a Merry Christmas" where the words are, "Now bring us some figgy pudding, now brings us some figgy pudding," we substituted a cruder version which went, "Now bring us some shitty pudding, now bring us some..." The third verse then took on a special meaning when we sang with increased gusto, "We won't go until we get it, we won't go until we get it." Alec never caught on to the lyric change, but did, as the words were sung, exhibit a noticeable frown and cast quick glances around the choir to determine the source of something that seemed to be amiss, never quite sure what it was or from whence it came. We felt quite pleased with ourselves.

Choir proved not a complete waste of time, for I enjoyed singing and music held a preeminent place in our house. I learned vocal tricks such as taking a breath whenever needed rather than at the end of a line or lyrical pause when everyone else would take a breath. This ploy, if practiced by many others, avoided an audible gasp by the entire choir. Breath control became a challenge, for try as I might I consistently ran out of breath sooner than most other tenors. My parents sent me to our family doctor, who like my father migrated from east Tennessee, to determine if any medical problems were the source of the breathlessness. Medical history stored in the mind of the only physician I ever knew together with recent X-rays found the problem's source. Viral pneumonia at age six that confined me to bed for three months had left a scar across my left lung. Only later did I learn that antibiotics were ineffective against viruses. Wartime restrictions ruled out penicillin, the first and only antibiotic, as a treatment. My WWII pilot turned Sunday school teacher later told our captive audience that vials of penicillin were so plentiful in the military that they were often used as mouthwash. Civilians during the meantime had to do without. The scar on my lung permitted someone else to have better breath.

I also learned to sing with my mouth as wide open as sound and jaw permitted thus helping to form as large a cavity inside the mouth and throat as possible. Humming by keeping upper and lower jaws slightly apart to prevent the resonance of vibrating teeth produces the best sound. The final and most important lesson I learned was that I had very little future as a vocalist.

Five years earlier during the summer that I turned eight, Pop finally contracted with an architect-turned-contractor to build the new home Pop had spent the war years planning. Two vacant waterfront lots we owned on Stevenson Bay provided the site for the house. Resembling our former house on Cleveland Street, the new one was a modest, single-story, wood frame structure with white asbestos shingle siding and deep green shutters with a dark gray asphalt shingle roof. The old house, built by my father and grandfather just before Pearl Harbor, now belonged to an envious former neighbor who had grown tired of renting. The proceeds from its sale paid for the new house. To his credit and my envy, Pop never enjoyed the privilege of paying on a mortgage. While only a bit bigger than the old house, the new one, sited on an acre of water front property, overlooked the large bay between the mainland and the beach islands. Pop ordered the contractor to build the house with its front and rear reversed. Wishing to take advantage of the water view, the house's front elevation faced the water to the west where the living room, dining room, "front" porch, and master bedroom could overlook the water. There existed an additional motive for orienting the house in his manner in the days before home air conditioning. Pop wanted the master bedroom to benefit from the prevailing sea breezes during the hot summer nights. He was chagrined to discover, after we endured our first dog days of summer in the house that only during the daylight hours did the breezes blow off the water from west to east. In the evenings, the prevailing winds were from the southeast, and thus, it was I, with my bedroom on the east side of the house, who enjoyed the cooling breezes of the night while my parents perspired.

One Monday in December, after talking my way out of a command performance after school with Alec, I anxiously endured the long bus drive home. The bus never got any closer than three blocks to our house. For some unexplained reason, the school bus route never came closer than one block from my house. Some years I had to walk as much as a mile to the bus stop. I was worried because Laddie hadn't been seen for almost three days, an absence to which I had grown accustomed but one that still worried me lest, for whatever reason, Laddie did not return at all. Where Laddie would travel and what he would do, I learned through occasional remarks by friends to the effect they had seen Laddie sometimes miles away from our house. At first I refused to believe the reports, but as their frequency increased and spread to other people including some adults I became convinced.

When Laddie finally returned, he usually brought some token of his travels as though he had been on a shopping trip around town. On one of his sojourns he returned with a boot, a single leatherwork boot in flawless condition. I could envision him wandering innocently into an open garage and sniffing everything in sight. What was it about the boot? The smell of a human? The odor of new leather? Maybe it was the scent of another dog. Whatever it was, I can just imagine Laddie trotting so proudly home with the boot locked tight between his jaws. He undoubtedly didn't bring the companion with him because he couldn't figure out a way to carry both at the same time. Where he picked it up we never discovered. After inquiring about the neighborhood and not finding anyone missing one perfectly sound work boot, we faced a minor dilemma: what to do with it? It seemed in too good condition to throw away, but who would want just one boot if we tried to give it away? Thus it sat in the garage gathering mildew until it deteriorated sufficiently enough to warrant throwing it into the trash. This act had to be repeated several times because Laddie, being quite possessive about his treasures, consistently retrieved the boot from the trashcan. The first time Mother placed the boot in the garbage can, Laddie watched with close interest. No sooner had she entered the house when Laddie looked at me as if he were looking for a sign of disapproval. I just looked back at him and said nothing. He moseyed over to the garbage can and, using his nose, flipped off the lid with the same dexterity a human would display popping the top off a resealed Coke bottle with their thumb. He placed his front two paws on the edge of the can securing his grip with his extended claws. Burying his head inside the can, he jerked the boot out by one of its strings. He triumphantly marched over to where he slept, dropped it, and lay down resting his head on it.

Mother, after several more abortive attempts at throwing the boot away, became more cunning. She waited until Laddie wandered off and then wrapped the boot in newspaper, dumped all the other garbage out of the can, and placed the wrapped boot in the bottom of the can. The next morning, we awakened to find the boot back on Laddie's pallet and garbage strewn all over the side yard.

Mother had little time to be angry as the garbage men were rapidly approaching. She rushed out trying to put a blouse over her halter top as she ran. Frustrated, she discarded the top, hurriedly picked up the strewn trash, and stuffed it into the can, then turned to Laddie who watched all the while with boot dangling from his mouth by a shoestring. As mother tried to grab the boot, Laddie would duck and weave dodging mother's futile lunges. Finally, with garbage men laughing as they emptied the can into the waiting truck, the string broke. Mother snatched the boot and took off running toward the truck that already was moving down the street. She ran behind and with one last great effort flung the boot into the bin of the accelerating truck. Panting with sweat running down the cleavage in her bosom, her hair hanging down into her eyes and hands reeking of garbage, she muttered, "That dog!"

Monday afternoon there was still no sign of Laddie. I was more than a little worried, as he seemed to have been gone longer than usual. I opened a can of dog food, shook out the contents after punching a small hole in the unopened end, and placed it in Laddie's dish, freshened his water in an adjacent dish, and crossed my fingers that Laddie was all right.

Early the next morning, awakened by my mother's loud voice calling Pop and I from our respective beds, I jumped out of bed, rubbing sleep from my eyes, and yelled back, "Is Laddie here?"

"Yes," Mother said in a very perturbed voice, "and that's not all that's here. Reid, come here I want to show you something." She was standing in the opened front doorway, hands on her hips, glaring toward the side yard.

Whenever Mother spoke with the tone now present in her voice, both Pop and I knew that something worth much recrimination had happened. We drew on our pants and lumbered together to the front door. At the front corner of the house and garage lay Laddie midst a bundle of large white cloths. I rubbed my eyes again and ran over to Laddie who was just as excited to see me as I was to see him. The large white cloths were but a few of many such items that lay scattered over the lawn. Attached to over sixty feet of stout clothesline were sheets, pillow cases, towels, wash cloths, underwear of all varieties, and several men's work shirts. How Laddie managed to tear down a clothesline full of linens and clothes and drag it who knows how far home—with all still firmly attached by clothespins mind you—I couldn't imagine.

"Reid!" Mother exclaimed. "What are we going to do with all of these things?"

"I suppose Dean will have to canvass the neighborhood after school to determine who's missing a clothesline full of wash," he explained.

"I know that. I'm more concerned about what we're going to say to the people if we find out who they are. If they find out what happened to their wash before we can return it, I'll be mortified."

Taking a moment to compose herself she added, "I'm going to have to spend the entire day washing, drying, and ironing these clothes and bed linens—I only hope they're not torn." Turning to me, she said, "Young man, you come home right after school and spend whatever time it takes to find where this wash came from, do you understand?"

"Yes, ma'am," I replied, more elated at Laddie's return than intimidated by Mother's scolding. I openly laughed as Mother tried to wrestle the items away from Laddie who didn't cotton to relinquishing his hard won booty. The harder she pulled, the harder Laddie pulled back. It was a classic tug of war with Mother falling to the ground and being dragged along by Laddie's determination and sheer strength. After some loud guffaws, Pop told me to tell Laddie to stop. I couldn't wait to get to school to tell my friends.

I made a point to tell about Laddie's misadventures to friends in each of my first two classes. I was in the process of repeating the story to Denny, who sat next to me in choir, when suddenly I heard, "Mr. Collins!" The sharp, loud cry caught me by surprise. I turned and looked up into the darting eyes of Alec who hovered above me.

"Yes, sir?" came my startled reply.

"This is the second time in as many days and goodness knows how many others this term that I've had to stop practice to address your incessant chatter. I'll have no more of it, you'll report here after school today. Do you understand?"

"But I have to—""There will be no buts. Just be here!

"Yes, sir. I will, sir," I sheepishly replied. What a time to have to stay after school, I thought. I've got to get home to find the owner of the clothes Laddie so laboriously dragged home. The way my luck was running, the clothes probably belonged to Alec's sister. I worried all day how I could juggle the commands of both Mother and Alec.

It rained that afternoon thereby prohibiting the normal activities of my last period PE class. Because there was no indoor gym in the old schools, our class could only stand or horse around the locker and shower rooms that reeked of sweat that had accumulated during the morning classes and who knows how many days before then. The few painted over windows in the room were kept closed for privacy preventing any ventilation. The odor was one only a coach could love.

I approached Coach Smith for permission to go to the choir room across the street. Reasoning that it would mean one less sweaty body in the already crowded locker room, Coach gave his consent. Waiting for a moment until the rain reduced to a drizzle, I dashed to the choir room and entered its back door. The room was empty except for Alec who was working on some student papers at his desk with a space heater on the floor a few feet away. He looked up and said, "What are you doing here now, school isn't out?"

"The rain canceled PE today and Coach Smith said I could come over," I answered.

"Sit down," he said, pointing to the chair at the side of his desk. "I'll be with you in a minute." After checking through the paper he was working on, he dropped his red lead pencil on top of the remaining papers and said, "I want to ask you a question. Why is it that you are so bent on being disruptive during class? I constantly have to come down on you because you're talking, joking, or not paying attention. I know how important music is to your father, but obviously you don't share his enthusiasm."

"No, sir. I mean, yes, sir. What I mean is that he is much more interested in music than I, but choir is okay I guess," I replied, squirming a bit in my chair.

"Why is it we don't seem to be able to get along? Your dad and I don't seem to have any difficulty." Alec's voice was much softer than his usual sharp class tone.

"I don't know, you're all right, I guess. I get into trouble for talking too much in my other classes too," I confessed.

"Do you think that if you try real hard you could manage to curb your tongue during class, except to sing, of course?" he said with a laugh

"I could try, I mean, I will try," I replied with a broad smile but secretly wondering why Alec was suddenly being so friendly.

"Let me ask you one other question. I seem to get along with your dog even worse than you. Why does he charge at me barking so viciously?" Alec asked.

"Laddie's very protective and doesn't like strangers, he defends us against anyone he considers an intruder," I explained.

"But I've never done anything to warrant the way he comes at me with his fur raised and barking ferociously every time I walk past," Alec said, pressing for a better explanation.

Thinking for a moment I replied, "Do you remember the very first time you came by our house?"

"Yes. Why?"

"When Laddie first charged at you, you yelled at him and raised your fist. If you had just called to him and extended your hand, he would have stopped barking, wagged his tail, and trotted over hoping you would pet him. Instead, you acted like he was the intruder and not you. That made him fearful and more protective."

Alec grunted. He mulled over what I said and was about to respond when Tracy entered the back door. The rain stopped and the sun broke through the clouds turning the darkened room into a lighted stage. I quickly understood why she was the darling of the high school. She was strikingly beautiful and seemed to glow in the reflected afternoon sun. I stared.

"Alec...ah, Mr. Driver," she corrected herself when she turned and saw me sitting in a nearby chair. "Oh, hi, Dean. I didn't see you sitting there." Shaken out of my stupor, I had little trouble smiling in return but barely managed to get out an audible hi in return. Tracy turned to Alec and said, "Mr. Driver, we need you to come over to the auditorium to help with the senior play rehearsal, when you're through here, that is. Eddie Harlow needs a little coaxing and coaching to take the male lead. Will you come?" She asked in a way Alec would never consider declining.

"Certainly, but just a minute," he said, turning to me and returning to his usual stern voice, "Mr. Collins, you may go, but don't make me have to reprimand you another time or I'll go to your father, understood?"

"No sir, I mean yes, sir," I responded with a sign of relief. I could see out the opened back door that my bus hadn't yet left school as the final bell rang while Alec and I were talking. I looked in Tracy's eyes as I skipped out the door passed her and at that instant I was sorry I had to leave. I remember feeling embarrassed that Alec, reverting to his usual authoritarian tone, had scolded me in front of Tracy.

Upon arriving home, Jimmy and I combed the neighborhood trying to establish just whose laundry Laddie had purloined. We were approaching several of the last houses within what we considered Laddie's dragging range.

"Oh, shit," I muttered.

"What's wrong?" Jimmy asked.

"This house belongs to Mrs. Hooker, Driver's sister."

"Maybe it's not her laundry," Jimmy countered.

"Not with my luck," I responded with a sigh.

Reaching her front door, I knocked timidly. When she answered I said, "Mrs. Hooker, are you missing some laundry?"

"Why yes, how did you know?" came her puzzled reply.

"My dog took it from your clothesline. My mom rewashed and dried them for you. I'm sorry."

"Oh my, I wonder how he managed to do that?"

"He manages to do a lot of things we don't understand."

"Well, please thank your mother and thank you for returning them. I wondered what could have happened to an entire clothesline full of wash."

"You won't tell Mr. Driver, will you?" I replied.

"You needn't worry, he would just laugh his head off. I haven't been very sympathetic about your dog barking at him—he could avoid walking by your house if he wanted to."

*****

By midmorning of the Monday following Alec's concert date with Tracy (the same day as the first of my two successive encounters with Alec at school), rumors ran rampantly throughout the high school about Alec and Tracy. Alec, being isolated in the choir building at the far end of the campus, conducted his morning classes unaware that the gossip mill ground hard at work. On the other hand, Tracy found herself in the midst of the gossip whirlwind just as soon as she stepped off the bus that she rode when she didn't need her mother's car for after-school commitments. She was quickly engulfed by a number of her friends as well as curious acquaintances. The circle of news-hungry teenagers twisted its way around Tracy like a human tornado.

"Tracy, I hear you had a special date Friday night," cried one shrill voice. The voice slurred the word special while the remainder of the sentence sounded singsong.

Tracy knew immediately that the inevitable moment had arrived. She soon discovered she wasn't quite as prepared as she thought she would be.

"I gather you're referring to whom I was with rather than where we went. It was a nice evening. Alec and I enjoyed the concert very much," she stated, not realizing what she said until after she said it.

"Alec?" came a chorus of replies.

Immediately Tracy realized her error. No student, but no student ever referred to a teacher by their first name. She tried to correct herself by quickly but quietly adding, "I meant Mr. Driver."

It was too late, the slip was irretrievable. Her friends asked in rapid-fire succession the questions that interested them most.

"What's he like?"

"What happened?"

"Did he do anything?"

"Are you going to see him again?"

"What did your parents say?"

Tracy decided the slip didn't matter; she would have had to admit at some point that the evening constituted a bona fide date. Tracy decided to answer the questions in a calm and matter-of-fact tone in the pretense that nothing extraordinary had happened. The charade only served to whet the girls' appetite for information.

"Nothing special happened other than the concert itself. He's very polite, thoughtful, and gentlemanly even when Mother at first objected. Daddy assured her that I'd be okay, and they haven't forbid me seeing him again if I choose. And absolutely nothing happened after the concert."

"Well," the voice drawing out the four letters as far as possible, "are you going to see him again?"

"Yes, we're going to see the new Gene Kelly film, *Singing in the Rain,* and then go to the church choir Christmas party," Tracy stated, continuing her matter-of-fact tone.

Before noon, this last statement had been translated into "Tracy and Mr. Driver are going together and her parents say it's okay."

When Alec walked into the teachers' lounge for lunch, he hadn't caught wind of the morning's events. He saw Tracy in class and spoke to her only briefly. She didn't have a chance to mention any of her earlier conversations. Thus, he was unprepared for the reception he received when he entered the room. The usual cheery "Good morning, everyone" met with only muffled responses from a few of the male faculty members and only cold stares from the female faculty. Alec thought little of it until he sat down at a table with two other male faculty and opened his bagged lunch. After a minute or two, the English literature teacher who tried to sound more erudite by speaking with a forged British accent said, "I say, Alec, what's this I hear about you dating the Ashbury girl—robbing the cradle a bit, aren't we?"

Alec stopped mid-bite of his sandwich, looked up, and then looked around the stone silent room where every eye was fixed on him. He cleared his throat, took a bite of his sandwich, hoping no one would want to stare at his eating and giving himself a chance to collect his thoughts. After taking his time chewing his food he answered, "I just escorted Miss Ashbury to the Roger Wagner Chorale concert in Tampa on Friday night, that's all."

"That's all?" came the reply adding, "Look, ol' boy, this sort of thing is just not done. Please tell me you didn't kiss her."

"I don't see that this is any of your business—"

"Oh my god, he kissed her."

Alec glanced around the room and, as he suspected, every eye remained fixed on him, or nearly every eye. Herb Dudley sat at a table in the corner quieting eating his lunch and reading from a small black book opened in front of him. Two female faculty members abruptly rose from their table and stormed out of the room.

Becoming irritated and increasingly defensive, Alec decided to take another tack.

"Look around this room. How many faculty here are males? Outside of the principal, the athletic coaches, the shop teachers, the band director, you, and me, there are damn few. High school teaching is still a female-dominated profession, and when I look at my paycheck I understand why. How many of the male faculty are single? One! That's me! I may be the first because I'm probably the first single male faculty member this school has ever had."

By the end, Alec was nearly shouting. He looked around the room apologetically. Herb Dudley, seemingly unperturbed, continued his reading and eating.

"You may be right about that, ol' boy. That's all the more reason to exercise some restraint, you could very well make it more difficult for the next single male to get a position and make the rest of us married males look suspect during the interim.

"Look, I took the girl to a concert with her parents' full knowledge and consent. If I take her out again, it will also be with her and her parents' consent. I'm not a lecherous old man. I happen to find Tracy an engaging, charming, and attractive young lady who's intelligent and mature enough to know what she's doing. I can't imagine anyone being able to take advantage of her, and I certainly don't intend to try."

"You may be able to convince us, but you have an entire town out there that must also be convinced. What you do and say will affect their perceptions of all-male faculty members. You may be biting off more than you can chew," came a reply from the basketball coach-history teacher sitting with them.

"But—" Alec tried to rebut.

"You don't have to convince me," continued the coach. "I married the prettiest cheerleader this school ever produced who also happened to be the town's beauty queen, but she was twenty-two and long out of high school."

"What we're trying to say, Alec," the literature teacher said, dropping his improvised English accent and whispering, "is that you use some discretion and be prepared. This discussion won't be the last you'll have on the subject."

Alec watched Herb Dudley get up from his corner table after finishing his lunch and reading. Alec's eyes followed him as he walked to the door, opened it, and left the room. Alec, aware of Herb's strong convictions, knew Herb didn't approve of his actions even though Herb had been very friendly to him when they met the first week of school. Alec watched and wondered whether Herb would say anything.

The basketball coach followed Alec's eyes and correctly read his thoughts. He said to Alec, "Herb Dudley won't lecture you on morality. It's not his style to preach uninvited. However, I wouldn't ask his opinion because he'll tell you just what he believes. I suspect you already know that."

Alec did know how Herb felt, and he realized that Herb's silence had more impact than all the expressed recriminations and glares of the other teachers. Alec also realized that he would find little support among his colleagues for any further dates with Tracy.

The events of the next two weeks placed special emphasis on Saturday's date for Tracy and Alec. Each knew they were the subjects of close scrutiny by their respective peers but neither felt particularly nervous, for the evening's itinerary was similar to their previous date, innocent, and wholesome. Lloyd, his usual relaxed cordial self, met Alec at the door that Saturday night. Nancy was gracious but remained distant when she greeted Alec. The school gossip hadn't been serious enough for anyone, including Tracy, to bring it to the senior Ashburys' attention.

After the film they drove to the choir party already underway for over an hour. Alec warned the organizers that he might be a bit late due to a previous engagement, a subject on which he didn't choose to elaborate. While driving the short distance from the theater to the party, they talked of the film agreeing that Gene Kelly, Donald O'Conner, and newcomer, Debbie Reynolds, were better dancers than singers and that while Gene Kelly was more graceful, Donald O'Connor was more acrobatic. They agreed Cyd Charisse was stunning and that the movie should win an Academy Award.

They arrived at the host's house all smiles and ready for whatever revelry a church choir Christmas party provided. The hostess greeted them at the door with a warm "Merry Christmas" but with her eyes darting back and forth between them. She looked past them into the night to see if they were part of a larger group arriving together. Seeing no one else, she led them to a spacious family room generously decorated for the occasion where most of the choir was gathered. She announced, "Look, everybody, Alec and Tracy are here."

Stare is more what everybody did, for no one expected the two names to be mentioned in the same breath. Alec and Tracy's meetings after choir practice had always taken place after the other choir members departed. The room fell silent for one quick instant until some understanding soul rang out in a jovial voice, "Merry Christmas," that everyone repeated in unison.

The choir expected Alec to attend the party that was given, in part, as a testimonial to his work in reshaping its performance and musical format. Few expected Tracy to appear because she was by far the choir's youngest member and most thought the adult choir's slow-paced parties would bore her. No one expected the two of them to show up together.

Full of the season's spirit, no one openly displayed any more concern after the initial surprise. In the kitchen and the master-bath-turned-powder-room, however, whispers of speculation circulated among some of the female guests what meaning, if any, should be given to Alec and Tracy arriving together. One thought naively that it was just a coincidence, another was sure she heard one of them say something about an earlier engagement, still another said she heard that some high school teacher was dating one of his students, and do you think?

Having arrived late, Tracy and Alec stayed until they were the last to leave. They bid their host and hostess good night after Alec took special care to thank them for volunteering to host the party. As he had done for the first time during the movie, Alec held Tracy's hand while they walked to the car that, due to the number at the party, he had to park a block away. She seated herself halfway between Alec and the passenger side door that left Alec undecided whether to continue to hold her hand or put his arm around her. He chose the former as the latter seemed, for the moment, to be more awkward. They chatted enthusiastically about the film, the party, and the choir. They behaved as though neither wanted the evening to end.

When they reached Tracy's house, Alec got out, walked around his sister's car that he had again borrowed, opened the door for Tracy, and walked her to the lighted front porch. They suddenly grew silent each not knowing exactly what to say because they knew they wouldn't see each other again until Alec returned from his trip to Mexico. Alec had another reason for being silent: his mind searched for a way to tell Tracy what she now had a right to know. He wanted to give her a chance to think about his previous marriage and divorce during his two-week hiatus. Not only did it seem the fair thing to do, but also the two-week absence may cushion her initial reaction. He shuddered not knowing whether it was the chill of the evening or the thought of how she might react. He clasped her hands in his as they reached the porch and said, "Tracy, I like you very much, as if that isn't obvious. I cannot ask you to continue seeing me, however, without telling you something about me you're entitled to know."

"Yes," she said, quietly looking up into his eyes.

Clearing his throat, he began, "There's no easy way for me to say this, so I'll be blunt. Tracy, I've just recently been divorced from my first wife—it happened almost a year ago."

Not taking her eyes off his for an instant, not even to blink, she replied calmly, "I know."

"You know? How could you, you—" he stammered.

"Remember the first time we met I told you I worked in the school office? The faculty files are in Mr. Furst's office and one morning last month after he left school for an off-campus appointment, I looked at your application form and saw that you wrote 'married' for your marital status. Your withholding statement listed only one dependent, which meant that you must have been divorced sometime between filling out the application a year and a half ago and when you arrived last August."

His mouth dropped open and his eyes widened. He wasn't sure whether he was more surprised at her reaction, her ingenuity, or her obvious interest. He finally managed to gasp. "You don't mind? It doesn't bother you?" He hoped he already knew her answer.

"Not really. I thought about it for a while and decided that it was probably a wartime romance that didn't survive the peace," she explained.

"Why didn't you ask me about it?" he asked, hoping to probe further her thoughts.

"I felt that when you were ready to tell me you would without me asking. I just trusted you would before things went too far and... you did."

If there ever was a time it is now, he thought. He dropped her hands, removed his glasses and, never taking his eyes off hers, grabbed her arms and kissed her as passionately as he had ever kissed anyone.

Tracy responded by placing her arms around him and rising on her toes to meet his lips with hers. She had never been kissed with so much passion and tenderness. Her body, closer to his than it had been to anyone else's, could feel every curvature, swell, and indentation in his. The boys she kissed mostly leaned into her, lips puckered and necks craning and arms pawing at her from all directions. As Alec finished he kissed her neck just below her right ear that sent chills down her neck and arm and a rush of blood to her face.

He wanted desperately to say how much he loved her but hesitated lest he pressure her to respond before he had an opportunity to develop their relationship further. He resisted the temptation. He simply said, "Thank you for being so understanding. You don't know how much it means to me. You don't know how much you mean to me."

"I think maybe I do," she answered adding, "maybe after you return I'll know better how I feel about you."

That was good enough for him. He kissed her again, more delicately this time and not as long. He drew back and said, "I'd better say good night before I get in trouble with your parents."

"Good night," she replied adding, "would you like me to drive you to the airport tomorrow?"

"Thanks for asking, but Denise has offered to take me. I'll call you when I return."

He reached into his left coat pocket and withdrew a small, bright, neatly wrapped package and added as he handed it to her, "Merry Christmas, Tracy."

Chapter 7

Christmas, an especially festive holiday for the Ashbury household, meant friends and neighbors frequently dropping by,
often unannounced, to sample Nancy's special eggnog and
Tracy's fudge that she dared make only at Christmas. Nancy labored
for days over her traditional Christmas Day dinner that she gave
for close friends and family. With Alec traveling in Mexico, Nancy
relaxed for the first time in over a week and seemed to put him out of
her mind. She concentrated on her family's holiday plans and directing her church's annual food and toy drive for families in need. Tracy
slept late each morning enjoying not so much the extra rest as staying
up later than her school day schedule permitted. She rose in time to
help her mother some each day with the food drive and her family's
Christmas preparations.

Tuesday evening before Christmas Day, Ruth Ann Douglas,
Tracy's best friend, appeared at the Ashbury's front door bearing a gift
to exchange with Tracy, a routine they established when they were
very young girls. While Ruth Ann didn't share Tracy's beauty and
talent, she possessed the qualities of a good friend: loyalty, sympathy,
concern, and respect. In addition, she possessed the twin qualities
of a good nature and sense of humor. Physically, she carried more
weight for her medium height than what the health charts in her
hygiene class suggested. Her face, while not quite round, exhibited
rosy cheeks that had not lost their entire baby fat. She possessed one
physical characteristic that drew the attention of most adolescent
boys—large prominent breasts. At the rather young age of eleven,
concern for modesty and school etiquette forced her elementary
school principal to send her home with a note informing her parents that Ruth Ann should not attend school again without a bra.

From that day forward she never suffered from any lack of attention from her male peers or older males for that matter. It didn't take long for Ruth Ann to realize that her breasts were the primary cause of the attention she received from members of the opposite sex. Rather than be embarrassed, as some girls were by this type of attention, Ruth Ann decided to use her one outstanding physical feature to attract boys then selectively turn away those, for whatever reason, she didn't like. Tight knit sweaters in the winter, sundresses and low-cut bathing suits in the summer all served their purpose. One of her castoff boyfriends coined the often-repeated phrase that Ruth Ann's reputation always preceded her. By the time she reached seventeen, she became engaged to a senior in college with a promising future in his family business. Her early successes with the challenge of handling the incessant attentions of males with hyperactive hormones undoubtedly allowed Ruth Ann to keep events in perspective and cope with whatever problems she faced.

Tracy met Ruth Ann at the door and immediately escorted her to the family room where the large lavishly decorated Christmas tree stood and extracted Ruth Ann's gift from the stack under the tree and replaced it with the one Ruth Ann had given her. They quickly retreated upstairs to Tracy's room on the second floor where they knew they could enjoy privacy for the conversation each knew would ensue. Tracy hadn't yet told Ruth Ann the details of her dates with Alec. But what is more important, she hadn't shared her reasons for dating Alec. An omission that would soon be corrected, for Tracy was just as eager to confide in Ruth Ann, as Ruth Ann was to listen. Tracy felt a need for the confidence and support that she knew Ruth Ann would provide.

After entering Tracy's room, Tracy closed the door signaling to Ruth Ann that a serious discussion was imminent. Ruth Ann unabashedly jumpstarted the conversation with, "Well, how did it go?" obviously referring to Tracy's last date with Alec. Both girls positioned themselves crosswise on Tracy's double bed, a habit Tracy's parents hadn't been able to get her or her friends to break.

"We had a terrific time, just like the concert," Tracy explained.

Quickly getting down to brass tacks Ruth Ann asked, "Well, what happened?

"He gave me a Christmas present," Tracy answered, trying to sound nonchalant.

"What is it?" Ruth Ann said excitedly, her curiosity piqued to the breaking point.

"I don't know. I haven't opened it yet, it's under the tree with the rest of the gifts," Tracy answered, still trying to sound cavalier.

"Aren't you curious?" Ruth Ann quizzed, her voice reflecting greater excitement than Tracy.

"Yes, but I think that I'll wait until Christmas Eve after my parents go to bed," Tracy replied, adding, "I actually enjoy the anticipation and mystery. It's more exciting that way."

"I don't think I could stand the suspense, but I don't blame you for wanting to open it without your parents peering over your shoulder. Promise you'll call me just as soon as you open it," Ruth pleaded.

"You didn't have to ask, you know you'll be the first person I'll tell," Tracy answered with a trace of a smile.

"Well, did anything else happen?" Ruth Ann resumed her quest for more details.

"I kissed him," Tracy said, trying not to sound like she was bragging but the pretense of indifference had faded.

"You did?" Ruth Ann shrieked.

"Shhh!" Tracy urged, placing her index finger over her mouth.

"You did!" Ruth Ann whispered this time and added, "What did he do?"

"He kissed me back."

"He did?" Ruth Ann again shrieked in a slightly less loud voice. "Was this before or after he gave you the present?"

"This was after the concert," Tracy corrected.

"After the concert? But that was your first—"

"Date," Tracy finished Ruth Ann's sentence. "He kissed me first after the choir party before he gave me the present."

"What did you do?"

"I kissed him back, of course."

"And?" Ruth Ann urged.

"He was very passionate yet tender." Tracy recalled the chill bumps that ran down her neck and arm. She remembered how she blushed; at least she thought it was a blush she felt. Continuing her description, "It was really different from how the guys kiss," Tracy said, finding some difficulty deciding what feelings to reveal or not reveal to Ruth Ann.

"Oh?" responded Ruth Ann, waiting for an elaboration.

"Yeah, you know, the guys are so awkward and their hands so... so busy. Poor Buster, I hurt his feelings last night when he came over. While he was kissing me I shoved him away and told him to stop pawing at me. I told him it was as if he had eight arms. He said he bet I didn't say that to Mr. Driver."

"What did you say?" Ruth Ann grew more interested.

"I said, 'Buster!' and he dropped the subject," Tracy answered with a wink and a broad smile.

Turning more serious, Ruth Ann asked, "The big question everyone is asking around school is why you decided to go out with him. I guess I wonder, too, although I think I already know."

"I've thought about that a lot lately, and I think that at first I was flattered by his attentions, being an older man and all." Tracy's finger followed the quilted patterns on her "drunkard's path" quilt she used as a bedspread as she talked. "I also admire his knowledge of music, and now that I know him better I find that we have many interests in common. Besides, he's rather good-looking in an athletic sort of way."

"What did your parents say?"

"Mother isn't exactly pleased and Daddy, well, Daddy is Daddy. He likes Alec, even feels a little sorry for him. He has a pretty good idea what Alec is in for once our dating gets around. Daddy believes Alec genuinely likes me and is sincere about the promises he made to them. He says Alec has been too open to have any ulterior motive. Daddy would be more worried if Alec and I were seeing each other secretly."

"I really like your Dad, he's always so cool," Ruth Ann said, holding her chin in her hand on a propped elbow and staring into space.

"Daddy did scold me for not thinking about the problems he and Mother would have to face because of our dating. I suppose he's right. I didn't consider them. I guess I thought that no one except the kids at school would ever say or think anything about it. It's just that I can't believe that anyone cares, or that it's anyone else's business. I don't mind answering to Mother and Daddy, they're reasonable, but I just hate to have to answer to anyone else."

"Your dad's right, Tracy. This town is so small that everyone knows what everyone else is doing. People are going to talk, you know that. But don't worry too much about it, your dad is perfectly capable of handling anyone or anything, no one is going to get the best of him," Ruth Ann assured Tracy.

"I suppose you're right," Tracy responded, sounding somewhat resigned.

"But what about all the kids? Everybody is talking about you two."

"I can handle that. That's not what bothers me. What I don't like are the whispers and stares. I don't know how to handle them, so I simply ignore them hoping that after a while they'll go away," Tracy answered with a sigh.

"You should be used to being the center of attention by now," Ruth Ann responded.

"Attention, yes; scorn, no. But I've made my decision. I'm going to see Alec again and will do so until I decide not to. I'll do as my parents ask, and as far as anyone else is concerned, I couldn't care less," Tracy ended, sounding defiant.

"I don't believe that last statement for an instant. But don't worry, you're right. After a while the kids will stop talking and staring and some of the girls may even envy you. I think some of the girls in choir already feel that way."

Ruth Ann's remarks made Tracy feel better. She had a way of turning Tracy's despair into hope whenever the occasion arose, which it rarely did. But when it did, Tracy was glad to have Ruth Ann as a friend. Ruth Ann's curiosity still not satiated, she asked, "But what about your mom? How does she feel?"

"Mother says I have a father complex," Tracy sighed.

"What does your father say?" Ruth Ann pursued.

"He said, 'What's so bad about that?'" Tracy smiled.

They both broke into loud laughter with Ruth Ann falling off her elbow landing on her back and adding, "I love your father, he's a gas."

Continuing her thoughts, Tracy added, "I didn't tell them this, but I guess curiosity caused me to accept that first date and the first kiss. I wondered how I'd feel and react when we actually went out together. I also wondered how I'd feel when he touched me and kissed me. I felt a sense of importance and being grown up after that first date—I felt accepted into the adult world. I know this all sounds so very logical, but I'm having a hard time sorting everything out," Tracy confessed. By this time, she and Ruth Ann were sitting on the bed legs crossed and facing each other as they talked.

"It's probably because your folks have forced you to think about it a lot," Ruth Ann offered. "Besides, you obviously had to feel something to go out with him in the first place."

"I suppose so," Tracy responded, recalling how she had covertly looked at Alec's personnel file in Mr. Furst's office weeks before he asked her for their first date. She chose not to reveal her initiative to anyone other than Alec, not even her parents or Ruth Ann. Ruth Ann was not aware that Tracy had made it easy for Alec to approach her and even tacitly encouraged his advances. Tracy knew it was only a matter of time before he asked her out.

Ruth Ann, wanting to return to the more romantic details, stated, "Tell me about the kiss."

"Ruth Ann, I've told you all there's to tell. I didn't know what to expect. When the guys kiss me I feel cold and even sometimes repulsed. I tolerate it only because I know they expect it. Even the boys who don't affect me that way leave me feeling… well, unfeeling and indifferent. The truth is I haven't found anyone I really like—maybe that's why I never agreed to go steady. I know I hurt Buster's feelings when I refused to go steady. I think he just wanted to use going steady as an excuse for other things he had in mind, if you know what I mean." Tracy gave Ruth Ann that all-knowing stare.

Ruth Ann nodded and continued her foremost interest at the moment, "But what about Mr. Driver's…ah, Alec's kiss."

"I didn't feel cold, repulsed, or indifferent if that's what you mean. Maybe it was just the occasion or the novelty or the excitement of doing something that would shock everyone, I don't know."

"I gather you wouldn't object if he tried it again?" Ruth Ann continued giving Tracy her total, undivided attention.

"No, I wouldn't," Tracy answered without hesitation or elaboration.

"What about anything else he might try?" Ruth Ann teased.

"I've thought about that," Tracy answered with a wry grin.

"Tracy!"

"Well, after all, he's a man and he looks sexy in his running shorts—his legs are strong and powerful-looking," Tracy answered, recalling how he looked as he ran with the track team.

"Surely you're not thinking what I think you're thinking."

"No. It's much too early for that. Besides, he seems too polite to try anything until we get to know each other better. It's Buster that I have to fight off."

"And just how is it you know how he looks in running shorts?" Ruth Ann queried with more than passing interest.

"The cheerleading squad practices some days down at Green Field. I watch when Alec runs with the track team. He's very good, at running that is," she said with a grin.

"Were you watching by the locker room?" Ruth Ann asked, not trying very hard to hold back a broad grin.

"Ruth Ann, shame on you. You know I wouldn't do that." Tracy and Ruth Ann both laughed. Tracy blushed.

The locker room at Green Field enjoyed a notorious reputation. Although the new football field served as the game site that fall, the Green Field facility, only a scant four blocks from the old campus, remained the practice field for both football and track. The old building that contained the locker room sat in the southwest corner of the practice field close enough to the sidewalk to touch through one of the numerous holes in the chain link fence that separated them. The decaying facility suffered from years of neglect and overuse. Maintenance on the old facility ceased when plans for the newer campus were announced three years earlier. Large, gaping holes perforated the sides of the building allowing clear visual access to the locker room and showers. There was scarcely a teenage girl that, upon a dare or otherwise, hadn't walked by the locker room when the teams were showering and dressing and hesitated just long enough to view the boys inside. The less brazen waited until late in the fall when the teams showered well after sunset. The most unabashed viewers were the junior high girls, undoubtedly a result of their recent passage through puberty. The incidence of viewing by senior high girls, reflecting their maturity, appeared to decline with their age. Maybe it was because they had seen it all before. The boys knew the girls watched and delightfully tease and taunt those they caught.

As blatant as some of the ogling was no one did anything about it. The holes remained uncovered, and no one bothered to patrol the walks to discourage gawkers. Administrators probably reasoned that the facilities at Green Field would be razed upon completion of the new campus and that any funds expended for maintenance would be wasted. For over three years, however, the locker room at Green Field spiced many a teenage girl's fall evening.

The blush on Tracy's face belied her words, for she watched Alec on several occasions enter the locker room after track practice. One particular evening, darkness engulfed the field by the time she reached her car that she had subconsciously, or perhaps consciously, parked next to the locker room. Upon walking past the pocked facility at the finish of practice, she hesitated a moment, looked about, and then cast a quick glance through one of the larger openings in the cracked side boards. She didn't see Alec, but she did get an eye full of Roy Peters and Butch Crawford. Embarrassed by the thought that someone might have seen her adolescent actions, or perhaps disgusted by what she saw or didn't see, she jumped into her car, slammed the door, and quickly brought the car to a roar. Its tires screamed halfway down the block.

Ruth Ann chose not to pursue the subject lest she be forced into an admission of several indiscretions of her own. She changed the subject by asking, "What do you think is going to happen when you go off to college next fall?"

"I'm not sure whether Alec and I will still be dating by that time and I'm not sure whether I'm going to college."

"You're not? Your dad expects you to go I'm sure." Tracy's announcement surprised Ruth Ann as she presumed that not only would Tracy go to college but would attend only the best of schools.

"Yes, and Mom too. But I'm not interested in becoming a schoolteacher, nurse, or librarian. I love art, music, and literature, but there doesn't seem to be a future in any of these fields for me," Tracy said with a hint of disappointment, adding, "I'd like to do something with music though even if it were in local theater or choral groups."

"What about engineering or science like your dad?" Ruth Ann suggested, not quite believing that Tracy was serious.

"I have no desire to be the only female at a male engineering school. Can you see me at Georgia Tech or MIT?"

"Maybe not, but I wouldn't mind being at either one with all of those guys," Ruth Ann smiled.

"Ruth Ann, you sound like Buster. He says that the only reason girls go to college is to find a husband."

"Buster's a creep," Ruth Ann scowled.

"Don't be too harsh on him; he's just saying what many others think and what's pretty close to the truth. How many girls go off to college and return with a husband and no degree? How many return with a degree and no husband? And how many return with both? Most of those who do graduate end up teaching school—something I absolutely have no desire to do," Tracy explained.

"I see what you mean, but Buster's still a creep," Ruth Ann responded.

"If I end up married and with children, a career is almost out of the question except if I want to be a secretary or something like that. No, I think I'll attend St. Pete JC and take courses in art, music, literature, and history and hope some opportunity comes along to pursue my interests in music. Are you and Bob still planning to get married?" It was Tracy's turn to be inquisitor.

"We want to. I can get a job at the university and maybe take a course or two each semester. Bob needs the financial help to finish school and get his accounting certificate. I really don't mind though.

He'll have to support me for a long time after he starts a practice. At least, I hope I don't have to end up being a secretary for the rest of my life." Ruth Ann possessed a clear vision of her future as a wife and mother; she had never considered anything else.

There was a knock at the door, Nancy opened it a crack, peeked in, and said, "Tracy, Susan's on the phone. Oh hi, Ruth Ann, I'm sorry I didn't see you come in."

"Merry Christmas, Mrs. Ashbury. Oh, I forgot, Tracy," Ruth Ann exclaimed, clasping her hand over her mouth. "Susan wants us to come over to her house. She's invited a bunch of kids over for a party."

"Thanks a lot for telling me," Tracy answered sarcastically.

"I couldn't help it, the conversation was so interesting I forgot," she said with a sparkle in her eye.

Nancy looked puzzled but resigned herself that no one could understand what teenagers meant.

*****

After Christmas, a series of telephone calls from friends disturbed the Ashbury holiday respite. Rumors had reached them that Tracy had dated one of the high school teachers and were calling to verify the gossip. To these calls, Nancy's end of the conversation consisted of:

"Yes, she has seen him on two occasions."

"But Tracy seems determined and to forbid her to see him at all would result in a vote of no confidence and a confrontation neither of which we want."

"Well, we've always allowed Tracy some discretion and don't intend to change now that she is practically grown. We would rather sanction limited and restricted dating than to worry if she and Alec were meeting secretly. We don't want to place her in a position of having to be deceitful."

"We just hope and pray the fascination and novelty will soon wear off. If it weren't for the vast age difference...Alec is really not a bad sort. He doesn't smoke, and if he drinks, he hasn't said. He's neat, courteous, well mannered, and certainly well educated. Poor soul, you should've seen him eat grits for the first time—he deserves some sort of award for gallantry."

Their friends, polite and sympathetic, offered to do whatever she and Lloyd wished. They emphasized that they liked Tracy and didn't want to see her hurt, but were confident that she was mature and intelligent enough to come through this episode and be the better for it.

After fielding her third call, Nancy hung up the phone, turned to Marie Davies, best friend and confidant who sat at the breakfast table having coffee, and said, "Marie, the next time that damn phone rings, either you answer it or I'll rip the darned thing off the wall. I'm tired of pouring out my heart and soul!"

The local area network was working at peak efficiency for no more than a dozen heartbeats separated her words from the next ring. Marie with a wry grin rose and dutifully answered it. This time it was their minister who wanted to express his concern over the "situation" between Tracy and Alec.

"Hello. Oh, hello, Reverend Williams. No this is Marie Davies, Nancy is indisposed at the moment. May I take a message?" Marie listened for a moment and responded, "Oh, but what are best friends for?" She smiled and winked at Nancy who had buried her head in her arms when she realized who had called.

"Yes, I'll be sure to tell her to call you."

Turning to Nancy she said, "Reverend Williams wants—"

"Yes, I heard. I'll tell Lloyd to return the call, it's his turn. Meanwhile, let's go shopping. I need to get away from the phone before it rings again."

Lloyd did eventually return the call and assured the good reverend that he wasn't to blame by hiring Alec as interim church choir director. Lloyd further assured him that the "situation" so far was well in hand. Although concerned, he and Nancy decided to set limits rather than say no. Lloyd felt it best to maintain an open mind until or unless something happened to threaten Tracy's welfare.

"Besides," Lloyd told the reverend, "I kind of like the guy. He's forthright, above board, and says what he means—even if he thinks the other person won't like it. I respect a man for that. I dislike and distrust anyone who only says what they think the other person wants to hear. Maybe that's why I can't stand politicians."

Lloyd didn't satisfy the concerns of the pastor, who chose not to pursue the issue any further. Knowing Lloyd's resoluteness after he had reached a decision, the minister politely ended the conversation by reassuring Lloyd that he would carefully monitor the "situation" to prevent the possibility of any embarrassment for Tracy. Lloyd started to say that wasn't necessary but realized the minister thought otherwise and would be undeterred by Lloyd's request.

The next day, the minister made a series of calls to John Furst and Walter Goss, the school district's assistant superintendent for music and art instruction and the church's former choir director. They arranged a meeting for the morning after New Year's Day in the principal's office to discuss the "situation."

*****

When Alec stepped off the airplane, at what was once Drew Air Field but converted to civilian use and renamed Tampa International Airport after the war, he bore all the trappings of a serious traveler: a camera and photo bag dangled by straps from his neck, a backpack strapped across his shoulders, and in each hand he carried a small traveling case. He wore a bright print short sleeve shirt, khaki walking shorts, the type with six pockets that either zipped, buckled, or snapped, white ankle high socks (two pairs), canvas topped and hard crepe sole walking shoes, and finally an oversized straw sombrero on his head. The camera and bag of exposed film banged against his chest in cadence to his gait. He had the look of a "flat land tourister" a la Barney Google. How he managed to navigate the shallow, steep metal steps leading from the plane's door to the airport tarmac is testament to his athletic dexterity.

Denise waited patiently for Alec to collect the bags he had checked and noted ironically that he carried more on his return trip from Mexico than he did on his trip from New Jersey to Florida. Despite their gender difference, Alec and Denise bore remarkable resemblance to each other. They shared the same angular features, sharp cheekbones, rather pointed noses, and dimpleless chins. Denise wore her hair short and when she donned her sunglasses, her profile could easily pass for Alec's. Although two years younger than Alec, their mother relied on Denise to mentor Alec in her absence. Alec's feelings to the contrary, their mother felt that Denise possessed the more level head and even temper.

Mark and Denise married the week after his graduation from medical school at the University of Connecticut. During Denise's first two years at the university, she spent many nights studying in the medical school library where she and Mark met in the checkout line. They dated for more than a year before Mark proposed. Denise finished her studies in sociology while Mark served his residency at the university hospital. It was during this time that Denise, relying on Alec's advice, medical directories and census data, painstakingly researched and ultimately confirmed central Florida as the site with the most potential for her husband's forthcoming medical practice. Their mother appreciated Denise's savvy.

Denise, with a semblance of pity, told Alec as he lumbered and lugged baggage out of the claim area, to wait while she pulled the car around. Alec gratefully accepted. Once in the car, she drilled him with all the usual questions of one returning from a holiday trip. Alec answered them with the relish and enthusiasm of a dedicated traveler. He enjoyed the ancient ruins and magnificent countryside and said that he fully intended to return one day and travel along El Camino Real just as the ancient Aztecs and Spanish Conquistadors. He ended by revealing his planned trip through Canada next summer that would include a visit with their mother and brothers in Providence on his way back.

The late afternoon winter sun stood just above the horizon in a bright orange ball enlarged by the double effect of the earth's atmosphere acting as a magnifier and the thin layer of high-altitude clouds diffusing its rays. Driving west across Tampa Bay was both strikingly beautiful and blinding as the sun sat at an angle that make the car's visor of no use and Denise's sunglasses of marginal value. She squinted as she drove. Having been preoccupied with thoughts of Christmas when she drove Alec to the airport two weeks earlier, she hadn't mentioned his sudden use of her car. Despite her repeated offers he didn't use it until December first, when he borrowed it twice in as many weeks. At the time he explained that he needed it for social engagements that she readily interpreted as dates. Denise moved to Florida before Alec's divorce and only learned its circumstances and the emotional drain it placed on him secondhand through their mother. In their home away from home, Denise decided to assume, as her mother had requested, a maternal role toward Alec. Out of fear of upsetting Alec, she had successfully avoided asking him specific questions about his divorce, a practice she intended to pursue regarding much of his personal life, but curiosity over his sudden need for her car overcame her reticence. She asked, "Tell me about this lady you've obviously been seeing but not talking about."

"I guess it's silly for me not to have mentioned her. I suppose I should have." Pausing for a moment to reflect on Tracy, he continued, "She's the most beautiful girl I've ever met. She's bright, talented, and very charming. I'm transfixed by her dark, penetrating eyes. She—"

"Whoa! I thought you're just having a simple date or two; it sounds like you're in love again."

She bit her lip knowing she should not have added the word again. She heaved a sigh of relief when Alec's responded, "No, it's the first time I've been in love. It's as though I've never been in love. I feel like what's in the past never happened, it's simply a nightmare from which I've finally awakened to discover it was only a bad dream." Alec's words were slow and deliberate.

"Who is this lady and where did you meet her?" Denise asked with a keen sense of interest.

"Her name is Tracy Ashbury, a name as melodic and beautiful as she is—she's in my choir," he answered innocently.

"Ashbury, that name has a familiar ring. Where does she sit in the church choir?" she queried.

"She sings soprano in both choirs."

"You're dating a member of your class?" she asked, trying to remain calm but not succeeding very well.

"Calm down, sis. I thought you'd understand—I have her parents' permission—it's no big deal," Alec tried to explain.

"No big deal?" she shouted.

"Don't mock me," he insisted, perturbed at her reaction. "Besides, everything is innocent. I haven't been anything but a perfect gentleman."

"Would you have me believe that a thirty-seven-year-old, divorced, war veteran's relationship with an attractive seventeen- or eighteen-year-old school girl is strictly platonic?" she asked with a decided tone of disbelief.

"Yes. No! I mean, of course part of the attraction I feel toward her is sensual, but I've no intention letting those feelings get out of hand, at least while she's a student in my class," Alec answered defiantly.

"During the meantime, everyone else in town will think otherwise. Look, Alec, I dearly love you, but you've got to understand that this community is not exactly liberal and open-minded. People here are churchgoing, Bible-toting, God-fearing moral idealists. It makes little difference what you or I think, after all we're related. You must consider what this town thinks, for it is these people who will determine, to a large extent, what happens. Don't be surprised if you hear from them and soon." Denise shook her head in disbelief at her brother's attitude and feeling sorry that she had asked. She muttered under her breath, "I don't believe this."

Denise correctly anticipated the town's reaction. Upon arrival at school the next morning, Tracy went straight to the administration office where she worked each day before school and during the homeroom period (the first twenty minutes of the school day). Before she had a chance to begin fielding telephone calls and assisting students with their usual back-to-school problems, John Furst quietly asked if she would come into his office. After closing the door behind her, he asked her to sit down, for he had a delicate matter to discuss. He began, "Tracy, what I have to say, I want you to understand, has absolutely nothing to do with you or your conduct in school. You're an exemplary student with an impeccable record both in and outside of the classroom and I want to keep it that way." John's voice sounded his age. The sound was comforting though, like that of a grandfather. It's difficult to sound angry with a voice like John's no matter what the subject.

Looking puzzled, Tracy attempted, "Yes, but what—"

"Please, let me finish and then you may ask any questions you may have. This session we're having is purely informational and I asked you in here as a matter of courtesy. It's common knowledge that Mr. Driver has been seeing you socially—"

"It has only been twice—" Tracy tried to interrupt.

John simply held up his hand, palm turned toward her, and she stopped.

"I also understand," he continued, "that your parents have consented to these…ah, shall we say, meetings on a limited and restricted basis. This arrangement, as far as the school is concerned, is purely a matter between you and your parents and, of course, Mr. Driver."

By this time Tracy was at attention in her chair, sitting bolt upright her back not touching the chair back. Her mind raced to what Mr. Furst might say next.

"I'll be meeting with Mr. Driver later today to advise him that the district administration and I will not allow him to…to fraternize with you on school property, during normal school hours, or at school-sponsored functions. Should he attempt to do so, his contract will not be renewed or, if necessary, he will be dismissed." John's voice echoed so much empathy that it diffused the threat, and Tracy scarcely took notice.

"But, Mr. Furst, Mr. Driver has been a perfect gentleman; he hasn't done anything to warrant anyone's concern. I don't see—" Tracy tried to rebut.

"My concern," John interrupted, "isn't just with you, but with how parents of other girls will feel about sending their daughters to school if the situation is left unchecked. Parents need to feel that their daughters are not going to be subject to undue or unwanted pressure from those who are in a position of authority. The school is placed in a position of trust, and school policy must foster that trust. I'm sure you understand."

"Not really," she murmured.

"I believe you'll understand that what he does after school hours and off school property is his own business as long as he breaks no laws, but recall you're underage and your parents continued consent is, therefore, essential."

Tracy slumped back into her chair, thinking about what the principal said, her reaction, and Alec's possible reaction. Sensing the consternation in Tracy's mind, John offered, "Tracy, place yourself in my position. Is there any other position I could take? School policy cannot condone open season on young girls by teachers, or administrators for that matter, twice their age. I'm actually doing Mr. Driver a favor—for I do like the man—I'm trying to head off a potentially serious problem before it develops. Just remember, in five months, you'll be a graduate of this school and as such beyond school policy. What happens to you after June may be of personal concern to me, but no concern to the school board—just bear with us for five more months, okay?"

"I suppose so. I guess I see your point, but I still feel your concern is unwarranted, at least in our case." Her reluctance was subdued by his logic and the compassion in his voice.

"Just trust me. You're a very fine young lady and I only want the best for you. Now get out there and get busy before first period begins." He rose and escorted her to the door.

During choir that morning, Tracy penned a note to Alec fearing any conversation with him might be misinterpreted by all the eyes that followed her every move. After class, she casually dropped the note on his lectern making certain he, but no one else, noticed. She tried to smile but didn't succeed very well. Alec opened the note and read its simple two-word message, "Brace yourself."

*****

Alec, puzzled by the note, received a message ten minutes later from John Furst asking Alec to meet with him and Walter Goss during sixth period. Alec knew Walter from the monthly district meetings on music and art and from the church where Walter once directed the choir. *Oh, dear*, he thought, putting the pieces together, *the shit has hit the fan.*

Following Tracy's advice, Alec braced himself as he entered John's office. After the usual pleasantries, John deferred to Walter the point of the meeting. Walter Goss was a trim, balding man only four years Alec's senior in age but many years in experience. He also possessed an advanced degree in music education. Until the draft age was raised toward the end of the war, he had been too old to serve in the military. By the time he received his induction notice and took his physical, the war ended. He spent the war years and the years since accumulating experience in the school system ultimately, rising to his present post six months earlier. He had two school age children from a ten-year marriage to his wife, Janice. His tenure as choir director for the school and the church, posts presently occupied by Alec, spanned his entire pre-administrative career.

Walter explained the concern he and John had for Alec's interest in Tracy and the policy of the school board covering virtually the same ground John Furst did in his earlier discussion with Alec. Walter elaborated on the need for the school faculty and administration to be above reproach. Therefore, Alec would not be permitted to associate socially with Tracy during school hours nor at school sponsored events. He relayed the minister's concern about the church choir and suggested that in the best interest of all concerned that either Tracy or Alec resign from the church choir. Walter offered to retake the reins of the choir until a full-time paid director of music could be recruited should Alec choose that option.

Throughout the discourse Alec sat uncharacteristically silent, studying carefully the expressions on Walter's face and listening attentively to what he said. When Walter finished there was a prolonged silence broken finally by Alec, "Walter, I've never entertained any notion in my capacity as a member of this faculty to cause any embarrassment to Tracy, the school, or myself by behaving in a manner unbecoming my position. I'm too much of a professional to allow that to happen, I trust you know that. I'll abide by your decision to avoid any further potential embarrassment to Tracy for whom I care very much. I also value my position on the faculty and want to do nothing to place it in jeopardy." Alec paused for a moment and then continued, "I will, of course, step down as interim choir director at the church so that Tracy may continue to be a member. I'll simply state that my school duties require more of my time than I anticipated and I can't do justice to both choirs," Alec said resolutely.

Alec's contriteness didn't fully reflect his thoughts. He did care very much for Tracy—that was the primary reason he responded as he did. He resented, however, being double-teamed and lectured like one of the school's students. He especially resented being asked to resign from the church choir and felt the ultimatum given to be grossly unfair and unwarranted. He was aware that as interim director he would be replaced before too much longer anyway. It was the circumstance in which the resignation was to be given that bothered him most. He vowed never again to resign under circumstances he felt were unjustified.

"Fine, then it's settled and finished. As far as we're concerned, it need go no further than this office," Walter said, looking to John for his concurrence that was given by a nod of the head. Walter then added, "Alec, it goes without saying, but I want to say it anyway, that you're entitled to conduct your affairs…ah, social life outside of school in any manner you deem appropriate subject only to the wishes of those with whom you choose to associate. As long as you break no laws or violate board policy, your private life lies outside the jurisdiction of the board."

Not appeased by Walter's last statement, Alec rose from his chair and started toward the door, stopped, turned, and said, "Perhaps you're right. I guess I just don't like being lectured."

Chapter 8

*D*espite their mandates and entreaties, Alec realized, after the initial shock of the meeting wore off, that his relationship with Tracy would not be significantly altered. He never seriously entertained any thought of escorting her to any school functions and did not wish to place Tracy, nor himself for that matter, in an embarrassing position by being excessively friendly to her during the school day. Thus, in essence, the restrictions imposed by John Furst would not result in any further constraints than those already dictated by Tracy's parents. Alec even felt a sense of relief to be rid of his church choir duties even though he missed the Thursday night meetings with Tracy. She also resigned the choir because of conflicts with school activities, or so she told Walter Goss. They dated mostly on Sunday afternoons that often lasted well into the evening and only occasionally on Friday or Saturday night.

Sunday afternoons, weather permitting, consisted of picnics and trips to the beach. If sufficient time lapsed between successive winter cold fronts, the weather in central Florida would clear and the temperature would rise into the low eighties. On such days, Tracy and Alec walked barefoot for miles in ankle-deep water along the white sandy beaches talking, collecting seashells and sand dollars, or simply holding hands. They shared the gorgeous sunsets that the clear skies afforded often sitting on the sand and watching the sun settle deeper and deeper into the blue-green Gulf waters and hoping to catch a glimpse of the Green Flash.

The Green Flash, known almost exclusively by ardent sailors, is a natural phenomenon that occurs just as the sun disappears below the horizon on a hazy but cloudless evening. Only visible over water, the phenomenon occurs on very few days as the atmospheric conditions must be just right. If all the conditions are met, the rapidly disappearing last tip of the sun produces a distinct green flash of light if for but a brief moment as it sinks below the horizon. This rare refraction of light is taken as a good omen as it indicates that "God is in his heaven and all is right with the world."

On their way to the beach, Alec, driving either Denise's 1951 Plymouth or Nancy's 1952 Buick, frequently turned off the causeway and drove as far as practical onto dredged up bay bottom that was fast becoming Island Estates, a large residential development interlaced with numerous canals that would allow many future home buyers to enjoy "waterfront" property. They walked on the white, sun-bleached sand dikes that were formed by huge draglines throwing their large buckets into the bay and dragging them along the bottom scooping up sand in immense dripping gulps and dumping it in front of the monstrous machine. Two score throws and a little time for drying provided enough fill and support to allow the drag-line to crawl forward forty or fifty feet where it stopped and repeated the process. After enclosing a carefully surveyed area by the dike, a dredge equipped with a snout-like device in the shape of a large eggbeater, was towed into a position near the dike. The dredge dipped its beak into the bay and with the help of anchors and pulleys it oscillated from side to side grinding and sucking the bay bottom into its snout. It then discharged the heavy wet muck through large linked pipes placed on empty oil drums in a snake like fashion into the area encircled by the dike. The displaced water drained through weep holes inserted periodically in the dike. As the soupy sand-and-water mixture dried, a crust of harden sand formed on top, giving it the appearance of a hardened surface. More than once Alec pulled himself or Tracy out of the waist-deep muck that lay beneath the broken surface.

On some days they sat for hours watching the dredge that, because its rental charge was by the day, operated around the clock and on Sundays. The operation became a source of fascination and concern for Tracy as she watched the once clear bay waters turn murky. Because seaweed disappeared with bay bottom, the bay waters remained that way for many years. They agreed that it seemed a high price to pay for progress measured by the number of new water front lots created along the maze of canals being formed by the development.

Alec used these excursions to talk openly of his wartime experiences and his first marriage to a hometown girl. He told Tracy that she was correct when she surmised that the marriage occurred because he felt a need to be close to someone. After the war was over, the marriage lasted for several years while he attended Princeton. As time passed, the difference in their personal interests became prominent because the wartime nexus that held them together vanished. He told Tracy how impressed he was with each of the places where he was stationed during the war: the west coast of Florida, England, and Germany for a short time immediately following VE day. He not only swore he would return to Florida to live but to visit the English and German countryside he grew to love. Traveling during the service stirred a passion within him to see the world as he had seen England and Germany. His first wife, he confessed, didn't share his passion for travel or living in Florida. It came down to a choice between her and Florida. She made Alec decide, but Alec felt that it was she that had made the choice. Alec's revelations of his prior romance and subsequent marriage didn't bother Tracy. Instead, they seemed to draw her closer to him as did Alec's encounters with John Furst and Walter Goss. The encounters and discussions made Tracy feel more a part of the adult world, a world that she eagerly sought to join. They also served to demonstrate the deep affection Alec felt for her.

On inclement Sundays, Alec and Tracy wandered into the Ashbury living room where Lloyd placed, over Nancy's strenuous objection, his newest gadget, a television set brandishing a nine-inch oval screen. The first television station within receiving range began broadcasting in St. Petersburg bringing the new media to central Florida for the first time. Lloyd did not so much purchase the set for viewing as for tinkering. Lloyd relieved Nancy's concern for living room decor by keeping it most of the time in his garage-turned-shop where he took it apart and reassembled it on several occasions just to see how it worked and, of course, improve upon its design and performance. Sunday evening fare consisted of Jack Benny, Alec's favorite because of Jack's deadpan humor and parsimony; *Private Secretary*, Tracy's favorite because she loved the way Ann Southern was able to finagle her boss, Mr. Sands; Walter Winchell, and the *GE Theater*. Lloyd preferred viewing on Monday nights when he could catch George Burns and Gracie Allen, *I Love Lucy*, and Red Buttons. Nancy thought the invention an intrusion and rarely deigned to watch.

The Sunday dates came midst Alec's intense rehearsing for his first spring concert. Despite what some people thought about his relationship with Tracy, he knew he would be judged professionally by how well the choirs performed at the annual public concert. He followed Tracy's advice and planned a "pops" theme for the concert using the more popular songs from the Rogers and Hammerstein productions, *South Pacific, Oklahoma,* and *Carousel*. He planned to end the concert with the *Battle Hymn of the Republic*; the Mormon Tabernacle Choir version was enjoying a surprising run at the top of popular charts. Tracy would provide the only accompaniment on the piano.

Following his previous plan, he carefully selected the twelve best voices in the choir including Tracy and Eddie Harlow and scheduled throughout the school year short programs with monthly luncheon meetings of one civic club or another. He hoped to accomplish two goals in the process. The presentations provided exposure for the choir's best voices that he hoped boded well for the entire choir. They also allowed the twelve to gain experience and poise as well as provide an opportunity to meld together into a well-coordinated and synchronized singing group. The twelve formed the core for the musical numbers in the concert with the remaining students (including the junior high choir) providing the choral background.

The concert, held in the high school auditorium in mid-March, received rave reviews by parents and Alec's fellow teachers. Many took the time to congratulate him personally after the performance. Tracy delighted the audience with her choreographed performance of "I'm Gonna Wash That Man Right Outa My Hair," while the boys in the chosen twelve brought the house down with their rendition of "There Is Nothing Like a Dame." Clearly the best performance of the evening belonged to Eddie Harlow who sang in his natural baritone voice, "Some Enchanted Evening." Alec found Lynnda Sharp's performance of "When You Walk Through a Storm" particularly moving.

However, the *pièce de résistance* had to be the Battle Hymn number. Not only did our combined choirs perform well, Tracy's piano accompaniment brought down the house. Alec knew she could play well, but her performance that evening exceeded even his high expectations. All in all, he thought with some satisfaction that the program couldn't have been better tailored for its audience or its performers. He had Tracy to thank for that. The concert gave Alec the musical credentials he sought.

Honoring her parents' wishes, Tracy continued to date on other weekend nights, boys in her class including and almost exclusively Buster Forbes. She drew the inevitable comparisons between the boys and Alec and each time the boys, and especially Buster, suffered markedly. Most of them possessed large egos and exuded an adolescent bravado, but they lacked the confidence, the maturity, the knowledge or *savoir-faire* of Alec. Only in physical looks could she say that they compared favorably with him. In terms of strength, stamina, and statue, however, she felt Alec could match them muscle for muscle, stride for stride, and pound for pound. She concluded that Alec's twenty-year head start had not placed him at any physical disadvantage to her seventeen- and eighteen-year-old male cohorts.

As the weeks went by, their lowered dating profile dampened the community's concern over Alec's interest in Tracy. Their lives seemed to settle down to something approximating normalcy. Telephone calls once or twice a week replaced the Thursday night diner visits. Tracy's parents and Alec's sister became reconciled to the calls and Sunday outings although none, except Alec and Tracy, felt entirely comfortable with their continuing relationship. By the time of the concert, Tracy virtually stopped dating anyone else even though she still honored the once a week limit on dates with Alec that her parents imposed.

Early March marked a milestone for Tracy. On her birthday Lloyd light-heartily remarked that at eighteen she had reached the age of consent, but would have to wait three more years to reach the age of majority, a difference he failed to understand. Alec, choosing not to intrude on the family celebration, didn't attend. Instead he made the occasion special several days later by taking Tracy to dinner and the Thornton Wilder play, *Our Town*, in St. Petersburg.

As her birthday passed, nothing else seemed to matter to Tracy except the relationship she and Alec were establishing and what they would do the next weekend. It seemed to both that life consisted of Sunday afternoons and all else was filler for the space between successive Sundays.

Tracy's growing affection for Alec went unnoticed by most who knew her as she considered her feelings toward him private and declined to discuss them even with Ruth Ann. She felt the community reacted poorly when it first discovered Alec's interest in her, and she was not going to reveal her true feelings and give the community another chance to react in a similar way. What was not obvious to the community did not go unnoticed by Alec. He felt her coming closer to him, such as how she squeezed his hand when he held it, the way she looked at him when she smiled at something witty he said, or the way she lay her head on his shoulder when they sat silently watching the sunset or listening to moving music.

Sunday mornings Alec walked to Denise's house for lunch and then continued to Tracy's afterward. As it happened, Denise and Mark lived halfway between Alec's garage apartment and Tracy's house. Alec's route took him past our house twice, once about eleven in the morning when we were at church and there was no one home to restrain Laddie, and again at nine in the evening when it was dark. This "rite of passage" was the only dampener on Alec's Sundays. Alec and Laddie formed a mutual disrespect as each waited for the other to back down.

One Sunday evening in late March after Alec and Laddie confronted each other for the second time that day, Alec thought that a strange parallel seemed to exist between the problems he was having with Laddie and those with others in the community. Alec later confided those feelings to Pop at a reception following the schools' spring open house for parents. Until the spring concert, neither Laddie nor many people in the community seemed willing to accept Alec as part of it. He recalled our after-school conversation in December and reasoned that his attentiveness and behavior toward Tracy had caused teachers, minister, principal, and some parents to become suspicious and defensive much as I described Laddie's behavior toward him. If correct, he asked Pop jokingly, "Why am I still having trouble with your dog when all the other fuss over Tracy and me seems to have settled down after the concert? A superstitious man might believe the continuing problems with your dog prophetic. It's a good thing that I'm not a superstitious man." He laughed. Pop smiled.

*****

I thought it was an April fool's joke when I first heard the news from Will Coats, a good friend and choir mate. He told the story at lunch, and the rumor spread like a wave over the sea of students in the cafeteria during the junior high lunch period. The lunchroom, located across the street from the two schools, sat next to the PE facility. The small wood frame building looked like a converted church with large wood posts dotting its front porch and the single gable a perfect nesting place for a steeple. The dining area occupied the space where pews might rest. The back of the room contained the serving area with the line backing down its west side and ultimately out the front door and onto the sidewalk. There were far more tables and chairs than the space allocated could comfortably hold, but then, little concern was given to student comfort especially when no one spent, in a day before school breakfasts, more than fifteen minutes a day at the tables. For the unfortunate latecomers, the wait in line lasted twice as long and was never worth it.

The junior high lunch period, scheduled an hour earlier than the senior high, barely allowed sufficient time for stragglers to finish before getting caught in the onslaught of onrushing senior high males who delighted in crushing any junior high youth between them and the cafeteria line. I know the rush didn't result from the expectation of a delicious meal.

The junior high lunch period reached its peak with the room crowded to overflowing.

"I know," I said to Will, "April Fool!"

"No, dumb shit, this is no April fool joke," yelled Will over the din of the lunchroom. "Mr. Driver plastered some guy in the senior high choir. He took him to the school nurse who called his mother to take him to the hospital."

"Was the guy hurt bad?" I asked, realizing Will wasn't kidding.

"He was bleeding pretty bad from the mouth and the nurse said he might need stitches." Will seemed to delight in being the source of fresh information.

"How do you know all this?" I asked, somewhat envious that Will had learned the juicy gossip first.

"I was in the nurse's office when they came in."

"What happened when the guy's mother showed up?" I asked, knowing the wrath a mother could exhibit when her child had been wronged.

"She was really mad. She said she would be back to talk with the Mr. Furst," Will answered with relish.

"Where was Mr. Driver?" I queried.

"In Mr. Furst's office."

"Who's the guy he hit?" I finally asked. The details of what transpired superseded my curiosity of who had been the recipient of the blow.

"I never saw him before," Will said with some disgust at his ignorance.

I learned later that it was Tommy Strickland. Because Tommy had no younger brothers or sisters in my class, I only knew him by reputation. Will was right about Alec. After securing medical care for Tommy, Alec headed straight to John Furst's office. He didn't intend to let John hear the story secondhand, reasoning that Tommy's parents would soon appear with their version. Alec thought it prudent to get there first with his story rather than end up on the defensive.

Tommy Strickland, the younger of two brothers to attend the high school and serve in its choir, seemed to carry a chip on his shoulder and antagonized nearly all of his teachers. He considered choir a blow off class and expressed only contempt for Alec and his serious approach to music. Repeatedly Alec called him down in class for talking, not singing with the rest of the choir, or for reading comic books. The tension built during the school year as Tommy became more brazen in his responses to Alec's reproaches. No one knew for certain the source of Tommy's attitude but speculation centered on a growing irritation over Alec's romantic flirtations with Tracy.

Tracy and Tommy entered kindergarten together and subsequently shared many classes over the ensuing years. While neither ever expressed any outward romantic interest in the other, they grew to be more than just casual friends. In their high school years, Tommy's open hostility to teachers bothered Tracy. Tommy's in-class remarks to Alec embarrassed her. Undoubtedly it was this part of Tommy's personality that kept him, literally, at arm's distance from Tracy. Apparently Alec's interest in Tracy and, perhaps more importantly, her interest in him aroused something in Tommy. His attitude could, I suppose, have been sparked by teenage bravado, resentment, or perhaps, jealousy. Some speculated that he secretly adored Tracy and used their platonic friendship as an opportunity to get close to her without fear of rejection. Conjecture was the only recourse in the search for a motive for Tommy's behavior. Outside a few caustic secret comments to close friends, Tommy never revealed to anyone how or even what he felt toward Alec. Some teachers believed that the absence of a strong masculine image in the home explained much of Tommy's recalcitrance. His father never returned home after being drafted into the service during the war. Some said he died in action, but others insisted that he simply chose not to return home after the war. His wife, Shirley, listed him as "missing-in-action."

Tommy, slight of build and average height, was a close physical match to Alec. When they stood toe to toe, they were also eyeball to eyeball. Their encounters during and after class often turned into a contest of who would blink first. As the school year wore on, Tommy became less timid about what he said and how he said it and Alec less tolerant of what he would take and how he would take it. To most in the class, even to Tracy, a clash between the two seemed inevitable. Caught in the middle, she felt powerless to intervene.

On this Thursday morning, the inevitable happened. After several rapid fire escalating verbal exchanges during class, Alec demanded Tommy stay after class, to which Tommy muttered to those sitting near him, "The hell I will!"

When the period ended, Tommy tried to make his way to the door, but Alec, his face reddened, intercepted him with arm extended and index finger pointing in parental fashion directly into Tommy's face.

"Young man, you sit down, I want to see you!" Alec yelled.

"I thought the only person you wanted to see was Tracy," Tommy yelled back.

"Leave her out of this," Alec said coldly.

Tommy brushed Alec's extended hand aside and said, "You're trying to make her a member of your family—a real Hooker!" Like lighting, Alec's right fist struck and caught Tommy square on the mouth. The blow was so quick that lingering students could only recall seeing Tommy reel over and blood pour from inside his mouth. No one, other than Alec, heard what Tommy said and it didn't appear to matter.

John listened carefully as Alec recounted the morning's events, jotting down a note here and there as Alec spoke. After Alec finished John remarked that while he understood, he did not agree with Alec's reaction. He further noted that the timing of this incident was most unfortunate for the list of faculty recommended for the new campus was due in the district office the next day. Given the potential gravity of the situation, he would have to omit Alec's name from the list until the matter was settled. Crestfallen, Alec lamented to John that he looked forward to working on the new campus where his duties would consist of instruction to senior high students only. John promised to address the matter immediately and attempt to resolve the issue quickly. However, he warned, striking a student, no matter how justified the provocation, constituted a serious infraction of school policy that allowed only limited corporal punishment administered by the principal or his delegated representative.

Alec left the principal's office with a sick feeling in his stomach and much less confident that his reaction to Tommy's insolence was justified. He wandered into the teachers' lounge where rumors of the incident, in swift course, preceded him. Naturally all in attendance wanted to learn firsthand what happened. Alec recounted most of the details. He thought about not revealing the specifics of what Tommy said, but the few students that witnessed the incident had already spread the word. John and Alec agreed not to officially quote Tommy but to state that he had been "provocatively disrespectful." It hardly mattered as striking a student was against school policy no matter the provocation. They decided to be cryptic for fear of fanning the flames over Alec and Tracy's relationship. They did not wish to subject Tracy and her parents to what would undoubtedly be additional embarrassment. They agreed that if provocation were to be his defense, it would be kept from the public. They could think of no reason to involve Tracy.

After Alec finished, Abe Jordan, the boy's wood shop instructor and a balding, mousy-looking little man with teenage sons of his own, offered his heartfelt support.

"I know the frustration you must have felt. Sometimes I want to reach out and knock some heads myself. Some of these boys' behavior borders on the criminal. I know few will actually end up in jail or on the wrong side of the law, but many have no respect for other people or property and are downright destructive. I have this one junior high class with the Collins kid in it. He isn't a gang leader, but he always seems to be in the middle of every disruptive incident that happens, unfortunately he's not the only one! Just let me tell you a few things that have happened to me."

Alec, being very familiar with my name, formed a receptive audience for any sympathy or reinforcement he could get. He nodded attentively for the shop teacher to continue and then withdrew a tuna fish and tomato sandwich from his lunch bag and sat back along with the others in the room to listen.

"One day," Abe began, "I noticed several boys gathered around the soldering irons in the back corner of the shop with Collins and the Coats kid in the middle of the group. They stayed there for some time, looking around occasionally as if to keep an eye out for me. I decided that I had better check on them. The soldering irons have tapered metal heads and are attached by a long metal shaft to a wood handle. The wooden box I made to store them in has a nice carved handle on a top that's countersunk into the four sides. I'm rather proud of the job I did. Anyway, the irons are heated in a small gas furnace until they are hot enough to melt the solder. As I walked toward them, they began to scurry about, so I shouted, 'What's going on?' When I reached the site I asked them to stand aside. I looked around and didn't see anything amiss, but I smelled the odor of burning wood. I looked to see what was burning and could find nothing obvious, but it seemed to be coming from the box on the workbench. I lifted the top off and peered down into it, and as I did a puff of black smoke engulfed my face so much I almost choked. I turned the box around and saw two large gaping holes in the backside of the box. They were heating the irons until they were white hot and then having a race to see who could burn through my handmade, finished tool box first."

"What did you do?" Alec asked more than passively interested in other teachers' reactions to unruly students.

"I made them pay for the materials to build a new box and stay after school for an hour a day for a week."

"Why didn't you have them make a new tool box?" Alec asked innocently.

"Are you kidding? Have you seen their work? Not on your life. But that's not all." He drew a deep breath and continued, "I've always extolled to my students the properties of Weldwood glue that provides a bond which, when dried, is often stronger than the wood itself. Well, someone in my sixth period class decided to put what I said to the test. The class is the last of the day and I noticed with some surprise one day last week that all of the tools were in their proper places on their wall hooks in the tool room without my calling for them to be returned. Pleased that the cleanup had been already accomplished, I closed and locked the tool room door. The next morning when the first period class began work, a student said the wood rulers were stuck to the wood paneled walls. I said, 'What?'

and inspected the rulers and found that all twenty-four eighteen-inch rulers had been glued to the wall with Weldwood glue. In addition, mind you, the pencil sharpener was full of hardened glue."

Again Alec asked in complete sympathy, "What did you do this time?

"I had to rip the rulers off the wall with a claw hammer and send in a purchase request for new rulers. I soaked the pencil sharpener for two days and the glue came loose from the metal somewhat, but I still had to get another one.

Alec shook his head. The shop teacher said, "There's more! One day last week, the Collins kid, Jimmy Middle, and Denny Norms were working, or supposed to be working on their cedar chests in an adjacent room that used to house the machine shop. Instead, do you know what they were doing?"

"No telling," said Alec.

"They were playing baseball!" Abe fired back.

Alec's eyes grew big, and he cocked his head in bewilderment.

"How—" Alec started to ask.

"They had the door between the two shops closed, so I couldn't see what was happening. You have to get the picture: the old machine shop is rather large, about thirty feet across and sixty feet deep with at least a sixteen-foot ceiling. They wadded up several sheets of newspaper and wrapped it with six or seven layers of masking tape, a design, if packed tight, makes, believe me, a very hard ball. Denny Norms, remember, is the star pitcher on the junior high baseball team. It seems he was pitching to the Collins kid who was using a bat that the Moore kid in another class was turning out on the wood lathe. Norms pitched Collins a fast one and Collins pulled it in a hard shot that went through the glass transom above the door to the wood shop and scattered glass in a line some fifty feet down the aisle. Fortunately, no one was there at the time. After being startled out of my skin, I picked up the ball and slowly walked into the room tossing the ball in the air as I walked. I found Norms and Collins pretending to be busy sanding their cedar chests. The Middle kid I found hiding under his overturned cedar chest.

"Now I haven't included everything like the time I was sitting at my desk deeply engrossed in *The Woodworkers Press* while, I thought, the class was busy reading an assignment. Suddenly a piece of stiff square cardboard they had been sailing around the room rips through the paper I was holding up in front of me and lands in my lap just missing my nose.

"I tell you what, Alec, you've struck a blow for all of us. Not only the Strickland kid, but the Middles, the Collins, the Norms, and all the other little assholes we have to put up with. I'll tell you something else too. I make them pay for any damages, I make them stay after school, I make them do extra work, I lower their grades, but they still keep coming back. I'll bet you right now that you'll never have any more trouble with the Strickland kid, ever!"

*****

"I want to know what you're going to do about it?" the shrill voice demanded. The voice, trembling with emotion, bit angrily into the already heavy atmosphere of John Furst's inner office. John's office, with its hard wood floors, plaster walls, and ceiling, and curtain-less windows, reverberated with Shirley's words. To add to the discomfort, the unseasonably cool temperature outside necessitated keeping the windows closed causing Shirley's voice to bounce repeatedly between the walls. Physically, Shirley Strickland was only a mite of a woman, easily qualifying for Oscar Hammerstein's lyrical description, *"I'm speaking of my sweetie pie, only sixty inches high, every inch is packed with dynamite."* Mentally, emotionally, and psychologically, she possessed all the attributes of an instructor in feminine assertiveness. Undaunted by masculine mores, language, and attitudes, she raised and supported herself and two sons without the benefit of the "stronger" sex. Never asking nor giving any quarter, Shirley managed to hold her own in any encounter, especially those that she picked. Shrewd and savvy, Shirley picked her battles and battlegrounds carefully. She played to win—compromise, was no better than a loss.

Firing on all cylinders, she came prepared to see swift justice done for the injustice suffered by her son. An assault on her son was an assault on her—raging mad she was firing back.

Shirley's fiery reputation preceded her everywhere she went. Both genders cringed when they stood on the receiving end of Shirley's wrath. Had she been a man, her, or his, emotional outbursts would not have been perceived any differently. Previous meetings with John Furst consisted of cordial parents' nights and the graduation of her oldest son two years earlier. John knew, however, what her reaction would be even before calling to inform her of Tommy's injury. The assistant principal normally handled calls of this nature. John, not wishing to burden his inexperienced second in command with the coming confrontation, placed the call and requested Shirley come by his office to discuss the incident after she returned from the hospital. Although sympathetic with the plight of a parent of a mistreated child, he prepared a strategy that he hoped would defuse the emotion and passion of the moment and settle the matter amicably without violating justice. He knew he had a fine line to walk.

John waited patiently while Shirley Strickland voiced her outrage until he thought it time to assume command of the meeting lest her emotions and temper get out of hand and reckless ultimatums ensued.

"I understand your feelings, Mrs. Strickland, both as a father and a school principal, I'm concerned when any one is struck and injured, no matter how slight, by anyone else while at school. Because I am concerned, I'm first interested in getting all the facts prior to deciding what action, if any, is warranted." Turning to Tommy who sat next to his mother, Mr. Furst asked, "Please tell me, Tommy, exactly what happened between you and Mr. Driver this morning."

Looking first at his mother, then at John, then back at his mother, Tommy bowed his head slightly and began, "Well, Mr. Driver hit me in the mouth," he tersely announced.

"Would you explain what led up to the…ah, incident?" John asked.

"Mr. Driver…he stuck his finger in my face and grabbed me as I tried to go to my next class. He hit me when I tried to get past him," Tommy replied in a loud voice.

"Why did Mr. Driver try to prevent you from going to your next class?" John pursued.

"I don't know," came a meek reply much softer than Tommy's previous one.

"Tommy, didn't Mr. Driver reprimand you in class for talking and not paying attention not once but repeatedly this morning? And did he not tell you to remain after class?" John asked in rapid-fire succession.

"Yes, but I had to go to my next class I didn't want to be late. He shouldn't have hit me for it!" Tommy shouted.

Shirley Strickland sat stoically, her eyes darting back and forth between the principal and her son as they spoke.

"Tell me exactly what you did to try to elude Mr. Driver. Did you not brush his arm aside and say something?" He paused for a moment, giving his questions time to sink in before continuing, "What did you say, Tommy? What was it you said to Mr. Driver just before he struck you?"

"I…I don't remember," he stammered.

"Didn't you say something about what Mr. Driver could do because you had no intention of staying after class?" John persisted.

Tommy sat silently.

"Come on, Tommy. What did you say? Surely you haven't forgotten so soon. If you wish, I could ask Mr. Driver. What did you say?" John pursued his line of questioning, feeling confident that Tommy would not reveal his reference to Tracy. Nor, he suspected, would Tommy dare repeat his expletive. John clearly had the upper hand. Tommy's behavior in other classes combined with what he said to Alec could result in disciplinary action that would delay Tommy's graduation. John was subtly but forcefully driving the point home.

With his head buried Tommy muttered, "I told him that—"

"I don't give a darn what he said. This crazed man should not have hit Tommy," Shirley interrupted, her voice quaking.

Nearly thirty years of administrative experience and a quiet disposition enabled John to maintain his calm even in the heat of parental or administrative battles. It was a quality that unquestionably contributed to the respect he commanded from students, teachers, administrators, parents, and the general public. Invoking all these admirable attributes, John turned to Shirley and said in a calm but authoritarian tone, "Mrs. Strickland, I'm trying to get Tommy to see that he did his best to provoke Mr. Driver this morning, as he has done on numerous other occasions to other teachers as well. I don't hold with striking a student, but at the same time I believe that it's important for all of us to understand the pressures that came to bear on Mr. Driver when he struck your son. Tommy must realize that he bears some responsibility for what happened this morning."

"All I understand is that I was called away from my work to take my son to the hospital because Mr. Driver struck him in the mouth. It's just fortunate that the wound didn't require stitches. I still want to know what you're going to do about it," she again demanded.

"I'd like to talk with Tommy alone for a few minutes, that is, if you'll allow me," John quietly asked while looking Shirley straight in the eyes.

John hadn't blinked during Shirley's shrill discourse, and she found his stare intimidating. She answered in a voice several octaves lower than her last statement, "I'll wait outside."

"That's okay, Mom. Go back to work. I'll ride home with Tim Smith. I'll be all right," Tommy said to her reassuringly.

"If you would like to return to work, Mrs. Strickland, I'll see to it personally that Tommy returns home safely," John offered.

"All right," she answered. "We'll continue this discussion tonight, Tommy, when I get home from work." She left, closing the door quietly behind her.

John spent the next five minutes explaining to Tommy that he knew exactly what Tommy said and that both he and Alec had acted improperly. He told Tommy that he must bear his share of the responsibility for Alec's actions and that this wasn't the first time that Tommy had been in the principal's or the dean of student's office, but John intended it to be the last. He told Tommy that if he apologized to Alec, he was certain that Alec would reciprocate. If he offered not to pursue a charge of assault against Alec, John explained, Alec would agree not to reveal what Tommy said. Tommy replied that he would think it over and let him know his decision the next day. John replied, "Fine."

After arriving late to his office the next morning, John smiled when he saw Tommy waiting for him. Tommy immediately announced that he had thought over John's suggestion and decided to accept. He just wanted to forget the whole thing. John advised him to see Alec immediately and to report back what happened between Alec and him.

John, while pleased with Tommy's decision, believed that fear of reprisal wasn't the sole motivating force in Tommy's apparent change in attitude. If hallway scuttlebutt proved correct, Tommy didn't enjoy much peer support. Many students believed something like this incident inevitable. For reasons most students had not discerned, Tommy seemed bent on antagonizing Alec, forcing, eventually, some type of showdown. Perhaps, John thought, if Tommy's actions were a cry for someone to provide him with guidance, he got it. Undoubtedly, John thought, the shock of being floored by a sharp blow to the mouth also had something to do with his change of attitude. It also appeared that other students didn't want to put up with Tommy's disruptive behavior any more than the teachers. He smiled to himself at that prospect.

Tommy soon returned and reported that he apologized to Alec and, as John had predicted, Alec returned the apology. As he left, John felt pleased with the outcome. There were only two things left to do: stop by the choir room on his way to deliver the list of recommended faculty to the district office and confirm Tommy's story with Alec and then pencil in Alec's name in the blank he had left for it. He thought this final act would thereby lay the entire matter to rest.

Shirley Strickland was furious at what she regarded as John's cavalier attitude when Tommy related the events that transpired that Friday at school. Tommy did not reveal to her what he said to Alec, and it mattered not. Nor did it matter that Tommy and Alec had resolved their differences. John Furst may consider the matter settled, but she remained determined to pursue her case the following week with the district superintendent, Christopher Fletcher. On Monday morning, she arranged an appointment with one of Mr. Fletcher's assistants for the following afternoon.

Tuesday morning Shirley dressed in her new business suit, intending to present her appearance and arguments in the best professional manner. After twenty determined minutes that afternoon, the assistant decided Mr. Fletcher should hear her story personally. After excusing himself and conferring for three or four minutes with him, the assistant returned and escorted Shirley into the superintendent's office where she spent another thirty minutes. At the end of the meeting Mr. Fletcher admitted that he hadn't heard of the incident, but if the facts confirmed her account of it, Alec would be asked to resign. With a great deal of smug satisfaction, Shirley Strickland strutted in her high heel pumps out of his office and back to her car.

Until this point, John Furst had successfully kept the incident confined to campus away from the local press. Shirley ended the journalistic silence. Before meeting with Christian Fletcher, she called *The Sun* and notified the reporter normally assigned to school board matters of her meeting and the reason for it. She scheduled an interview with the reporter immediately after her meeting with Fletcher. She reasoned that win, lose, or draw with the school board, the publicity could only help her cause. The next afternoon, the story was front-page news. The reporter quoted everyone involved, everyone that is except Alec and Tommy. Neither agreed to meet with *The Sun* reporter nor any of the reporters from the *Tribune* in Tampa nor the *Times* in St. Petersburg.

Three days later, after nonstop articles in all papers, Shirley received a telephone call from Mr. Fletcher telling her that he had verified her story to his satisfaction and that Mr. Driver would be asked to resign effective at the end of the school year. He told her that teachers are hired on a probationary basis during the first three years' service and that no reason need be given for not renewing their contracts during that period. If Mr. Driver refused to tender his resignation, there appeared to be sufficient grounds not to renew his contract for another year. To justify an immediate dismissal, a hearing would have to be held, a process that could last until the school year was over given the late date. He further told her that a press release covering the same conclusions he relayed to her would be distributed to the press after all parties had been informed. She thanked him for his concern and quick, decisive action. She smiled as she replaced the telephone receiver.

Walter Goss and John Furst received their notice from one of Christian Fletcher's assistants at the same time Christian phoned Shirley. The task of asking Alec for his resignation fell upon them. They reluctantly accepted the task and scheduled a meeting with Alec during his second period break the following Monday. A press release of the superintendent's action would be distributed that day at noon. By the time of the meeting, ten days had elapsed since Alec and Tommy resolved their differences. Alec thought the matter was closed. When Walter informed him of the superintendent's decision, Alec's jaw dropped in total disbelief. He recovered sufficiently to respond clearly that he would not resign. He had been forced to resign the church choir and accepted it partially out of deference to Tracy, but he would not resign this time. The issue had been resolved among the primary participants, including the choir to which Tommy had openly apologized, and John Furst. Alec thought, *Why should I resign simply because some irate mother wasn't as mature as her teenage son?* Suddenly he understood one of the sources of Tommy's attitude and behavioral problems and he sympathized with him.

Walter told Alec that even if he didn't tender his resignation he wouldn't be reappointed next year. Alec still refused, insisting that the issue should have remained resolved. Alec walked slowly back to the choir building at the other end of the campus. He thought of Tracy and his deep desire to remain in the community and build his career and, perhaps, start his own family. He saw his dreams being swept away by the harsh winds of a bitter woman's bent for vengeance. Yet he remained resolute; he would not give up without a fight.

He stood motionless in front of our, that is, the junior high choir, silent for the longest time. The normal before-class chatter that Alec often had to quiet with a loud whistle slowly ebbed as the young students sensed something was different that morning. A hush fell; the room grew so quiet that it drew even my attention. Alec simply said, "I've been asked to resign."

Everyone knew why, and whispers of confirmation spread throughout the large crowed room until silence filled the room as if by an invisible hand signaling quiet. Alec said no more on the subject during class, choosing to busy us in a methodical review of the most recent musical scores we had learned.

After class, a large number of students remained, expressing how they thought it was unfair for the school system to ask for his resignation. They pondered what they could do to help, and someone suggested they ask their parents to sign a petition to the superintendent requesting that Alec be retained because of his success with the choirs. Alec noticed a familiar head at the back of the crowd and was clearly taken aback when he realized who it was. I was the last student he thought he would see come to his defense. I know he thought I was there solely to gloat. In all the turmoil, Alec thought no more of it.

John Furst belatedly told Alec of another factor bearing on the school district superintendent's decision. The same week that Shirley Strickland talked with Christopher Fletcher, Arthur Oats, the parent of another senior high choir member, called on John to discuss the "distressing" incident. When John informed Arthur that the matter had been resolved, he became angry, saying that he and other parents were clearly opposed to Alec's reappointment. John suggested that Arthur and the others could put their objections in a signed letter and deliver it to him and he would forward it to Christopher Fletcher. To John Furst's surprise Arthur did just that. Two days later on Thursday morning he hand delivered a typed note signed by a half dozen parents requesting that Alec not be reappointed by the district the following year.

The local papers quickly learned of Arthur's petition, and a counter petition requesting that Alec be allowed to continue in his post was quickly circulated. Despite the Cold War, the local papers seemed preoccupied with Alec's story and carried numerous stories and editorials on both sides of the issue. The papers waffled on their positions reflecting the division within the community. No school in the district, in anyone's memory, had experienced a similar incident. The lack of precedent undoubtedly contributed heavily to the growing controversy. During the entire process Alec, John, and Tommy maintained their tacit agreement not to reveal the exact contents of Tommy's remarks. The longer the controversy dragged on, the less relevant those contents became. After a while no one seemed to care, positions had become entrenched.

For the most part, I remained reticent choosing to listen and watch my friends plot ways to get their parents to sign the petition supporting Alec. To most of my friends the petition was excitement, a chance to conspire against the school district and rebel against authority, or so it seemed to me.

I knew Tommy Strickland only by reputation and in that regard all too well. I guess I saw a part of Tommy in myself, and it bothered me. It also bothered me that a teacher who finally would no longer put up with disruptive behavior would be fired. Recall that at the time I, too, was unaware of what Tommy had said. What a difference two years makes, I remember thinking. My sixth grade teacher had transferred from a school in the South Bronx. She was a heavyset woman in her late thirties and as strong as an ox. I asked myself, how many times had Miss Charlot slapped students with no more provocation than normal lack of discipline and drew no one's ire except, of course, the students. There had been no outpouring of indignation, no press reports, no meetings with the superintendent of schools, or principal for that matter; it was simply her way of maintaining order. I was on the receiving end of her wallops on two or three occasions that year but didn't hold the record. Wally Deacon was the recipient of her powerful swings so frequently that he learned the signs of a forthcoming blow. On one occasion Wally buried his head in his arms on his desk to protect his face from what he knew was coming not just by what Miss Charlot did but also by what he had done. She tried to pry one of his arms free from his head, but it took two of hers to do so. When she freed one arm to deliver the blow, Wally yanked his arm back over his head for protection. Before long, both teacher and student were rolling on the floor while the rest of us watched with glee. She continued to try to wrestle his arms free for a clean, sharp blow. She finally settled for numerous glancing strikes about Wally's head.

Miss Charlot started the year by apprising us that she had taught the toughest hoods in the world and the students in our class were no match for them or her. The irony of her bravado was that after five months with our class, she entered the city hospital for three months suffering from a "nervous breakdown." When she returned to class for the last month of school, she was a different woman, never again raising her voice or striking a student. That summer she married an Egyptian and left town never heard from again. No, I thought, it's unfair for Alec to have to resign. I knew all too well what teachers like Alec had to endure and I guess I secretly admired any one of them who fought back rather than capitulate.

Pop shared my concern for Alec but for different reasons. Having never taught children, he was unaware of the pressures teachers had to endure, but he did recognize unruly behavior. Clearly the description I provided of Tommy Strickland's behavior fell into that definition. Pop also understood the temperament of dedicated musicians that sometimes caused their behavior to become quite emotional. His thoughts weren't just the results of stereotyping, but resulted from what Pop obviously recognized in himself and his musical mentors.

Pop decided against signing any petition. That was not Pop's style. Newspaper reporters followed the story closely quoting parents on both sides of the issue. Pop didn't wish to become part of, nor contribute to, the growing public spectacle. Instead he called his long-time musical colleague, Walter Goss, and upon Walter's advice, wrote Christopher Fletcher on his own business letterhead. The letter read:

April 21, 1954

Dear Mr. Fletcher:

I understand, through my son, Dean, a student of Mr. Alec Driver, that Mr. Driver has become involved in a rather embarrassing incident at school. From the information Dean brought home, Mr. Driver was entirely within his rights in protecting himself. According to my son, Mr. Driver gave the boy in question a rough time, which he, no doubt, well-deserved.

It was my special privilege to attend the Spring Concert of the junior and senior high glee clubs, which demonstrated the good work Mr. Driver has done since coming to the schools. I believe he is doing an excellent job and is extremely conscientious in his work. Frankly, I believe his efforts at the schools are a definite asset to our community and in the lives of his students. No doubt, Alec is rather emotional, but most good musicians suffer from the same fate.

I sincerely trust you will give Mr. Driver the consideration he has earned and allow him to continue in his capacity.

Yours very truly,

Reid Collins

Walter Goss, reacting to Pop's call and his own professional judgment, wrote an internal memorandum to Christopher Fletcher fully supportive of Pop's position on retaining Alec. Walter agreed with Pop that the progress Alec had made in the choirs far out-weighed the negative effects of what he believed would undoubtedly be an isolated incident. After all, he thought, both parties directly involved had reconciled. Walter saw a net loss for the school system if Alec were not retained.

Fearing that mere memos were insufficient, John arranged a lunch with Pop and Walter after which they descended upon Christian Fletcher's office to deliver their opinions personally. The meeting had its desired effect as Christian responded to the advice of his assistant superintendent of music, his principal in charge, and Pop's compassionate logic and rescinded his request for Alec's resignation and even approved Alec's appointment to the new campus for the coming school year. Mr. Fletcher undoubtedly took comfort in the fact that, despite the publicity, there wasn't an overwhelming public outcry for Alec's dismissal. It was not that people were willing to tolerate either type of behavior; it just seemed that few paid any attention and for those that did, opinion was split. I believe most people viewed Alec's and Tommy's actions as offsetting fouls, a type of educational do-over.

Following Pop's decision to write Christopher Fletcher in support of Alec, I asked him why Arthur Oats, a member of Pop's church choir and neighbor to my grandparents, would oppose Alec's reappointment. His own son benefited by Alec's tutelage and, as a consequence, was voted most talented by the senior class. Pop felt that Arthur's resentment was more likely directed at Alec's association with Tracy than the incident with Tommy Strickland. Maybe, he said, Arthur senses that there is more to the story than what people knew. After all, Pop reminded me, Arthur has three daughters, the youngest of which was in the same choir with me. Perhaps, he conjectured, Arthur believes Alec's relationship with Tracy and his striking Tommy are not isolated incidents. Because Arthur has three teenage daughters he is particularly sensitive to male teachers taking advantage of their female students. But who knows for certain what motivates a man? he asked me rhetorically.

Chapter 9

Shirley Strickland was livid. She felt betrayed—double-crossed by Christopher Fletcher. The letter he sent explaining the basis for his decision did not mention his earlier verbal commitment. She had little recourse. For reasons Tommy never revealed to her, he refused to file charges or testify against Alec despite Shirley's admonitions to the contrary, and she could find no one else who could, or would, swear to exactly what happened. Her previous protestations to the press resulted only in her embarrassment when Christian Fletcher announced his decision to rescind Alec's dismissal. Her only recourse was to have the last word. She responded to Mr. Fletcher's letter by return mail. In no uncertain terms she stated that she didn't consider the resolution of the incident in any way satisfactory. Nevertheless, she felt thwarted in pursuing the matter further and let it die with her last letter.

Alec felt a great sense of relief and vindication. He knew that he had alienated much of the community by first openly dating Tracy and then striking Tommy. The decision to retain him only served to deepen the resentment of those who had opposed him. Those who aided his cause soon faded into anonymity. Many supporters thought Alec's dismissal too harsh a punishment for an instinctive response to an unruly student. That Tommy and Alec came to terms satisfied most who signed the reinstatement petitions. Alec discovered later that the support he temporarily enjoyed did not emanate from his personal charm. He could count only a handful of personal supporters, including Pop, Walter Goss, and a few others, who believed Alec's skill at orchestrating young voices superseded any isolated impulse. I wonder if people's attitudes would have been different if they had known what Tommy said. Alec's desire to protect Tracy from embarrassment may have cost him additional support.

Mr. Jordon, the shop teacher, had been prophetic. Tommy Strickland respected Alec for not revealing what he said. His sore mouth served as a reminder of the cost of disrespect. He never again disrupted class, and Alec went out his way to let Tommy know that he recognized and appreciated his change in attitude and behavior. The two quietly parted ways after the semester ended.

Throughout the nearly month-long ordeal, Tracy and, to Alec's delight, both Nancy and Lloyd were strongly supportive. Alec never mentioned the contents of Tommy's statement, for he suspected they already knew and if they didn't he had no desire to tell them. Nancy had known Shirley for a number of years through the PTA and felt sympathy for Shirley's general circumstances but not her attitude and emotional temperament. She understood the difficulty Shirley experienced in raising two sons without a husband (or anyone else for that matter) for financial and moral support. Though not in the position herself, Nancy appreciated the plight that a woman faces in trying to obtain employment at a salary that allows her to support a family. She felt empathy for the frustration that a female single parent faces in trying to cope in a man's world. She believed that Shirley's encounters with the school system's male administrators only served to reinforce the bitterness she felt in being abandoned by a man to fend for herself and her male children.

Alec said that he felt no malice toward Shirley realizing that her frustrations and the desire to protect her son had led to her actions. He expressed disappointment that the school district responded to her emotions rather than the reason of his and Tommy's reconciliation. Wishing to depersonalize Shirley's response, he readily agreed with Nancy's assessment that Shirley's actions resulted more from the frustration she felt in coping in a man's world than from himself. Finally, Nancy said how difficult it must be for Shirley to provide for her family on a fraction of the income that men her same age earned.

Lloyd sat quietly listening to what Nancy and Alec were saying, passively agreeing until Nancy made this last statement. He shifted in his favorite chair, indicating to Nancy that he wanted to say something. Lloyd asked, "She works at the bank, in the bookkeeping department, doesn't she?"

"Why, yes. At least I believe so, why?" Nancy asked in return.

"Think about it for a minute," Lloyd began. "Bank bookkeepers, school teachers"—turning to Alec who sat on the sofa with Tracy—"present company being a notable exception, nurses, dime store clerks, telephone operators, librarians, what do they all have in common?"

"Well," Nancy started as she mulled Lloyd's question for a moment.

"They're all female-dominated professions," Lloyd answered for her.

"And they're all low-paying," Alec chimed in with what he considered a sore point.

"Yes, and do you know why?" Lloyd challenged.

"Perhaps they're victims of discrimination," Nancy suggested.

"Perhaps, but even if all discrimination were ended, pay differentials would still exist. The real problem is that women seem willing to work for pay levels less than what attract a comparably qualified man. Look at schoolteachers for example. It's still a female-dominated profession and will be as long as men feel the pay is insufficient to support a family. Consider for a moment Alec's position and those of most other male teachers. What jobs do they hold? They hold positions that provide, for the most part, additional pay for particular skills. Coaches, band directors, choral directors, shop teachers either earn income supplements or can earn additional income in off-time employment."

"Lloyd, that sounds too simple. Why would women be willing to work for lower pay?" Nancy rebutted.

"Women, eager to achieve their career goals and enhance their family's finances, accept positions at pay levels that experienced or otherwise capable males wouldn't accept such as those that exist in financially beleaguered institutions like school districts, banks, hospitals, and public utilities," Lloyd concluded.

"I'm still unconvinced. I don't think you can blame women for their own plight. I'm sure Shirley Strickland would not accept one cent less than she had to," Nancy countered.

"Not specific women, women in general—those who want to work outside their homes—acting together, not in concert, they collectively push down their income by their eagerness to have careers. They're willing to accept these pay levels because their income supplements that of their husbands'. As barriers to women in the workforce come down in the future, it's conceivable that the rush to careers will be sufficient and concentrated in a few select occupations to offset any increased income due to their greater acceptance in the workforce. They could end up with no greater income, relative to men, than they currently enjoy, at least for a considerable period of time. I'm no economist, but I'm sure this argument makes good economic sense."

Lloyd's argument greatly impressed Alec. He recalled reading about the flood of immigrants to this country that kept their wages low in certain industries for many years. Here's a man, he thought, trained in one highly technical profession hypothesizing, in a defensible way, about laws and principles in another complex discipline. What a fine mind this man has, Alec concluded.

"I hate to interrupt this intellectual discussion with more mundane matters, but now is as good a time as any to tell Alec that Buster asked me to the prom, and I said yes," Tracy interjected. She cast a glance at Alec to determine his reaction as she had deliberately waited until such a propitious moment when her parents were present to tell Alec of her decision.

"That's great! You'll be the most beautiful girl there—the 'belle of the ball'—and I'll know. I'm going to help chaperon, can you imagine that? John Furst asked me. And I thought everyone considered me the Rocky Marciano of Clearwater High."

"I guess John figured that no one would dare dance out of step with you around," Lloyd said with a broad smile.

Everyone laughed.

"Lloyd, that's awful for you to say," Nancy pleaded.

"That's it! John asked me because he wants me to be the bouncer," Alec kidded. They laughed.

*****

Until construction of the new high school, the prom took place each year on the third Saturday in May in the ballroom occupying the top two floors of the old Fort Harrison Hotel—now the educational center of the Church of Scientology. Built of Spanish-style architecture in the late twenties, the cream-colored building with red tiled roof is one of the tallest structures in the upper county, standing fourteen stories high. It served for many years as the winter headquarters for the Philadelphia Phillies and every other notable group who came to town. The meeting place for civic clubs and political parties, it also served as the site for many social activities and prominent dances and balls. The terrace off the ballroom presented a magnificent view of the entire community, the bay, the beaches beyond, and the Gulf of Mexico. The two-story ballroom, ringed with a balcony, provided a comfortable place where more passive guests could view the dancers below. It formed the perfect setting for significant events like proms for graduating seniors. Most graduates had never visited the ballroom and its adjoining terrace.

Organizers arranged the ballroom floor with tables and chairs along the walls, three deep at some points, with the center area reserved for dancing. By seven in the evening, the guests nearly filled all the available tables, but Tracy and Buster had not appeared. Alec, having arrived long before the first guests, assisted with the many last-minute touches while keeping an eye on the elevator doors for Tracy. He watched with increasing anxiety as couple after couple arrived but no Tracy and Buster. Perspiration either from the mounting temperature in the room or from nervous energy began to soak through his dress shirt and he feared for his white dinner jacket. Not having air conditioning, the windows on three sides of the ballroom were open as were the doors to the terrace but, as usual, Florida was intolerably hot in late May.

As the time approached for the prom to begin, the sun settled into the horizon just slightly north of due west in a brilliant display of oranges, yellows, reds, and violets. The sky's colors melded into the blue-green waters of the Gulf forming a panoramic rainbow. Few graduates noticed, each more interested in who came with whom and who wore what than the panorama of nature's magnificent colors.

After what seemed to Alec an interminable time, Tracy and Buster emerged from one of the elevators. Alec's prophecy became reality, Tracy was stunning. She wore a white chiffon gown full to the floor with pink ribbons interlacing the edge around the capped sleeves and deep neckline. A pink sash graced her tiny waist and, as was her habit, she wore a matching ribbon through her hair. Her dark complexion stood in stark contrast to her dress as revealed by her bare shoulders down to her cleavage clearly visible above the gown's neckline. As Alec's eyes drank in every bit of Tracy's radiance he noticed in the midst of the deep crease in her bosom something he had almost forgotten—the solid gold chain necklace and pendant the shape of the major clef symbol that he gave her for Christmas. Upon reflection, he thought, the gift was probably too expensive for a man his age to give to a schoolgirl he had dated only twice. Tracy told Alec how beautiful it was and graciously expressed her thanks when he returned from Mexico. She said she would save it for special occasions. She never told Buster that Alec gave it to her. Thankfully, Buster hadn't bothered to ask. Knowing Buster, it probably didn't occur to him that the necklace was a gift.

The gold sparkled in the bright lights of the entry and set off Tracy's entire appearance. Alec thought it a fitting and elegant adornment to her radiance. He slowly made his way through the throng of excited students, and finally reaching his destination he stopped and stared into her eyes for what seemed to Buster an eternity. Alec finally said, "Tracy, you're simply stunning. You complement the sunset, with or without the Green Flash." He made no pretense to disguise his delight in seeing her.

Without taking her eyes off his, Tracy responded simply and quietly, "Thank you."

Alec then turned to Buster and added tersely with extended hand, "Good to see you, Buster."

Buster grumbled and limply shook Alec's hand.

Alec had every intention of dancing several dances with Tracy, but the admonition of John Furst and Walter Goss also weighed heavily on his mind. The solution, as he saw it, lay in dancing with a number of different girls from the choir to dilute the impact of dancing with Tracy.

It soon became apparent that Alec's musical talents extended to the dance floor. His movements were fluid and flawless flowing in graceful rhythm perfectly timed to the music. Even the clumsiest girls seemed to glide around the floor as each took her gleeful turn. The basketball coach, who considered himself the best stepper in town, confessed privately to his wife that Alec had him beat. Much to the coach's consternation, his wife readily agreed. Alec's dancing demonstration didn't escape Tracy's notice. She tried, discretely at first, to watch Alec out of the corner of her eye or by quick glances. Finally, his performance became a topic of conversation at her table and provided her the opportunity to devote her full attention to his graceful movements.

Swing, jitterbug, Charleston, rumba, cha-cha, two-step, waltz, Alec performed each to accomplished perfection. His dancing raised the question in everyone's mind, if not on their lips, who would be next. No one, including Buster, doubted that Alec was slowly but deliberately plying his way toward his ultimate target, Tracy. When he would make his move remained the only issue. Midway through the scheduled dance hours as if by cue, Eddie Harlow, who won raves for his performance as Sir Joseph Porter and especially for his rendition of "When I Was a Lad" in *H. M. S. Pinafore*, stepped to the band platform and announced that he had been asked (by the sympathetic and sentimental basketball coach, Eddie, later revealed) to sing a special number, a recent release by Doris Day that had just made the hit list. Alec, sensing the significance of Eddie being asked to sing, made his long-anticipated move to dance with Tracy. Politely requesting Buster's permission, he asked her to dance never giving poor Buster a chance to respond. Alec and Tracy danced to the music and words of "Secret Love."

Hardly aware of Eddie's words, they danced never allowing their eyes to wander from each other's. They became oblivious to everyone and everything else. As close as they had ever been, they glided over the floor as one; their movements so graceful and smooth, they appeared to be skating on ice.

When Eddie finished, a loud round of applause broke out that Alec and Tracy thought intended for Eddie. When they looked about they realized that they had been the only couple dancing, the others had ebbed and flowed to the sides of the dance floor where they watched Alec and Tracy while Eddie sang. Surprised, Alec smiled. Tracy beamed.

*****

Thirteen days after the prom, Tracy graduated in the last ceremony conducted at the old high school campus. The ceremony quickly became a sentimental occasion. Many graduates were children of previous graduates who had listened, laughed, and learned in those same halls. Even though the new campus, located on the eastern edge of town, was larger and long sought by most in the community, the tradeoffs were not all positive; concrete for polished oak floors, ten for twelve-foot ceilings, masonry for brick construction, single for two stories, and long for short distances between classes. The new campus did, however, provide a much needed utility: air conditioning for its gym (including the band and choir rooms), library, cafeteria, auditorium, and administrative offices but not the classrooms. As a sign of the changing times the plans included an expansive parking lot to accommodate the growing number of students who were driving their own cars to school.

The junior high would expand into the abandoned senior high building but only temporarily, for planning of a new junior high had already begun. The old structures would serve as the up-county special education center for nearly ten years before being abandoned to vandals and arsonists. Those in attendance at the last graduation sensed the impending loss, and some even wondered aloud if they weren't losing more than they were gaining. The massive and physically sound buildings had housed thousands of students during boom, depression, world war, and the Korean conflict. It spanned the era of Hoover to Eisenhower: a time of maturing, a time of change.

The auditorium where most school events took place was impressive both in size and configuration. The main floor contained five hundred wood, curve-backed seats separated by two centers and surrounded by two side aisles. The horseshoe shaped balcony seated over two hundred. No posts marred or obscured anyone's view on either floor. The very large stage, the best equipped in the mid-county, served as the site for plays, concerts, musical productions, community-wide meetings, and numerous school functions.

On this day the graduates filed in and down the two center aisles, turning toward the steps at either side of the stage, then continued to the rows of chairs placed for them immediately behind the seats of the speakers. Invariably one or more boys tripped on their gowns as they ascended the narrow steps. Thanks to the fortunes of the alphabet, Tracy was the first to enter and had a front row seat. Alec sat with the faculty in the front row of the audience and smiled unashamedly at her throughout the ceremony.

Staring at her remarkable beauty and sparkling countenance, he thought of the first time he saw her; it seemed as though it were yesterday and yet, a lifetime away. He recalled the hypnotic effect of her dark, penetrating eyes. He believed they were her most stunning feature; it was as though she could see directly into his soul. Her dark hair and complexion complemented her eyes. At first he liked her hair longer, for it added beauty and innocence to her face. He soon discovered that the shorter hair added a touch of elegance and dispelled her look of innocence.

He found her appealing in many different ways. He found her slender without being skinny, small in stature without being short, assertive without being overbearing, vibrant without being silly, charming without being effusive, and young without being immature. In sum, he found her completely irresistible.

Midst the pleasure of his thoughts, he could not help wondering how his relationship with her might change after graduation. Since prom night she had been more affectionate than she had previously. She seemed to have committed herself to him. But what of her parents? he thought. Alec didn't have to wonder long. After the ceremonies ended, Lloyd pulled Alec aside and told him that he and Nancy had decided that their restrictions on Tracy's association with him would end that day. Lloyd saw little need to continue the limits because she was eighteen and no longer in school. He asked Alec for a personal commitment in return. He asked that Alec continue to temper his relationship with Tracy until she completed at least two years study at St. Petersburg Junior College.

Alec listened and recalled Lloyd's logical and rational attitude to his first date with Tracy, the same reason with which he approached every issue Alec ever heard him discuss. Alec agreed and told Lloyd that he would honor his wishes, for he respected Lloyd and his reasoned approach to life.

Alec reminded Lloyd of his planned two-month trip across Canada from Vancouver to Nova Scotia that would allow Tracy time to weigh whether she wished to continue seeing him after his return. They both agreed that giving her some breathing room served both of their best interests especially at this critical time in Tracy's life. They shook hands. Lloyd put his arm around Alec and wished him good luck and a safe trip.

Tracy spent the remainder of the evening with parents and grandparents and then joined her classmates for an all-night beach party. Alec left her to family and friends, for it was their day as much as Tracy's. He and Tracy planned to spend the next afternoon and evening together, his last before leaving on his summer trip.

He spent the next morning packing and making last-minute preparations. After lunch, Tracy picked him up and drove, as planned, to the beach where they spent the remainder of the afternoon. That evening she dropped Alec by his apartment and returned an hour later as Alec had made dinner reservations at the Palm Garden Restaurant five miles south of Largo in a remote area surrounded by numerous orange groves.

Scores of palm trees and large oaks flanked the restaurant on all four sides. It lay on a narrow winding road that led to Indian Rocks Beach. The road carried little traffic because all those lacking a sense of adventure avoided the rickety old wooden bridge that crossed the narrow channel beyond the restaurant. The old timbers cracked and popped as each vehicle made its way slowly over the decaying structure.

They both ordered shrimp stuffed with crabmeat, an entrée for which the restaurant had achieved notoriety. Lingering over their meal, they savored their newly acquired freedom to enjoy each other's company without the fear of public censure. They talked as though they were seeing each other for the first time. Alec laughed when Tracy told him of the strange look his landlady gave her when she returned for him that evening. He said Mrs. Smith watched his movements very carefully during the past year, leading him to believe that she was suspicious of single men.

"I hope she'll be asleep when we get back," Alec said, glancing at Tracy to observe her reaction.

"I hope so too," she answered, looking up from her coffee into his eyes.

Alec did his best to suppress his obvious delight over her response. He planned to ask her up to his apartment when they returned, but was uncertain how she would react. That uncertainty seemed relieved, as did even the need to ask. He thought, *Please, Mrs. Smith, for one night please be asleep.*

*****

Mrs. Annie Smith, or Miss Annie to all who knew her, lived alone in her aging house and had done so for most of the ten years since her husband died. Her sons teased that it was a race between her and the house to see which could outlast the other. Her husband of fifty-five years left her little except the house and two grown children scarcely able to provide for themselves and their families. She had never been gainfully employed, but to say she had never worked belied the many hours of the many days, months, and years she toiled on their farm before moving to Florida from a rural Tennessee Valley farm. Up before the sun, she tended the cows and chickens before fixing breakfast for her husband and young sons. She managed the truck garden while her husband plowed and harvested the fields. As my grandparents, she and her family migrated late in life to Florida after being chased off their farm by the TVA. Her sons, never giving higher education a moment's thought or encouragement, did achieve something that eluded both parents—a high school education. The younger followed the older and began work for the telephone company immediately upon graduation. Had they remained single or their wives worked gainfully, they might have enjoyed a reasonable standard of living. Instead, each chose, with no resistance from their wives, to have four children and non-employed spouses. Wages paid by the phone company were fair, but simply inadequate to support a family of six.

She occasionally rented a room and bath in the house to single older ladies but primarily gained needed income from young couples renting the apartment over the garage. She agreed to rent the apartment to Alec only because he wouldn't require access to her house. She wasn't about to spend one night in a house alone with a strange man. Suspicious of strangers, especially men, she feared for her safety ever since her husband died. The need for rental income to supplement her meager social security check overcame her fears, at least as long as Alec confined himself to the apartment.

Her eighty-one years and the experience of the depression taught her to be frugal. Even though the house, half her age, had no mortgage her income barely covered groceries, utilities, and growing medical bills. Her entertainment consisted of tending a small garden—frequently on her hands and knees for she was no longer able to bend or stoop—and her ladies circle that met every two weeks in a neighbor's house. She had long-abandoned attending church on Sundays, for she felt her health wouldn't permit the energy and effort required for prolonged stays away from home. She listened to "services" over her radio and read from her well-worn Bible daily. In the heat of the day and after dark, she often sat in her favorite chair by the front window in the parlor where she could watch any who traveled the street by her house. She would be there day and night often late on many nights as her back would only allow occasional restful sleep in bed.

Early mornings and late evenings she spent on the front porch combing her hair now an even consistent silver. She wore it tied in a circular knot on the back of her head except for washing, combing, and sleeping. When unraveled it reached her waist. Despite many offers by both daughters-in-law, she steadfastly resisted any attempt to cut her hair. Whether from her front room or front porch, there was hardly a passing sole that escaped her attention.

At first she watched Alec's every movement both out of curiosity and suspicion. As time went by she learned her lone male tenant was quiet, unobtrusive and harmless. Best of all he paid his rent regularly on the same day every month without her asking. Her mind relieved of fear, she continued to watch solely as a matter of curiosity and little else to do. She felt gratified that the only female visitor to his apartment was Denise who stopped by periodically to bring odds and ends to make Alec's life and apartment comfortable. Miss Annie not only feared for her safety but worried lest Alec entertain certain ladies of questionable virtue, such shenanigans she would not tolerate on her property. Her fears had been allayed during the past ten months on both accounts.

On this day in June, however, she witnessed, for the first time, a female other than Denise Hooker drive up to her house, park, and climb the outside steps to Alec's apartment. *She looks so young*, Miss Annie thought. This event occurred twice that afternoon, but on neither occasion did the young lady enter the apartment. On both occasions Alec met her at the door and escorted her back to the car.

At nine o'clock in the evening, Miss Annie sat, back in pain, in her darkened parlor. A car pulled into the driveway and continued up to the front of the garage. She turned the best she could and looked out her side window in time to see a figure emerge from each side of the car. From his lean angular frame, she could tell that one was Alec and the other was obviously the silhouette of a female. They slowly climbed the stairs where Alec in the dim light unlocked the door after a few abortive attempts, reached inside, and turned on the light in the front room and stood aside to allow his guest to enter. Miss Annie heard the door close and watched as lights in sequence went on in each room of the apartment. She could see shadows through the draperies as the figures walked back and forth in the apartment. The lights stayed on for as long as she watched.

Miss Annie twitched abruptly and suddenly realized that she had dozed off for an indeterminate time. She looked up at Alec's apartment and at first thought all the lights were still on, but a second look revealed that his bedroom was dark. She sat back in her chair and wondered what time it was. She could not see the tall grandfather's clock on the other side of the room and had not heard its last chime. The pain in her back had subsided, but she was too tired to rise and move to her bed. She gradually drifted back to sleep in her chair only to be reawakened sometime later by a car's ignition outside her window. She watched as the car backed into the street where only then were its headlights turned on. *I wonder what time it is*, she thought.

Chapter 10

August 1955

A lbert Einstein died. Even at the tender age of fifteen I recognized that 1955 marked many changes in American life. Culturally, the mid-fifties gave birth to a new musical sound given the name Rock and Roll. According to lore, the term was first popularized by a New York disk jockey, and undoubtedly emanated from the song "Rock with Me Henry, Roll with Me Henry," later renamed "Dance with Me Henry" to make it suitable for radio broadcast. A bit different from "U2," isn't it? An earlier song, "Rock and Roll," appeared in the score of the 1934 Jack Benny film, *Transatlantic Marriage-Go-Round.*

A white kid from Mississippi cut his first record singing "That's All Right Mama," a black song that he sang slower, more relaxed and sensual than the original version. Thus began a revolution whose conception may have been the musical score behind the credits of the Glenn Ford film *Blackboard Jungle*, "Rock around the Clock," the first true "rock and roll" hit and still one of my favorites. The film introduced Sidney Poitier and Vic Morrow. Despite the impact of rock and roll, the number one broadcast song in 1955 was "The Ballad of Davy Crockett" and the best-selling record single was "Cherry Pink and Apple Blossom White." "Rock Around the Clock" placed second with a three-way tie for third—"Sincerely" and revivals of "Sixteen Tons" by Tennessee Ernie Ford and "The Yellow Rose of Texas" by Mitch Miller. I liked them all. James Dean died.

The changes in Florida proved even more dramatic than those in the rest of the country. The fastest growing counties in America lay along Florida's west coast. Our Sunday afternoon drives, no matter the direction, took us passed numerous developments carved out of once expansive citrus groves. Thousands of acres of grove land gave way to Easter egg houses as we called them because they were painted alternating pastel shades of pink, yellow, green, blue, and occasionally for relief, white. The developments crammed as many small concrete block and masonry houses as possible in the once flourishing citrus groves. Each house contained a carport, a bath, two or three bedrooms along with a kitchen and a recent innovation, the Florida room—a den or family room that consisted of an enclosed back porch with jalousie or Miami-styled windows. Developers left scattered clusters of citrus trees as token reminders of the mighty groves that once covered the sandy soil. The developments, along with burgeoning trailer parks containing thousands of immobile mobile homes, served the rapidly growing population of retirees fleeing the cold and expense of their northern origins.

The fast growing population of older migrants placed a strain on the local infrastructure leading to the construction of some long needed projects such as large scale sewer treatment plants that replaced near universal reliance on septic tanks and the horrific practice of dumping raw sewage into the once pristine waters of Clearwater Bay. The installation of the modern facilities ripped up older streets to accommodate the required lines. A host of other projects including road widening and extension, new hospitals and parks, a second and then a third fire station, and greatly expanded police protection all followed in a never-ending chase to keep up with the burgeoning population. It seemed that everywhere I went, by car, bicycle, or on foot, I encountered traffic snarls and detours around one type of construction project or another. The rapid development turned many ordinary grove owners into wealthy land developers reaping returns far more than those they enjoyed as growers. Land values soared rapidly causing property taxes to rise and further discourage agriculture production and encourage real estate development. The increased demand for city services forced tax rates to rise along with the property values making the growing tax burden for undeveloped property to rise even faster. These economic forces led to the continued and ever-expanding conversion of nurseries, dairy farms, and citrus groves into subdivisions whose populations far exceeded those of the original communities they now surrounded. As my Italian friends would say, "*Non mi piace.*"

Air conditioning infiltrated Florida on a massive scale. Undoubtedly, without air conditioning Florida communities would still be winter playgrounds and summer ghost towns. Winter tourists formed a solid seasonal base for Florida's economy for many decades. Numerous hotels, restaurants, and other tourist services would close the week following Easter and not reopen until the day after New Year's. Summer tourists and permanent migrants in large numbers paralleled the widespread installation of air conditioning in both homes and public places. Florida from May to November is simply too hot and humid for most people native to northern climes. Air conditioning also provided an escape from the mosquitoes that managed to survive the increased regularity of DDT spraying. The joys of air conditioning never graced my presence while I lived with my parents—that luxury would wait until I emptied the nest. Cynical friends accused my parents of using the lack of air conditioning as an inducement to usher me out the door.

Not all the effects of air conditioning were positive, at least at first. Metallic duck work and louvered vents marred once beautiful interiors of churches, schools, civic buildings, and stores. The alternative, chosen by many property owners, consisted of pocking the exterior of buildings with dozens of window units each dripping condensation making the buildings resemble large honeycombs. The buildings seemed to weep. Despite the aesthetic monstrosities created by the new luxury, citizens readily made the transition for the welcomed comfort the *nouveau* necessity afforded.

Four-lane bridges to the beach replaced the two-lane bridges built during the twenties. The street where we lived during the War was widened to four lanes as it carried an increasing burden of vehicles to the beach and back. Telephone numbers now had five digits, and more people could choose private lines. The Clearwater Bombers won their second national championship with the help, for the first time, of a few nonnative players. Herb Dudley and a new, young left-handed pitcher from Nashville, Johnny Hunter, were considered the best in the sport. The Sunshine Skyway connecting the peninsular of Pinellas County with Manatee and Sarasota Counties replaced the old ferry across the lower portion of Tampa Bay. More cars traveled the new bridge in one week than the ferry carried in an entire year. Dredging, filling, clearing, and developing were not only signs of progress but of upheaval, stress, and strain as the communities struggled with the change that many sought but for which few were prepared.

*****

Nancy Ashbury endured the most difficult two-year period of her life; the period began with tragedy and ended with triumph. The tragedy she bore, the triumph belonged to Alec. One month after Tracy graduated from high school, Lloyd, age fifty-three, suffered a fatal stroke. Nancy was not prepared mentally or emotionally for her husband's sudden and unexpected death. She depended on him for guidance and counsel that she sorely missed during the next twenty-four months. His death didn't catch her financially unprepared; the royalties from Lloyd's numerous patents would support her for many years and provide a handsome residual for Tracy upon Nancy's death. She had always been in charge of the household and certainly had the capability of continuing in that capacity, but that remained the least of her worries. She missed the reasoned support that Lloyd always provided, the confidant he had been, and the empathy he felt for her hurts. He had been more than a husband, he had been a friend.

She felt inadequate as the sole source of advice and counsel for Tracy. "If only I knew what Lloyd would say," she confided in friends on numerous occasions. "But then," she would conclude, "I never knew what he'd say when he was alive, how could I possibly know now that he's gone?" Nancy lamented not for herself but for Tracy because she too had to bear the loss of Lloyd's counsel. Nancy took solace in the fact that Tracy stood poised at the threshold of adulthood when Lloyd died. The responsibility for the remainder of her life would be up to Tracy. Nancy prayed that Tracy had enough of her father in her to fill the gaps. During the interim, Nancy would do the best she could in Lloyd's absence.

In retrospect, Nancy thought, Alec had not pushed or pressured them and discreetly left them alone when they needed or wanted to be. It appeared to her that Alec was honoring some unspoken commitment, and she often wondered what Lloyd said to him at Tracy's graduation. Lloyd never told her the specifics of his last conversation with Alec. Nancy slowly accepted Alec and admired his musical abilities while remaining unconvinced that Alec and Tracy's relationship served either's best interest. On occasion, she admitted to the possibility that she could be wrong.

She simply ran out of excuses why Tracy should not marry Alec. The age discrepancy never seemed to bother Tracy. When she finished the schooling she promised her father, there remained little basis for Nancy's objections particularly in the face of Tracy's continued insistence that she loved Alec and wanted to marry him. This determination persisted despite Nancy's state of shock when Tracy finally told her of Alec's previous marriage and subsequent divorce. Over the past two years Nancy frequently recalled the dispassion in Tracy's voice as she retold the story. To Tracy, it was as though his previous marriage and divorce were irrelevant. Mother's view differed appreciably from daughter's, but even that difference seemed irrelevant to Tracy.

Held on the kind of hot and sultry July evening when people dressed only for special occasions, their wedding was impressive without being elaborate. Tracy and Alec timed the wedding to enable Tracy to complete her studies at the junior college and allow six weeks for an extended honeymoon through England before Alec reported for the fall term. The date bore an unintended significance: it was the tenth anniversary of Alec's first wedding and two years since Lloyd's death.

In Lloyd's absence, Denise Hooker offered and Nancy graciously accepted her assistance in the wedding arrangements. They approached the same minister who became upset by Alec's attentions to Tracy while she was a student in his class and a member of the church choir. He also presided at Lloyd's funeral. The minister seemed relieved to hear they were engaged and readily agreed to perform the marriage ceremony in his church.

The church building provided an architectural relief to the otherwise brick and mortar look of the downtown area. Located on one of the two main streets in town, it was constructed in the style of a Spanish mission with masonry exterior painted a bright coral pink with an aqua green tiled roof. The sanctuary contained exposed dark wood rafters, columns, and beams against off-white plaster walls. Three large chandeliers hung over the center aisle of the long rectangular room. Arched stained glass windows lined each side of the room, swinging open to provide cross ventilation during the hot summer months. This year would be the church's last without air conditioning.

The July wedding provided many of Tracy's friends who attended college out of town an opportunity to serve as bridesmaids. Ruth Ann took off a week from her job in Gainesville where she supported her husband's graduate education. Excited to reciprocate as Tracy's maid of honor, Ruth Ann provided much needed reassurance to Nancy.

Nancy asked Lloyd's brother, Robert from California, to give Tracy away. Alec's younger brother, Richard, came from Rhode Island to be best man. Tracy selected Denise's daughter to be the flower girl.

Nancy felt a little apprehensive about the wedding for what seemed to her as two contradictory reasons: she remained uncomfortable with her decision to honor Tracy's wish to marry Alec and yet, she worried lest some of her long-time friends would decide at the last minute not to attend. She reasoned that having consented to the marriage she wanted and even needed the support that her friends' attendance could provide. Ruth Ann's presence and positive attitude calmed Nancy's fears.

To Nancy's relief, most of her long-time friends appeared on schedule with but few exceptions. She could not, however, count among her guests, a single person who had signed Arthur Oaks letter requesting Alec's dismissal. John Furst, one year into retirement complicated by unexpected heart trouble, made a pleasant surprise appearance. Walter Goss and the new high school principal and their wives arrived together followed by the basketball coach, the band director, and Alec's newest and best friend, Jack Winslow, and his wife, Cynthia. A newcomer, Jack assumed a teaching job in the junior high while awaiting assignment to an administrative position. He and Alec became friends after meeting in a district-wide teacher's meeting.

Despite the heat, Tracy looked radiant as she floated down the aisle to the echoing sounds of Mendelssohn. She wore a long, white satin wedding gown and carried a bouquet of yellow roses. Her bridesmaids, eyes fixed on Tracy, wore pastel yellow gowns and corsages of white roses. Alec smiled broadly and proudly as she neared and changed from her uncle's arm to his. He appeared relaxed and comfortable in his tuxedo while poor Richard constantly tugged at his collar and pulled on his jacket either out of nervousness or a bad fit.

Nancy took pleasure in the warmth and openness her friends displayed as they greeted Alec and Tracy during the reception held in the church's educational wing. Eddie Harlow relented to Alec and Tracy's entreaties to sing "Secret Love" as he had at her prom. The eight-thirty time of the wedding allowed most of the day's heat to dissipate from the building. However, the humidity remained. Tracy and Alec left the reception early and spent their first two nights together in a hotel on the beach. From there they drove their rental car to the airport for their flight to New York where they boarded the Queen Mary for passage to England.

Memories of Lloyd's death, the events of the following two years, and the wedding occupied Nancy's thoughts as she sat in Lloyd's old chair in her living room with Tracy's unopened letter in her lap. Almost three weeks had lapsed since Alec and Tracy left for England. Were it not for Alec she would never have conceived that her daughter would spend her honeymoon hiking through the English countryside. She had been eager to hear from Tracy, but when the letter finally arrived she became uncharacteristically hesitant to open and read it, choosing instead to reflect for a moment on the events of the past two years.

She had been watching the sunlight dance on the water and became mesmerized by the reflections. She sighed, looked down at the envelope in her lap, picked it up, and tore open one end, removed the lengthy letter, and read,

Dear Mother:

I wanted to write much sooner, but the pace Alec set for our trip hasn't allowed the time to do so. We're on the train to Scotland, and Alec is asleep. To make up for the delay I'll write a longer letter.

I didn't get a chance to tell you how wonderful the wedding was and how marvelous you have been. I know Daddy's death affected you deeply and that you only tolerate Alec for my sake, all of which makes you special for the graciousness you displayed toward us. I miss Daddy awfully and Alec does too. Daddy and Alec did seem to hit it off. I know Alec sincerely respected him, and Daddy seemed genuinely to like Alec. I hope someday you will feel the same way.

I'm having a wonderful time. Even though we seem to move quickly from one village to another, Alec is considerate and has given me something for my poor tired feet. If our entire marriage is like this trip, I know I'll be very happy. So far we've traveled through Thomas Hardy country after visiting Cornwall and King Arthur's haunts. We stayed in the village of Ashbury, and it was as beautiful as Alec said it would be. It's exciting visiting the places of our ancestors. I would have liked to have stayed even longer, but we traveled to Oxford on the third day—what an impressive university. We're almost at the halfway point of our

journey, so I may not be able to write a long
letter again.

As much as I am enjoying the trip, I'm anxious to get back to our new house and get settled.

Nancy looked up and thought about the house Tracy and Alec
selected some weeks before the wedding. To call it modest in size
would be charitable. *It's tiny,* she thought. Its low, slightly sloped roof
only made it appear smaller. The lot, barely large enough to accommodate the house, had, as so many new inexpensive masonry houses,
no garage, only a carport. The rooms were small with the low ceilings
serving only to emphasize the house's lack of space. Even to Nancy's
short stature, it made her feel like ducking each time she walked in.
However, it was new, located on a freshly paved asphalt street, sans
curbs, along with a dozen other matchbox houses just like it. It's odd,
Nancy thought, for a man who professes to like trees to choose a
house on land with only an occasional orange tree left over from the
bulldozer's blade. Nancy suspected Alec's meager salary had a great
deal to do with their choice of residence. After asking Nancy's permission to marry Tracy, Alec revealed, after some subtle prodding, that
he started with the district at a ten-month salary of thirty-two hundred dollars. The coming year, the first of their married life, he would
earn the grand sum of thirty-six hundred dollars plus a ten percent
supplement for his extracurricular duties as choral director. Another
ten percent he could earn from occasional duties as choir director at
churches and musical director of local little theater groups. No one
even discussed the possibility of Tracy working outside their home.

Nancy again sighed.

Alec and I really appreciate your and Denise's
help in furnishing the house. You have made it
so comfortable right away that I feel it's truly a
home. Alec said to be sure to also thank you for
letting us keep your old Buick. I know that one
of the biggest adjustments Alec will make to our
marriage is getting used to the idea of owning a

car—he has never owned one before, but then I guess you already know that. I also appreciate the wardrobe of clothes you purchased for me; it is simply beautiful and should keep me dressed for some time. I hope I won't have to accept your offer of continued help with my clothes; Alec and I want so much to make it on our own.

What I want most to thank you for are not the material things, although heaven knows we need them and would be strapped to buy them all ourselves. What I want most to thank you for is the love and trust you have shown me ever since Daddy died. You never tried to hide your reservations toward Alec but even so you never made me feel like I was wrong or that I had let you down. Your support has meant more to me than any money you could give, and with Daddy gone I know providing it was especially hard for you. We all miss Daddy; Alec still decries his loss and feels that he too has lost a friend.

I want to give to our home what you gave to yours and Daddy's. I also want to help Alec with his music, help him plan and work with him on the special projects he has in mind for the high school choir. He has accomplished so much since he started and wants to do so much more, and I want to work with him and share in that work. He believes I can be so much help now that I have added two years of college to my musical education. I just want to contribute and share his experiences even when we have a family of our own.

I love you, Mother, and wish Daddy were alive so I could tell him the same although I'm sure he already knows. Alec said to tell you he loves you too, but don't tell anyone—they might get the wrong idea. Doesn't that sound like some-thing Daddy would say?

I'll fill you in on all the details of our trip when we return. Alec has taken ten rolls of slides and is already planning a European trip next year.

Love,

Tracy and Alec

Tracy, so young, so full of enthusiasm and hope, Nancy couldn't bear the thought of her not realizing her goals. She refolded the letter and inserted it back into the torn envelope from which she would extract it repeatedly over the next five years. She pledged that what-ever she could do she would do for Tracy. She would tell Tracy in the coming weeks and months, "As long as I live, I will love and support you even if I think you're wrong and if I think you're right the support will be absolute." That promise became a commitment for Nancy.

Jarred by the sudden ringing of her doorbell, Nancy glanced at the ship's clock on the mantel. She had completely lost track of the time. The bell jogged her memory of Marie Davies's visit to discuss plans by the garden club to landscape a small park abandoned by the city to sand spurs and Johnson grass. The club signed an agreement with the city council that if the club would provide landscaping and maintain it, the city would agree to clear and maintain the remainder of the park and its equipment.

Marie, noticeably older than Nancy and a more recent migrant to the county, stood ever ready to brag about her son, James, a Cornell graduate, who recently entered the University of Florida's Law School. Nancy suspected that Marie's constant inquires of Tracy were simply a pretext for volunteering scores of anecdotes of James's accomplishments, which Nancy always politely acknowledged. But then James did live up to his mother's boasting, for that Nancy gave him credit. Marie remained courteous despite her braggadocio and had been a friend since she and her family moved to Florida more than a decade ago.

Marie's husband suffered a paralyzing stroke in the midst of a high-pressure career as a highly successful investment banker on Wall Street. The family moved to Florida in an attempt to distance him from the pressure cooker of high finance in the hope of escaping repeated strokes. Mother and young son benefited from the relaxed pace the small community provided. It came too late for husband and father. He died of a subsequent stroke within a year of moving south leaving behind a large endowment for his family. Marie was thereby a particular comfort to Nancy when Lloyd died of his stroke seven years later. Her visits provided much needed breaks in Nancy's melancholy.

Chapter 11

August 1957

Three years passed before Alec and I again came face to face. Bigger and hairier, my body bore the obvious outward manifestations of coming adulthood. Inwardly, my values and attitudes changed course. No longer was I the mischievous adolescent who delighted in cutting classes, ambushing cars with paper clips shot with rubber bands, and upsetting teachers to no end with one prank after another. Even under the threat of death, I could not point to an exact moment when I became interested in achieving something besides how much havoc or chaos I could create. But it happened.

The change, in part, undoubtedly resulted from a series of events that occurred nearly two years earlier during my sophomore year. The Dean of Girls not only made a very unpopular decision but a clearly unexpected one. Upon the move to the new campus, the school board voted to create a Dean of Girls post and at the same time designate the existing assistant principal as Dean of Boys. The girls were permitted the unprecedented opportunity to vote for their choice for the post. They overwhelmingly chose their health and PE coach, the very same lady who mistakenly ordered the wrong style shorts two years earlier. She proved to be a good-natured, jovial, and hence a popular teacher. The school board honored the girls' wish and appointed the teacher to the post.

Her name was Pat Meeks, and she carried a great deal more weight than what one would expect of a PE and health teacher. Her stout frame escaped student ridicule as her good-hearted personality and warm manner endeared her to most students. However, as so many times happens, the sudden promotion to an administrative position produced a dramatic personality transformation. Pat's normal easygoing nature turned into a stern demeanor that exhibited zero tolerance for any infraction of the rules. During her first two years in office, the change of personality remained an unconfirmed rumor for few girls conducted themselves badly enough to warrant a trip to Pat's office. Rumor turned to ugly reality during the fall of her third full year of duty.

In a tough decision, Pat ruled one of the cheerleading squad's co-captains, a very popular girl, ineligible to serve for the remainder of the year. It seems the girl had the misfortune of receiving a grade of D in one of her six courses. Pat referred to the school board's policy that to engage in extracurricular activities, students must earn no grade less than C. Many students thought the decision to declare the girl ineligible for the remainder of the year, as opposed to the remainder of the current semester, unduly harsh. Despite the outcry, the principal upheld Pat's decision, but unfortunately the controversy did not end there.

Some of the deposed girl's male cohorts decided to seek revenge on Pat. On a particularly dark night, several boys sneaked into Pat's yard and scribbled numerous vulgarities and threw paint on her house and its white cement tile roof.

In a swift piece of brilliant detective work Pat, with help from the local police, ferreted out the boys' identities within days. The boys were suspended from school for a period sufficient to force summer school attendance. They were also precluded from any further extracurricular activities. Their parents paid to repaint Pat's house and roof. After the announcement of the suspensions most expected Pat to drop the criminal charges she filed to gain police assistance in solving the crime. She didn't.

The boys' parents questioned the propriety of the school's decision to suspend them. After all, they argued, the damage was to private property and despite being directed against a school administrator, did not occur at a school-sponsored function. Pat successfully countered that the time and place were unimportant. The district authorities decided that school administrators may discipline the youths reasoning that an attack against a school administrator was an attack against school administration and discipline.

The parents filed a formal but nonetheless futile legal protest against the school's action. During the interim, a less formal but highly formidable protest began among the students in the junior and sophomore classes. Posters and tags that fastened around buttons on shirts and blouses were printed clandestinely in a print shop owned by the parents of a sympathetic sophomore. They each bore the simple initials printed in red on white paper, DWFP or Down With Fat Pat. At first only a few students brandished the tags. Within only a matter of days, however, posters, tags, and graffiti began to appear everywhere including walls and sidewalks. School officials threaten to expel anyone wearing or posting the initials, but there were simply too many offenders to expel. The volume of letters to the editor of the town's paper exceeded those submitted during the flap over Alec striking Tommy Strickland. Again, a split appeared in local opinion over whom to blame. The division served Pat's cause. Without any overwhelming consensus, her view carried—the boys were punished twice. She won the battle for their hides, but lost the war for student respect. To her credit, Pat learned a lesson in the process. After all parties to the incident graduated, Pat's good nature gradually replaced the hardened obstinate attitude she had assumed. She later retired to endearing messages from many former students. I can't imagine any coming from any one I knew.

During the early weeks of the protest, I participated, not out of any conviction that the boys were unduly penalized but because I enjoyed the excitement, the chance to defy authority. As the protest drug on, my excitement waned, but my principle grew. Disappointed to see the months-long protest fail, I came away with the realization that some goals and ideas are worth serious effort and a long fight. I also learned that some battles are worth losing. Somewhere in the process I lost my taste for mischief.

During the long episode, Alec maintained a very low profile adopting a "better thee than me" attitude. The controversy, the talk, the threats, and the counter threats were all too reminiscent of his experience. He carefully watched from the sidelines with more than passing interest the events as they unfolded. He took particular note that the school's entire administration and the school board solidly backed Pat's actions from the beginning. It did not escape his attention that students mainly comprised the more vociferous objectors. He absorbed silently but bitterly the incongruity of this protest over his almost three years earlier. He failed to grasp the not so subtle and profound dissimilarities of Pat's protest from his. Right or wrong, he kept his feelings within the confines of his home.

As the end of my junior year in high school approached, I experienced great difficulty in deciding how to use my one remaining elective. English IV, calculus, physics, and social studies were required by the school's college-bound curriculum. I chose athletic PE as my fifth class; I would again be head manager of the school basketball team, a position in which I took a great deal of pride. I tried out for the baseball team during my sophomore year but lost out due to an unusually large number of returning senior lettermen. My size, stature, and lead feet made football out of the question. My failure to make the baseball team only slightly bruised my ego, for I played third base for the First Baptist Church fast pitch softball team. Our team won the up-county fast pitch championship four of the five years I played. Coaches and friends encouraged me to try out for baseball again, but I declined because I wanted to manage the basketball team as well as play softball two nights a week. Our basketball team won sixty games while losing only six in the two years I served as head manager. Our team won the school's first conference and district championships in my junior year and repeated the performance my senior year. But then I'm getting ahead of myself.

Study hall represented a possibility because I would have three credits over the graduation requirement, but my parents did not look favorably on wasting a credit. Almost by default I registered for choir after a three-year hiatus from music. Maybe Alec will have forgotten me I remember thinking. I didn't want to revive any memories of my lack of appreciation for Alec's no nonsense approach to music. Pop encouraged me to give it another try. Because it was a first period class I figured that it wouldn't be a very taxing beginning to the school day. Only a few survivors of our eighth grade choir remained, but there were an unusual number of my friends registered for choir.

As I mulled over my choices I realized that Alec hadn't traveled by our house with the same frequency he had in earlier years. I remembered that he and Tracy had married nearly two years earlier, and I suspected that had something to do with the decreased frequency of his passage by our house. When Alec did occasionally walk by, Laddie would give chase with the same vehemence that characterized their first encounter. Denise Hooker still lived in the modest-sized, older house at the end of our street where they had settled upon their arrival in town. Despite Dr. Hooker's successful medical practice, they had not chosen to move to a larger house in a more prestigious neighborhood. Rumor had it that Alec acquired a car and had actually been seen driving it, a story I had not been able to verify.

When school began, I quickly found that Alec conducted his class in much the same manner he did the first year he taught. There were the prolonged periods of vocal exercises, stretching, and posture drills along with the numerous handouts that formed a required choir notebook. Sporadic slide travelogues of Alec's trip the previous summer were the only breaks in Alec's musical regimen. Despite my turn toward serious study or, perhaps, because of it, I found Alec's classes a trying experience and looked for any relief that presented itself.

A notable difference existed in these slides from those Alec forced upon us in earlier years. The same figure, the same face kept popping up in slide after slide. At first Alec did not mention the omnipresent personage, but it didn't take me long to recognize that it was Tracy. Of course, I thought, Alec now has a traveling companion. Once I recognized the figure, I relieved my boredom of viewing innumerable slides of the European countryside and tourist haunts by looking for and scrutinizing Tracy and her travel attire, mostly khaki shorts, bright-colored knit tops, white, heavy socks, and leather walking boots, and the ever-present backpack. If anyone observed my eyes and expression, I suppose I could have been accused of ogling because, of course, I was. She had changed but then so had I and my perspective of the opposite sex. Whatever the case, I found her more alluring, more attractive, and more sensual than I remembered, for it had also been three years since I last saw her.

Not long into the semester Alec announced that he planned some special music for a concert scheduled shortly after the first of the year. At first I didn't pay much attention, for the concert was almost a semester away and most music Alec planned bore the label "special." The ordinary soon became extraordinary, for it turned out to be Beethoven's "Ninth Symphony" whose lyrics Alec insisted that we listen and learn the original German first even though the concert would be in English. We spent days listening to monaural LP recordings of professional choral groups performing the symphony and following along in the musical scores provided by Alec. Two weeks of listening and following in our scores transpired before we opened our collective mouth to sing the first note. When the time finally arrived for us to sing on our own, Alec broke the composition down into voice segments, practicing with only the portion of the choir affected in that particular segment. Apart from the incessant daily voice exercises, little other music graced our lips except for the traditional seasonal music that school assemblies required. Practices became grueling with Alec demanding much the same effort and concentration as the basketball coach. Were it not for the bell signaling the end of class each day, Alec's intensity would have carried him long after class officially ended.

After spending three painstaking weeks working, segment by segment, through the entire vocal score, Alec felt we were ready to rehearse it in its entirety. We consumed a week of abortive attempts before we finally made our way through the complete vocal score in one sitting.

The next day, on our third attempt, we again went through the vocal score in its entirety. The following morning we had a visitor in choir. Arriving late, I fast-talked Alec into believing that road widening work on Gulf-to-Bay had snarled traffic causing me to be tardy. Alec begrudging accepted the explanation but pointed out that no one else had been similarly delayed. I cleared my throat and quickly took my place in the tenor section without noticing the guest sitting to my left in the alto section. As Alec started the tape to accompany us, I looked around the room and discovered Tracy sitting one row in front of me, a distance of no more than six feet. Alec stopped the tape momentarily to work with the sopranos. I remember sitting with my eyes transfixed on Tracy whose real beauty far surpassed that revealed in Alec's slides.

For one brief moment, sensing she was the object of someone's concentrated attention, Tracy looked around the choir and her eyes met mine. She seemed much closer than the six feet that separated us. My hands broke out in a cold sweat, a chill went down my spine, and my mouth went dry. She smiled then looked away. The look wasn't much more than a glance and no more than a friendly gesture of recognition yet a strong feeling of emotion overwhelmed me. I sat transfixed thinking only of her striking sensuality and asking myself, what does she see in Alec? What did she ever see in Alec? How much longer can it last?

"Mr. Collins!" The sharp voice jolted me out of my romantic stupor. I looked to its source. "Does Beethoven bore you? I wish I could get you to pay as much attention to me as you do to others," Alec said in clear reference to my prolonged staring at Tracy.

Momentarily caught off guard, I recovered sufficiently to reply, "You're not nearly so pretty."

The class roared and Tracy smiled. Alec unamused said in a stern voice, "I want to see you after class, young man."

I grimaced. I don't deserve this, I thought.

When class ended Tracy filed out with the students, leaving Alec and me alone. While waiting for the rest of the class to leave, I became bellicose and belligerent. Maybe it was because this incident was the second time Alec chose to reprimand me in front of Tracy recalling the after-school episode three years earlier. Perhaps it was my resentment for Alec's humiliating reprimands of students' errant classroom behavior. Whatever the source, I was determined not to cower from Alec. After all I was older then and had a slight height and decided weight advantage over Alec. I remember thinking, I didn't do anything wrong and by God, and I'm not going to take any shit from him.

"Young man, I don't like your cavalier attitude and flippant remarks in class. I want it stopped!" Alec demanded.

"I'm not a big fan or yours either," I responded with a sense of justification.

"Don't be smart with me," Alec said in a raised voice, "I'm in charge of this class and I'll do and say whatever I wish."

"Then don't be surprised if you get as good as you give," I returned with an equally daring glare.

"I don't have to take this. Furthermore, I don't want you staring at my wife when she visits my class!" Alec declared.

"She didn't seem to mind. Look, Mr. Driver, I've known Tracy a lot longer than you have, and besides, there's no law against looking," I retorted.

"There is with my wife," Alec shouted as his face reddened.

"A temporary condition, no doubt," I responded defiantly.

A rush of rage ran through Alec's whole body. He clenched his fists and set his jaw. His eyes had fire in them. Poised to strike, Alec suddenly relaxed his jaw and unclenched his fists. He later confided in Jack Winslow, that the image of Tommy Strickland flashed through his mind, as did the quiet role that Pop played in saving his job. After what seem an eternity he finally said, "I'm going to forget you ever said that, but don't you ever give me any more trouble. And do not embarrass my wife again," Alec stated, his voice an octave lower but containing a noticeable quiver.

"It wasn't I who embarrassed her. I'm late for my next class." I brushed Alec aside and walked toward the door. I made up my mind that I would drop choir when the semester ended in six weeks and be done with this man whose personality I never really understood.

Three days later, the subject of the concert came up at the dinner table and I mentioned Tracy's repeated presence during choir but omitted my encounter with Alec and my plans to drop choir. Mother mentioned that she heard that Tracy was pregnant. My eyes opened wide and, in amazement I thought, why? Obviously I didn't mean the question literally. I simply wondered why she invested so much of herself in a marriage that seemed so incongruous. I recalled my remark to Alec in our after-class encounter and thought that instead of being flippant as I intended, the remark may have been prophetic. I felt from the very first that Alec's and Tracy's personalities and demeanors were disparate. Maybe it was Alec's reticence or obstinacy. It seemed to me that Alec had some plan or goal in life that made

Tracy merely a means to an end. It was as though she were one more accolade or adornment to the breastplate of his life. I wondered just how long it would be before she realized what was happening.

Pop broke my train of thought by mentioning that Alec must be visiting his sister less often or by car for only occasionally did he notice that Alec was the object of Laddie's vociferous barking.

"It seems," Pop remarked, "that Alec's avoiding the confrontations he experienced earlier with Laddie."

Too bad, I thought, he wasn't doing the same in class.

Laddie kept our household busy with various and sundry items he managed to drag home from his sojourns. I remember all too well the smelly task of having to bury an enormous Jew fish he dragged home from heaven knows where. Even though our house lay on the bay, Laddie couldn't have lugged it up to the house because of the five-foot-high sea wall. The large fish sat rotting in the hot sun for hours before I came home. Mother immediately assigned me the task of burying it. I nearly gagged in the process. During the interim, the whole neighborhood reeked of rotting Jew fish.

My most harrowing experience with one of Laddie's treasures consisted of trying to snatch a writhing water moccasin from between his jaws. He dodged my leaps and lunges and would whip the snake by shaking his head. The snake's head and tail would flop over and under Laddie's snout in rapid succession. By the time I grappled the snake from him, it resembled a piece of tattered rope.

As the semester wore on, Alec left me alone and I bided my time waiting for the term to end. Meanwhile, preparations for the Beethoven concert became more intense and demanding. Practices took place after school and included, with growing frequency, the Bay Area Symphony Orchestra that would provide the instrumental portion of the concert. The Bay Area Chorus, a group of amateur adult singers that Alec had helped form, provided soloists for the parts too difficult for our younger, less-trained voices.

Alec, at his best in preparing for and handling the evening's program, never hesitated—he knew where he wanted us to go and how to get us there. He deliberately rehearsed us, on numerous occasions, without the orchestra training us to take our cues from him and not the music. Most in-class practices used LP recordings for accompaniment but for only carefully selected excerpts, he demanded and received the choir's undivided and concentrated attention. He demanded and received total control. Several rehearsals were held during the holidays but after Christmas Day. The dress rehearsal was two nights before the concert on the third weekend in January.

After extensive discussions with the orchestra conductor and appropriate administrators, Alec decided the best facility for the concert was the high school auditorium where twelve hundred listeners could comfortably sit in seats with curved backs and armrests. To me, the choice of our high school auditorium weakened the importance of the concert. I felt a formal setting such as the old high school auditorium was more appropriate, but then Alec did not choose to consult me.

On the evening of the performance, the auditorium filled quickly as news of the unusual program had circulated in the community for more than two months. Not in the history of the district had a high school choir taken such a difficult composition as its concert theme and never had a concert been coordinated with a symphony orchestra. If for no other reason, the community could have responded simply out of sheer curiosity. Pop and Walter Goss were more than curious. They anticipated the significance of the performance long in advance and bought their tickets early. Christian Fletcher rarely attended individual school events lest he unintentionally showed favoritism to one particular school. The precedent breaking program planned by Alec proved too much for Christian to ignore.

The importance of the performance permeated the choir down to and including me. Everyone's mind focused on their specific individual part and one singular collective objective: the concern that everything be right. The level of concentration was intense.

White dinner jackets and evening gowns replaced choir robes. No stage settings were used except for standing bleachers for the choir and backdrops across the stage behind the choir and orchestra. The acoustics in the auditorium didn't require a sound amplification system. The choral portion of the Symphony begins with the fourth movement some forty minutes, give or take, after the beginning. I remember how long those forty minutes seemed.

The performance was a musical director's dream: everything fell into place at the appointed time. There were no missed cues, no unplanned breaks, no hesitations, the orchestra and chorus flowed smoothly from one movement to the next. Technically, the performance appeared, at least from my point of view, flawless. Qualitatively, little more could be expected from young amateur voices, and clearly no more had ever been achieved from any district choir.

The audience broke into a rousing, standing ovation responding in kind to the outstanding presentation that far surpassed their expectations. Pop caught Walter Goss's eye and each knew in their respective glances the vindication the other felt for interceding for Alec four years earlier. "What a pity," Pop later said, "to have deprived the students, the school, and the community of these moments because of a random, careless fit of anger." The community and the media were equally effusive in their praise.

Immediately following the performance, Alec and the orchestra conductor shook hands vigorously and smiled broadly. Many choir members, technicians, and stagehands gathered around Alec extending congratulations. Alec returned each compliment. Everyone smiled, everyone sensed the beauty of the performance, and each felt a deep sense of pride. Tracy, her pregnancy now showing, ran to Alec and kissed him. He held her in one arm while shaking hands with all those around him with the other. Through the sea of bodies and over the din of noise, I watched from across the stage. Alec must have sense me staring at him and Tracy just as Tracy had sensed my staring at her in class. He looked up and saw me staring not just at Tracy but also at him. We looked at each other for a moment before Alec nodded a gesture I returned. I turned and walked out the nearest exit to my car in the adjacent parking lot. I talked with Alec only one other time, but the music of and the passage from Schiller still echoes in my mind. I know I will carry them to my grave.

For this performance and others that followed, Alec received a citation the following year from the National Music Education Association for excellence in musical education. It came at the pinnacle of Alec's personal and professional life; he received awards not only from the NMEA and the school district in the form of a substantial increase in his salary, but also from Tracy with the birth of their first (and only) child, Richard, named after Alec's brother. Alec's dreams and aspirations were realized: he had a young, beautiful wife, a long sought son, and a successful career. He received numerous accolades for his musical and professional skills, and a secure position in the school system that allowed him plentiful time for travel. Alec had, at last, experienced his own Green Flash.

Chapter 12

August 1959

The late fifties marked a milestone for Clearwater and its internationally famous fast pitch softball team. Reflecting the city's changing composition, the Bombers, with almost half its players from out of state, won a third national title in an emotion-laden world tournament. Herb Dudley pitched for the Bombers after a two-year absence to play for a team in the mid-west, Aurora, I believe. Some thought that at age thirty-nine Herb had lost some of what had made him, perhaps, the best pitcher in the game. Herb proved the doubters wrong by almost singlehandedly winning the title for the team. In the process he gained all world honors and most valuable player of the tournament. I'll never forget the emotional speech he gave to a full house (the tournament was held in Clearwater that year) after the final championship game ended. He quoted *Isaiah 40:31* and led the hushed audience in prayer, something only Herb could have done.

Alec returned from a trip to Africa just in time to attend the final two games of the tournament. Jack Winslow urged him to attend as possibly the last chance to see Herb Dudley pitch for the Bombers in a world championship. Alec relented partly for Jack's sake and partly out of courtesy for a colleague. Whereas Herb had been cordial since Alec and Tracy married, their relationship remained mostly collegial and distant. Alec mused that Herb wasn't being aloof as that term simply couldn't apply to Herb. Alec told Jack that the memories of Alec's behavior toward Tracy and the Tommy Strickland incident probably still lingered disapprovingly in the back of Herb's mind.

The importance of the game, my participation and interest in softball, and maybe the last chance I'd have to see my former coach and Sunday school teacher pitch drew me to the stadium the night of the championship game. In an attempt to walk off nervous energy that the close defensive game generated, I wandered through the stadium crowd and spied Alec sitting with Jack Winslow. I knew Jack Winslow because he and his wife, Cynthia, served as guardians for an exchange student from Haiti I dated as a senior in high school. I couldn't count the many nights I spent watching television in their living room until the wee hours of the morning. Anita, born of French parents, lived in Haiti where her father owned a timber business. Her parents decided that a year in an American school would be a rewarding experience and a welcomed change from the French and Swiss schools Anita had attended most of her life. Anita had dark eyes and hair and possessed a beauty and maturity not normally seen in American girls of fifteen years. Very intelligent and well educated, she spoke five languages fluently. I envied her because I wasn't confident that I could speak English, that is, American fluently. But then Anita is another story.

I spoke to Alec and Jack and they moved over and invited me to join them. As we watched Herb put a finishing touch on what became a remarkable performance both on and off the pitcher's mound, Alec became uncharacteristically open and candid. Normally, at least in my presence, Alec was reticent. I remember being taken by his candor and glibness. He said that while watching and listening to Herb, it suddenly occurred to him that Herb represented all that was right about Clearwater and, at the same time, all that was wrong with it. Innocence, pride, strength, conviction, determination, and perseverance characterized both the man and his native community. In that sense Herb personified the community. On the other hand, Alec believed that Herb also embodied the parochial, provincial, or simply the closed minds of the community, the general reluctance to accept outsiders whose values and attitudes differed markedly from those of natives or naturalized residents who had easily assimilated into the fabric of the community. In a sense, referring to himself, Alec said that he felt he had rent that fabric rather than smoothed it and despite his apparent successes, still lingered like lint on cloth waiting to be picked off, close but never quite within its weave. Surprised at Alec's revelations, I recall Jack asked in response what had brought on his sudden attempt at introspection and its dismal outlook. Jack speculated that Alec's reflective mood was the result of his just completed trip to Africa. As Jack later learned, Alec's mood reflected the events that occurred in the ten days since his return.

Demographic growth provided other milestones for Clearwater. Outlying shopping centers robbed the old center of town of business. The town, now a city, progressed eastward into former countryside causing vacant storefronts to appear downtown. Traffic provided the only growth the downtown area experienced as numerous cars passed through on their way to the beach. Curbside parking gave way to four-lane streets that became thoroughfares. Located on what once was the edge of town, the medical clinic where I took my first breath was razed to construct the city's first shopping center. I teased with delight unknowing souls that I was born in the middle of the Cleveland Plaza parking lot. The first house my parents owned, just one block from the old clinic, had been purchased by the phone company as the site for a large mid-county equipment facility. Pop moved his office from Cleveland Street into a former Gulf service station that he converted into a small office building on the corner of Drew Street and North Fort Harrison Avenue. Telephone numbers expanded to seven digits, and most people had a private line, at least those who wanted or could afford one. Open wire slowly gave way to enclosed cable.

The population within the city limits doubled from 1940 to 1950 and preliminary estimates were that it had doubled again by 1959. Due to high differential property tax rates and annexation only by vote of affected residents, the population outside the corporate limits grew even faster. From a population of just over five thousand in 1940, Clearwater and its immediate surrounding area climbed to approximately fifty thousand by 1960. The average age, reflecting the large number of retirees migrating south, rose to fifty-five. One third of the population exceeded the normal retirement age of sixty-five. Retirement became an industry.

Meanwhile, rapid change came not only to the community but to people as well. Nancy Ashbury and I never talked, but we had something in common I later learned. We shared an intuitive feeling that Alec and Tracy's initial relationship and consequent marriage were fragile. Nancy's feelings undoubtedly stemmed from her first impression of Alec the night he came to call for Tracy for the concert in Tampa. My feelings came as a result of my encounters with Alec that fateful semester of my senior year. Despite our misgivings both Nancy and I harbored our feelings silently.

Nancy watched the changes taking place in her once small, peaceful village and those taking place, more subtly and quietly, in Alec and Tracy's relationship as the pressures of marriage and parenthood increased. The partnership Tracy so eagerly sought and enjoyed with Alec in his choirs slowly dissolved after Richard's birth. Nancy instinctively felt the birth of Richard would affect Tracy's role and responsibilities as well as Alec's attitude toward her. She tried to prepare Tracy for this change, but Tracy was equally certain that her mother's suspicions were unfounded.

Thus, Nancy was not surprised when she answered the phone early one morning in late June 1960 and heard, "Oh, Mother, I just don't know what I'm going to do," the voice sobbed at the other end of the line.

"What is it, dear? What's the matter?" Nancy responded with a definite concern in her voice.

"Things are so different and we're so poor. Alec doesn't even care, he's unwilling to change. I don't know how long I can stand it," Tracy managed to get out between sobs.

Nancy listened quietly and knew that the moment she feared had come. *What should I say? How should I respond?* she wondered. Despite her premonitions Nancy felt ill prepared. For the moment, she decided to encourage Tracy to talk not only to discover the source of her present difficulty, but also to allow her to vent what obviously were pent-up frustrations.

"I want you to come over and talk for a while. I'll fix a nice lunch and Richard can nap while we talk," Nancy suggested, hoping to lure Tracy away from her immediate environment and back into the comfort of her former home.

After a little coaxing, an hour later Tracy stood at the back door, Richard in one arm and her purse and baby paraphernalia in the other. She fumbled with the door. Nancy came to her rescue and opened it.

"Here, let me take Richard," Nancy said as she reached for the squirming infant. She took him in her arms and thought to herself how she would never cease to be amazed that Richard looked so much like Alec and not at all like Tracy or anyone else on their side of the family. Perhaps, she thought, it's fortunate he's not a girl.

"Now start from the beginning and tell me what's bothering you," Nancy said as they sat down in the family room where a playpen for Richard's visits occupied one corner.

"I've calmed down some since I called. I awakened this morning feeling greatly depressed. I've had these feelings for some time, but dismissed them as exhaustion or fatigue that a good night's rest would cure. It's frightening to awaken after a night's rest and find them worse instead rather than better. I must have had an anxiety attack. The realization that Alec left yesterday without me finally struck home. Oh, I know you offered to keep Richard and Alec urged me to go, but I couldn't, I mean, two couldn't go. The cost simply exceeded what we can afford and even if we had the money, I couldn't leave Richard with you for two months, it wouldn't be fair. I felt bad enough leaving him for almost a month last summer."

Tracy hardly took a breath as she spoke. She had composed and rehearsed her speech even before calling her mother. She hadn't told Nancy just how early she awakened and how many hours she lay in bed thinking about her plight and realizing that the vacant space next to her was not just for a few nights while the high school choir traveled for a concert. The absence would last two months. The more she thought about Alec's absence and attitude, the more depressed she became until finally she became engulfed in sheer panic. The call to Nancy calmed her enough to organize her thoughts. However, she no longer could keep them to herself.

"I thought it my duty to suggest that he go without me, but I couldn't help hoping he'd refuse. Then when he said he would go and I gave him my blessing, I sensed he felt relieved. Everyone knows how much he loves to travel and how much travel is a part of his life. I did not want to be the one that prevented him from going. Travel seems to be the only real vice he has. He does work hard to earn his trips. It would have been nice, however, for him to decline, at least just this once, but then I didn't ever tell him exactly how I felt. You would think that Richard's birth and his new responsibilities would make him alter his priorities without me having to prod him. I guess that's what bothers me the most: he tries to carry on his life as he always did. There's little change in his attitude in spite of our marriage, a child, and a house. I believe the reason he still walks most places rather than drive is that he resents even having a car. He seems to consider it an intrusion in his personal life."

Tracy rose from her seat in the family room and walked to the kitchen, withdrew a glass from the large polished oak cabinets, and poured a glass of water from the bottle kept in the refrigerator. She walked back and sat down, took a sip then continued, "He makes me feel less and less like a lover and more and more like a mother. I dearly love Richard, but I don't want to be considered solely a mother, a babysitter, a nanny—I want to be appreciated as a wife, a companion, a lover. He used to treat me that way: he was kind, thoughtful, considerate, and looked to my every need. Since Richard's birth, he has turned his affection and love to him, which is fine except that I'm no longer included. He denies all of this, of course. He claims he loves me very much and he probably does in his own way, but it's no longer my way."

Tracy paused for just a moment to collect her thoughts. Nancy took advantage of the break to suggest, "Let's have some lunch. Come into the kitchen and talk while I fix a tuna salad. The boiled eggs have probably cooled by now. What were you saying earlier about being poor? You knew all along that school teachers aren't paid very well."

"I knew, but then I didn't realize the sacrifices that would mean. Despite the sizable increases he has received lately, and he's so proud of them, his salary is so low that we can hardly make it. If it weren't for you helping with some of my and Richard's clothes...I would just hate to think what we would wear. We're still driving your old Buick—I don't know how we'll ever afford a new one. The worst part is that Alec has no ambition to better either himself or his family. He's content to live as we are forever just as long as he gets to make his trips. I've even offered to help by going to work, but he won't hear of it. I don't believe I can live the rest of my life this way; we're living hand to mouth. I haven't dared suggest that he forget about his two-month summer trips and find a job instead. We'd be better off two ways—no vacation expenses and more income.

"Oh, Mother, what am I to do?" Tracy asked, a tear running down her cheek. "I'm sorry you have to see me like this, but I thought for hours this morning and couldn't bring myself to talk with anyone else."

"Dear, you know that you can always talk with me, it's always been that way, hasn't it?" Nancy tried her best to be reassuring.

"Yes, but I'm trying to be more independent. However, I'm afraid I'm not succeeding very well. I guess the real reason I hesitated to call is that I'm embarrassed to admit that I've let matters get out of hand and then let them bother me so," Tracy confessed.

"You certainly needn't feel embarrassed, dear. Everyone needs someone to confide in, I guess that's why I miss your father so. You don't need any excuse to come talk with me about anything that bothers you. That's what I'm here for," Nancy continued her attempt to reassure Tracy.

Tracy thought about what her mother said. Her reluctance in coming to her mother for advice had been aided by the necessity it would require of another admission, one that would be, she feared, the most difficult of all to make.

"There's another reason why I didn't want to call you. You may already know what it is. The thought has haunted me for weeks. I've come to the point where you thought I would end up all along. From the beginning you foresaw this moment, a time when I finally would have to admit some reservation in Alec's and my relationship. I think you're just surprised that it took this long. I guess I just didn't want to admit that you were right and I was wrong," Tracy had great difficulty in forming her words. She took another sip from her glass.

Nancy stopped her lunch preparations and looked sympathetically at Tracy, giving Tracy her undivided attention. She responded, "While it's true I had serious reservations about you and Alec from the start, I believed it was I who was wrong. Lloyd always gave you two the benefit of the doubt, and I have to admit it was catching. Besides, you seemed so happy and despite my fears, your life together appeared to be going well.

"I know how difficult it must have been for you to call this morning, but I want that to end right now. I'm here whenever you need me and even when you don't need me." Returning the subject of their conversation to the concern at hand, Nancy asked, "Have you told Alec how you feel?"

"Not really, I've tried, but I guess I really didn't know how or I just simply didn't want to create an argument," Tracy's voice trailed off into a sigh.

Nancy finished preparing the salad and tea and placed them on the table. She would tend to Richard later, he seemed happy enough for the time being, she thought. She asked, "Do you still love him?" Nancy watched Tracy's expression for her reaction.

Tracy, pokerfaced, paused for a considerable time before replying quietly, "I don't know."

"If you can't answer that question affirmatively, then the answer must be no," responded Nancy, abandoning for the moment her role as listener.

"It's just not that simple, Mother," she rebutted, toying with one of the Saltine crackers on her plate. "For the first time in my life," she continued, "I'm looking at more than just the present, I'm thinking also of the future and I can't imagine how long I'll be able to survive living and feeling this way."

"It seems to me you have already made up your mind," Nancy interjected.

"Not yet. I have to tell Alec exactly how I feel and give him... give us a chance to work things out. I don't want to pack and leave at the first sign of depression. I feel I owe it to Alec, Richard, and myself to try to make things work. I may be just feeling a little low at the moment—I'm not ready to make any long run decisions yet." Tracy finally managed a bite of the salad Nancy had fixed.

"Would you feel comfortable talking with Cynthia Winslow?" Nancy suggested.

"No. Cynthia and Jack are good friends to both Alec and me. It would put them in an awkward position, besides, I'm a private person when it comes to my feelings, you know that. No, for the time being, if you don't mind, I would rather confine my thoughts to the two of us," turning and looking at Richard quietly playing in his pen, Tracy added with the hint of a smile, "and Richard of course." The tuna tasted good to Tracy and she began to feel better.

"Well then, I want you to do one thing," Nancy requested, reaching for Tracy's hand across the table.

"What's that?" Tracy grabbed her mother's hand and squeezed.

"I want you and Richard to come over every day for lunch. It's more pleasant here and you don't need to be alone when you're feeling this depressed, okay?" she asked as she returned Tracy's squeeze.

"Okay," Tracy responded, smiling openly for the first time that day.

For the next month, Tracy and Richard visited Nancy nearly every day for lunch. Mother and daughter talked for hours on one subject after another trying to avoid dwelling on Tracy's unhappiness and the direction her marriage was taking.

One such morning in early July, Tracy and Richard arrived later than usual, coming straight from an appointment with Richard's pediatrician. Tracy noticed the expensive Lincoln parked in front of her mother's house as she pulled into the drive and immediately recognized it as Marie Davies's.

Nancy heard Tracy come in the back door and rose to call her to the living room where she was entertaining Marie and her son, James, who had just returned home sporting an Ivy League education and a brand-new law degree. As Tracy later discovered, Marie was traipsing James around town showing him off to all of her garden club friends of which Nancy had always been her favorite.

"Tracy," Nancy began as she led her and Richard into the room, "you remember Marie Davies and James, don't you?"

"Yes," she answered, adding, "how are you?" James caught her eye. He looked older, more mature, and less gangly than she remembered from high school, but after all, she thought, that was over eight years ago and he was a year ahead of me. James fit the mold of medium height perfectly for no one ever described him at any age as tall or short. He possessed the type of face that always looked younger than his actual age. As a senior in high school, he often was mistaken as a sophomore. College and law school succeeded in maturing him physically if for no other reason than a significant loss of weight. Despite the maturing, he could easily pass for a younger age and frequently encountered requests for an ID well after he turned twenty-one.

James was the consummate student. Always there, always prepared, always coveted by every teacher and professor whose class he graced. Never known for his athletic abilities, he deftly avoided the nerd image with his sense of humor and witty, cutting remarks. To classmates, he was the comic relief of whatever course they shared with him. Teachers welcomed his wit and perfectly timed remarks as breaks in the tedium of their subjects. James accomplished what eluded most teachers, the ability to relax students, and teachers for that matter, just enough for pedagogical success.

It always perplexed Nancy and Marie that despite their closeness, James and Tracy scarcely seemed to notice each other. Maybe, they conjectured, it was the year's difference in age or perhaps the closeness of the mothers bred, if not contempt, indifference between the children. As James and Tracy's high school years drew to an end, Nancy speculated to Marie that perhaps the two families were so close that James and Tracy simply overlooked each other. In any event, those times were pre-college, pre-law school, and pre-Alec.

After exchanging pleasantries, Nancy explained to Tracy that James had just completed law school, passed the Florida bar exam, and started practice in Pasco County.

"Actually, Tracy," James interrupted, "I'll just be an assistant district attorney at least until I get my legal feet wet."

"Congratulations and welcome back home, I know you're relieved to finally finish your education," Tracy responded politely.

"Yes, for a while there I thought it would take forever," he added. "But it looks like you have been busy yourself—just who might this be?" he asked, turning his head in Richard's direction.

The four-way conversation took several turns over the next hour when Marie glanced at her watch and said, "Oh my, look how long we have stayed," she remarked with some alarm.

"Why don't I fix us some lunch," Nancy suggested. She wasn't anxious for Marie and James to leave as she thought the visit was having a therapeutic effect on Tracy.

"No, no, we won't ask you to do that, but we'll have lunch together. We want the three of you to be our guests at that nice Greek restaurant in Tarpon Springs. It's the least we can do for staying so long," Marie responded.

"Well—" Nancy began, uncertain how to address Marie's suggestion considering her own wishes.

"We won't take no for an answer," Marie insisted.

"Richard is not good company in restaurants. I'll keep him here while the three of you go to lunch," Nancy suggested, all the willing to make the sacrifice in order for Tracy to continue the visit with James and Marie.

"All right," said Marie, "but on one condition, I'll stay with you and Richard." Turning to James, she continued, "James, you take this lovely young lady to lunch and pick me up when you return and that will be that."

Tracy hesitated for a moment, but knowing Marie's reticence once having made a decision and hearing Richard let out a loud scream she relented. She glanced at her mother seeking some guidance that she received by a simple nod. Tracy secretly welcomed the respite from motherhood. Besides, she thought, it's only a twenty-minute drive to the restaurant and we'll be back in an hour and a half.

James and Tracy drove north on old Highway 19 through the old citrus communities of Ozona and Palm Harbor. James, having noticed Tracy's polite but emotionless demeanor during the hour-long visit, decided to coax her out of the formality she evinced.

"I guess we really weren't all that close in school being a grade apart. The last time I remember seeing you, you were May Queen and a very attractive one I might add." He grinned, hoping his compliment and smile would warm the conversation.

"Thank you," responded Tracy. "Right now that seems like such a long time ago. Your mother says you did very well in school," Tracy answered, finding small talk difficult with someone she knew mainly as the son of her mother's best friend, someone she had not seen since he entered the halls of Ivy.

"I'm afraid Mother gets carried away sometimes. I believe your mother said your husband is out of the country on some sort of trip. She also said he's the high school music teacher, should I know him? I only remember Mr. Goss."

"Alec came the year after you graduated and replaced Walter Goss. He is in North Africa visiting Morocco, French Algeria, and Egypt," Tracy answered flatly.

"Sounds fascinating, you didn't want to go?" James asked innocently, not knowing what emotions he stirred in Tracy.

"No," she sighed, "someone had to take care of Richard. Mother kept him last summer while Alec and I traveled, and I just didn't feel like asking her again," her voice trailing off as thoughts of her plight began to run anew through her mind.

"It sounds like your husband really likes to travel," he continued treading unknowingly on sensitive feelings.

"Yes, it's a passion he picked up in the service. It really means a lot to him," Tracy tried to hide the growing emotion in her voice.

"It must. I don't know that I could go halfway around the world and leave someone as attractive as you behind. I haven't yet met the man, but I already suspect his sanity," he said, trying to make his statement sound more complimentary to her than detrimental to Alec.

Tracy turned and looked out her side window at the passing houses and orange groves without responding. Tears began to flow down her cheeks. She quickly searched her purse for a tissue.

"I'm sorry, I believe I've upset you. Forgive me. I have a loose tongue—it comes with the legal training or else is a prerequisite, I don't know which," James said apologetically.

Tracy took a moment to collect herself before answering. "That's all right, I'm a bit out of sorts today, could we talk of something else?" she asked as she blotted her tears.

"Certainly," he immediately responded, "we could always talk about me, Mother always does, much to everyone's dismay I fear."

James had inadvertently struck a raw nerve and it became clear that it wasn't simply a matter of what he had said. He directed the conversation away from family to their present venture.

Fifty years earlier, Tarpon Springs had attracted hundreds of Greek immigrants who came to dive in the clear Gulf waters for the once plentiful sponges. In the late forties and early fifties, oxygen absorbing microorganism called the Red Tide for the red hue the bacteria cast on affected waters, ravaged fish, and plant life in the Gulf. The bacteria killed the lush sponges growing along the Gulf coast and, thereby, decimated forever, the sponge industry in Tarpon Springs. The sponge industry was dead, but the quaint shops and restaurants were quickly becoming tourist attractions along the old sponge docks. Pappas's is the largest and finest restaurant and sits in the midst of the old fleet area providing an interesting and romantic view for its patrons. Most recently, Tarpon Springs gained notoriety for being the site of the filming of *The Twelve Mile Reef* with Gilbert Roland, Robert Wagner, and Terry Moore.

James and Tracy ordered lunch and by the time they finished he had her laughing and smiling. For one brief but delightful hour, her mind lost track of all that troubled her. When they returned to Nancy's, Marie was ready to leave, so James did not linger. Before leaving, Marie invited Nancy and Tracy to a garden party she was giving for James. James urged Tracy to come, reassuring her that she already knew most on the guest list. "Anyway," he teased, "the party is just an excuse to pass out business cards for my future law practice." Tracy said she would consider it and thanked him for the lunch and invitation.

After Marie and James left, Nancy asked Tracy, "Well, are you going to go to the party?"

"Me? What about you? You're invited, too, you know," Tracy responded, watching for her mother's reaction.

"Dear, Marie only asked me to be polite. The party is for James and his friends, not for old folks like me. I'll be happy to keep Richard while you go though," she offered.

"I don't know whether I should," Tracy answered, hinting for some encouragement that Nancy immediately provided.

"Sure you should. It's an excellent opportunity to be among people your own age and get your mind off yourself for a while. Go ahead, you'll enjoy yourself."

"Maybe I will," she answered, reflectively pausing, then asking in a soft voice her mother did not hear, "I wonder if James is still dating Sarah Dawkins?"

*****

Marie Davies prepared a lengthy guest list, but James prevailed upon her to limit the invitations to mostly his old friends and only a smattering of hers. Even edited, the list was lengthy enough to justify what Marie wanted to do—have it in her garden. Despite the fact it was mid-July, Marie's backyard seemed to defy the heat and humidity and remained, day or night, unseasonably cool and comfortable. The large sprawling live oaks that shaded the property during the day and its site at the top of a small rise where southeasterly breezes cooled it at night created an oasis from the normal torrid summer heat.

Bordered on three sides by a lush, tall hedge of ligustrum banked with many varieties of azaleas, the garden encompassed her entire backyard, an area slightly less than an acre. Meandering brick walks wove their way among the many planter beds filled with Spanish ivy and jasmine and bordered with liriope. The beds circumscribed the massive oaks whose huge trunks were interlaced by the climbing vines. Large wood Lutyens benches offered the guests comfortable, spacious places to sit.

Nestled in a corner of the yard, a greenhouse, camouflaged by viburnum hedges, served as Marie's laboratory where she experimented with new varieties of day lilies that lined the outer edges of the beds along the sides of the garden. Behind the greenhouse lay a massive compost pile formed each year with the help of tens of thousands of falling oak leaves and hedge trimmings.

Extending from the terrace at the back of the house lay an impressive reflecting pool with three fountains that sprayed water in gentle patterns resembling hibiscus blossoms. The free form lawn formed by the walks, beds, and pool was a green keeper's dream. Planted in zoysia grass, it looked like a large putting green with its surface as flat and smooth as a billiard table and strong enough to bear the weight of her invited guests with only the slightest sign of wear. The garden, as Marie intended, served as an ideal place to entertain a large number of guests.

Marie took great pride in everything she had, but apart from James her garden remained her most prized accomplishment. Since the death of her husband nearly a decade earlier, she spent increasing amounts of time supervising her gardeners and planning future projects. Her election as president of the garden club for three consecutive years came as no surprise to anyone.

Perhaps boredom, loneliness, curiosity, or the desire for a momentary escape, prodded Tracy to attend the party. She made a few pretenses to Nancy about not feeling right going alone, but she secretly welcomed the expected resultant encouragement that her mother gave. She looked forward to reminiscing with old friends and catching up on everyone including the status of James and his high school sweetheart, Sarah.

By the time she dropped Richard at her mother's and arrived at Marie's, twilight had set in and the party was well underway. Forced by the large number of cars parked along Marie's street to park on a side street, Tracy took a shortcut through a hidden back gate that she and her mother used on previous visits to Marie's garden. As she emerged into the backyard, she stepped back in time eight years. Despite being a year younger than James and most of his friends, she knew nearly everyone there. Marie hired a band for the occasion that was playing "Wish You Were Here" as Tracy walked into the midst of a small group.

Marie and James had not seen Tracy enter the garden as they positioned themselves in the house to greet guests as they arrived at the front door. Tracy mingled among the guests for almost an hour before James, having abandoned his post inside the house, spotted her chatting with two of her former cheerleader friends. He did little to suppress the delight that came over his face. Marie, who hardly missed anything that happened around her, correctly read his expression and only a single glance in the direction of his eyes explained why.

"Now how do you suppose Tracy slipped passed us, James? Go down and welcome her and say she's not to leave without seeing me."

"Yes, I'm going to do just that." James's eyes remained riveted to Tracy.

"And, James," Marie paused, "her mother hasn't said so, but I suspect that all is not quite right in Tracy's life at the moment. Try not to complicate it further."

Recalling Tracy's reaction to his comment about her husband traveling alone, he wondered what gave his mother the same impression he received from Tracy. He asked, "How do you know that if Mrs. Ashbury hasn't said anything?"

"It's what she hasn't said. Ever since her husband left for God-knows-where, Tracy has been spending an inordinate amount of time at her mother's. Nancy has said little about these visits. I surmised some intimate personal problems."

"Mother, you missed your calling, you should have been a detective."

"Oh, but, James, I am," she replied with a wry smile.

James made his way among the small clusters of guests that separated the terrace where he left his mother from the place on the brick walk where Tracy stood talking with the former cheerleaders. As he approached her, she broke away from the group and started toward the house.

"There you are, you little sneak. How did you manage to slip in? I was afraid you weren't coming," he said, brandishing a broad grin.

"Good evening, James. I'm working my way to your mother. I arrived late and took the shortcut through the rose garden, thinking you and your mother were already back here. I just got caught up in sharing memories with some old friends. I think nearly everyone is here." Tracy turned and glanced over the numerous guests scattered over Marie's backyard.

"Yes, I should've had more business cards printed," he teased.

"Oh, you'll do well in law," she teased back.

"Yes, when I eventually set up practice, I plan to open my office next door to an ambulance service…and buy a fast car."

They laughed. It was a corny joke, but it served its purpose.

"You're awful," she said.

"I know. Can I offer you something to drink? Mother made her favorite recipe." He took her arm and escorted her toward the table set up on the terrace.

"Yes, if it's not too strong, I have to drive home alone."

"Pity," he mumbled under his breath.

"I haven't seen Sarah. Is she here?" Tracy asked, hoping that she made the question sound innocent enough.

"Not quite," he said with some relief, "she met some guy from Georgia while in college and is now Mrs. Robert Rogers living in Atlanta. I haven't heard from her since my junior year in college. She probably has gained thirty pounds and has three children by now."

"Oh, that's too bad. I know how close you two were in high school," Tracy continued her interrogation, trying her best to retain the innocence in her voice.

"Not really," he said without any elaboration. Tracy didn't ask for any further explanation.

They strolled toward the terrace where the caterers had provided an envious table of cakes, pastries, cut sandwiches, fruit, and cheeses. Marie planned something for everyone's taste or diet. As they reached the table, James said, "You look especially lovely tonight, but then you always have even way back then," he said with a nod of his head toward his guests.

Tracy caught his meaning and smiled, replying, "Thank you. I wore this sun dress thinking it would be warm, but the garden is quite cool, it's a little chilly."

"Let's take our punch into the library where you can warm up. Maybe we'll find Mother. She told me not to let you get away without seeing her."

"I wouldn't even think of it," Tracy joked.

James led Tracy into the library where the sound of the band playing on the terrace echoed quietly into the room. The clatter and chatter of the party were but distant echoes. Tracy sat at one end of an oversized sofa while James sat in a stuffed winged back armchair perpendicular to her.

"I've always admired your mother's library. The book wall with all the leather-bound editions is very impressive as is the oriental carpet; I don't recall seeing it before."

"Mother has a passion for decorating, or redecorating. She redecorated the library last year. The carpet is new, that is, it's old, but new, if that makes sense."

"Yes," she smiled.

"So how's the party?" James asked, searching for a subject that would keep the conversation moving.

"It's very nice. Your mother has outdone herself, if that's possible. The garden is beautiful, as always, and the way it's lighted provides a relaxing and even romantic setting. I'm glad you invited me," Tracy answered with a distinct tone of sincerity.

"I'm glad you came," he replied, trying to echo her note of sincerity.

Tracy smiled and said, "It's good to see old friends again. It's amazing how you can live in the same town with many of your old friends and go years without seeing them. Some of us were quite close in high school, but we have since drifted apart. I find that a little sad."

"I know what you mean. Most people here know me from high school, but after eight years living somewhere else chasing an education, I'm not the same, you're not the same, and they're not either," James responded, trying not to sound too introspective.

"That's true. It's becoming increasingly difficult to recognize old friends much less acquaintances. I notice something else as well. The band is playing all of the old songs we were so crazy about in school, but I wonder if anyone is really listening." Tracy turned in the direction of the French doors that looked out into the backyard.

"You're right about that. I've heard them play for over an hour, but I don't think I can recall the name of a single song," James replied.

They sat silently for a few moments listening to the sounds of the band through the doors.

"What are they playing right now?" Tracy asked, testing James's memory.

James paused, listened again for a moment, smiled, looked into Tracy's eyes, and answered, "You Belong to Me." Tracy blushed then James added, "By Jo Stafford."

For a moment James wished it had been another Jo Stafford favorite, "Make Love to Me." Deciding it was time to change the subject, James's tone became more serious. He said, "Tracy, I want to apologize for speaking out of turn on the way to Pappas's. I didn't mean to offend or embarrass you. I know it's none of my business, but if you have or ever have a problem that I could help you with, please don't hesitate to ask. You have my card," he added with a grin.

"Cute. Thank you for your concern. The problem's me, not you. I usually don't let down like that. Normally, I'm a very private person," Tracy answered. The inflection in her voice made James believe she might be willing to make an exception that night.

"Well, I won't pry, but if you ever need a little advice or counsel, not necessarily legal," he smiled then turned serious again, "please call me, or Mother," he added.

"Right now I'm up to here"—placing the edge of her hand just under her chin—"in advice about one thing or another. Alec thinks I should be traveling with him, and maybe I should; Mother thinks I need an interest of my own, and maybe I should; Richard wants me to pay constant attention to him, and maybe I should; some of my old friends think I should complete my education, and maybe I should; others think I should go to work, and maybe I should."

The suddenness with which Tracy decided to share some of her frustrations with James might have appeared to some who knew her as impulsive. But Tracy rarely did anything impulsive, and her decision that night represented no exception. As the evening of the party neared, she thought about James and the brief moment of relief she felt during lunch at Pappas's restaurant. James represented something comforting to her, and she felt drawn to him without really knowing why. He was a familiar face in a mass of strangers, something friendly and reassuring.

"And what does Tracy think?" he interrupted.

"Tracy thinks she's going to have an extremely difficult time pleasing husband, mother, son, and friends." She fell back against the sofa and placed her hand to her forehead resting her elbow on the sofa arm.

"Let me volunteer one more bit of advice," James pleaded.

"Go ahead, I'll just add it to the list," Tracy said sarcastically. Her sarcasm notwithstanding, Tracy dropped her arm on the sofa arm and gave James the courtesy of her full attention.

"You can't please everyone no matter how hard you try. What you have to do is please yourself. I know that sounds selfish, but look at it this way. If you're not happy you're not going to be able to make anyone else happy. You decide what's best for you and do it. If you need my help, remember you have my card." James smiled with that last remark.

"Right here," Tracy responded, but before she could say anything else the French doors to the library swung open and Marie entered.

"So there you two are. James, you're not keeping Tracy all to yourself, are you?"

"I was trying, Mother."

Chapter 13

*A*lec returned home in mid-August full of smiles, gifts, and stories of his trip to Casablanca, Tripoli, Cairo, the Suez, and the Sahara where he hiked for a full day under the hot July sun and spent a cold night just to imagine himself in some ancient caravan. Alec decided mid-trip that he and Tracy would travel to the Middle East and the Holy Land the following summer. Upon his return, Tracy gave him a week to settle down from his trip. By the end of the week his slides were ready and he insisted Tracy see them in their entirety, all one hundred and forty-four. As the last of what seemed to Tracy an endless stream of meaningless faces and objects clicked through the last cassette, Alec started to explain how and where they would travel next year.

Tracy decided the time ripe to reveal what had caused her much consternation, numerous consultations, a great deal of hand wringing, some soul searching, and many sleepless nights. With the generous support of Nancy and an assist or two from James, she had composed and rehearsed her appeal to Alec. As the time for her performance drew nigh, she grew increasingly nervous. She could not recall a single slide, not even the last one. They were images of people and places that vastly differed from those that held her current interest. She found the hour-long experience excruciating and only then realized the effect the slide travelogue must have on those captured by compulsory school attendance laws.

Before Alec left she had only alluded to her feelings, subtle hints that either went unheard or over his head. Her rehearsed revelations would be the first of their marriage as she always dutifully followed, albeit willingly in many instances, Alec's plans and schemes. She braced herself for the coming confrontation for, given the attitude he evinced since returning; she sensed he would be unsympathetic. Tracy genuinely disliked confrontations because of her encounter seven years earlier with her parents. After mustering sufficient courage, she interrupted Alec's discourse on next summer's planned travel.

"Alec, I've thought a lot about our trips over the past two months and I believe that we shouldn't plan a trip for next year or, perhaps, for any other year for a while." As she spoke her voice cracked and she cleared her throat.

"I guess I don't understand," he asked, sounding truly surprised and puzzled by her statement. "Why?"

"First, we can't afford long costly vacations anymore—"

"But—" Alec tried to interrupt.

Raising her voice, Tracy started over. "Trying to save enough to travel on your salary simply puts too much strain on our already overburdened budget. We can't afford decent clothes for Richard without Mother's help, and the car hardly runs and looks simply dreadful. We haven't any money to spare. I don't know about you, but I can't go on living from hand to mouth." Tracy paused long enough to give Alec time to respond.

Looking dumbfounded, Alec asked, "May I ask what brought this on? I thought you enjoyed traveling. You liked the trips to England, Europe, and Canada—I thought that traveling is as much a part of your life as it is mine. Are you upset that you chose to stay home this year?"

"Alec," she looked him in the eye and grabbed his hands in hers and in a tone barely above a whisper she said, "England was our honeymoon and Europe was before Richard. And if you remember we took a quick trip across Canada over my protestations to the contrary—I'm simply being realistic, how we live ten months is five times more important than how we spend two months. If we had more money, I would enjoy travel, but we don't. Don't you see that if we didn't travel and you found a summer job we would be better off financially all year long?"

Pulling back from her grasp, he stated somewhat indignantly, "I've planned these trips for you. Richard can stay with—"

"No, you haven't!" her voice suddenly turning to louder and sharper tones. "When have you ever asked me where I would like to go, or when, or how long, or even if! Don't be hypocritical, the trips are for you. You traveled before we met, since we met, and you'll travel after we—" She stopped mid-sentence.

"After we what?" he demanded.

"Alec," her voice modulated downward once more, "what I'm desperately trying to say, and I've thought about this all summer, is that our lives have changed. We have a home, a family, a mortgage, a car that needs replacement, and other countless needs. We're not two independent individuals any longer. Maybe someday in the future when Richard is older and on his own and your income is higher we can travel again. For now, we have so many needs." She gave Alec a quizzical look, as though to say, "Don't you understand?"

Alec's remarks were unrehearsed, but he answered quickly and decisively as if he knew the lines by heart. "Do you realize that when Richard is older and on his own that I'll be retired? I'm too old to wait until we've absolved all of our responsibilities before I can live again. Besides, we're doing okay despite what you say. We're not as well-off as your parents were at this stage, but we can make it," he rebutted.

"I know we can make it, but why must it be so hard? I'm not and hope that you're not satisfied with just making it. We need to have some leeway and be able to afford all of our basic needs without having to worry about a check bouncing. If only you could get a better-paying job, then maybe we could have enough money to travel. Our budget should reflect our basic needs, and if there is any money left over then we can travel. The problem is that you plan our budget the other way around, using what's left over from travel for basic necessities," she exclaimed.

He thought for a moment reflecting on what she just said and offered, "What if I took that music position the junior college offered last year, would that satisfy you?" he asked.

"That's a step in the right direction. The increase in pay would be welcomed, but would hardly represent a windfall. You'd still be in the same position, a low salary with increases over the long run that would at best match inflation. After ten years our standard of living would be no greater than when we started," she replied.

Alec thought he recognized something familiar in this latest demonstration of her intellectual capacity. Then it came to him: she's beginning to reason like her father. His curiosity piqued over the source of her knowledge he asked, "How do you know about that?"

"I learned that in my economics courses, which you said I would never use." She huffed, sounding indignant at his surprise.

Reverting back to his previous line of thought Alec added, "Anyway, I don't think I'd like teaching music as an academic subject. I enjoy working with people to achieve good vocal composition and execution—"

"What you need to do," Tracy interrupted, "is what Walter Goss and Jack Winslow did, go into administration. The salaries are higher and are for twelve not ten months, then...then we could live decently," Tracy pleaded.

"Administration! You've got to be kidding. That's the last thing I want to do—sit behind a desk in a shirt and tie day in and day out and get three weeks' vacation a year! I get almost that much at Christmas alone. There's no way I'd even consider it, no matter how much the job paid," Alec retorted.

"What are you doing to me?" Tracy screamed. "What are you condemning me to? Is this it?" she asked as she spread her arms apart to indicate their entire state of affairs.

"What do you want? I guess I don't understand," he asked antagonistically.

"I want to be able to write a check for what we need when we need it without the fear of it bouncing or encroaching on your travel funds. I want to be able to refuse financial help from my mother. I want Richard to have nice clothes, good health care, and the assurance of a college education. I want a home that doesn't have cold, hard, terrazzo floors, low ceilings, cramped rooms, and a single bath. I want to be able to buy my own clothes and dress nicely and drive a safe car that doesn't embarrass me. I want—" She broke down and cried. This part of her presentation was unrehearsed.

Alec stood motionless and quiet, not knowing what to say or do. He could try to reconcile or appease her but, in all honesty, he couldn't. He knew he could not or would not do as she asked.

He loved her very dearly, for she was the most beautiful woman he had ever met and until this very moment also the most vibrant and exciting. He thought that her youth would allow her to adjust to his world, his values, and his attitudes. He now knew differently. A product of her formative years, she couldn't substitute his values for hers. Before Richard's birth, the conflicts in their worlds remained beneath the surface as they somehow managed to meet each other's wishes without serious sacrifice on either's part. Richard's birth placed additional demands on already strained resources producing the inevitable sacrifice of some desires to pursue others. Alec realized that home and hearth, not travel and freedom, dominated Tracy's priorities.

Over the following weeks, Alec was more attentive to Tracy and her needs, at least the ones he felt willing or able to satisfy, in the hope that she would eventually convert or capitulate to his wishes. He certainly had no intention of converting to hers. With the exception of the tournament game he attended with Jack, he devoted more time to Tracy and less time doting on Richard and organizing his music plans. She responded for a while, giving him a surprise forty-fifth birthday party with their best friends and neighbors as guests. She occasionally laughed and smiled at little things that happened. They visited used car lots in a futile search for a better car that they could also afford. The cars they liked always seemed to be just out of their financial reach. Alec kept looking, kept promising, but also kept saving for what he was sure would be an enjoyable trip next summer. He gave Tracy the extra income he earned assisting churches with their music programs, but the sums were meager and offered little relief.

One Saturday in early October, while Tracy accompanied Richard to another toddler's birthday party, Alec, taking advantage of both their absences, walked to Denise's house for the first time in months. Still uncertain whether Tracy would eventually come around, Alec thought that Denise would provide him with a sympathetic but yet feminine point of view as well as some much needed advice. As he passed our house, Laddie charged out with what seemed to Alec renewed energy. Already feeling irritated by what he considered Tracy's recalcitrance, Alec yelled and shouted back at Laddie until neighbors looked out their windows to see what the commotion was. Jimmy, who witnessed the episode from his bedroom window, said that if we had been home instead of out shopping, Alec appeared upset enough to extend his vehemence personally despite the debt he felt he owed Pop. Alec must have thought that his record since the incident with Tommy Strickland had long since vindicated Pop's recommendation. Evidently Alec decided that he wasn't indebted to Pop forever.

"Alec," Denise began after listening patiently to her brother's marital problems, "Tracy's very young and the only child from a highly stable, financially sound family. She's used to having her way and anything she wanted when she wanted it without having to sacrifice. Let's face it, she was spoiled and still is. She doesn't like worrying about things that she never had to bother with before your marriage. She's not used to sacrificing what she deems is most important to her. For that matter, neither have you. You knew you were older and set in your ways. You knew or should have known that those ways are, in many instances, radically different from hers or her family's. The problems you're having should come as no surprise, they don't to me, or did you really believe they wouldn't matter?"

"We got along so well while we dated and during the first years of our marriage. Everything seemed to change after Richard's birth. She says that I see her primarily as a mother and not a partner. To me that's her role in the partnership, I don't know what she expects." Alec huffed and crossed one leg over the other in his chair.

"The presence of children, and I speak with good authority, does cause many changes in married people's lives: responsibilities change, goals change, attitudes, habits, and feelings change. Frankly, I don't know what we would do if Mark were anything but a doctor and have the income that comes with it. Thank God for Saturday mornings when he takes the kids out to give me the house to myself." She sighed then added, "Children do make a difference, you want them, you love them, but then you have to adjust to them. They make the future so much more important than the present. You have to plan housing, medical care, friends to play with, schools they'll attend, birthday parties, college, and even Little League. Tracy's concerns have shifted back to those things that are important to her, and she sees that your present finances and habits are inconsistent with these values. It seems her main complaint is that you haven't recognized these changes or even worse, chose to ignore them. In either case she feels they've fallen upon her and she feels inadequate to cope," Denise answered, feeling confident that she had correctly summarized Tracy's feelings, but not so confident that she convinced Alec.

"I guess I was just naive, I thought we could go on forever doing as we were—and I believe I could. Tracy just doesn't seem able to accept the consequences of that. We could do it, I know we could do it, if only she—" His voice trailed off as he simply drew a blank and couldn't finish his sentence.

"You might as well face the situation, Alec. Tracy's values are different from yours. Before Richard, it didn't matter nearly as much as it does now. Unless you two can get together and resolve these differences you risk losing the two people that mean the most to you."

"Ah, come on, sis, it won't come to that. Tracy's upset, but she'll get over it. We love each other too much to let these temporary problems destroy what we have together. Joe Brown at Brown Motors is going to give me a real break on a good used car, she'll like that," Alec said confidently.

*****

While Alec visited Denise, Tracy drove Richard to the birthday party and rather than stay and assist the hostess with the party as she told Alec, she left Richard and drove to her mother's. Tracy called Nancy earlier in the week and said that she wanted to talk with her on Saturday. Tracy resisted Nancy's entreaties to disclose the nature of her visit over the telephone. Instead she begged off by saying she wasn't ready to discuss it, but would be on Saturday.

Tracy decided to take charge of her life, no longer would she be at the mercy of anyone. The time had come for her to make decisions; no longer would they be deferred to parents or husband. She began the process before Alec returned from Africa and felt she had given Alec and their marriage every chance she could. Each time Alec let the opportunity lapse by only responding superficially to her concerns. She could discern no change in his attitude. Alec only seemed to placate her wishes. Once she realized that her present situation was hopeless, she knew what she must do and had little difficulty in making the decision. She had given so much thought to her alternatives for so long the actual decision came easily and seemed anticlimactic. She wanted to tell Nancy first as Tracy counted on her assuming an important supporting role in the unfolding drama. The message Tracy carried for Nancy was far too important to confine to a telephone call, so Tracy decided to keep Nancy in suspense until they could meet alone.

Thus, Nancy waited with more than idle curiosity for Tracy to arrive Saturday morning. While waiting, Nancy busied herself by addressing envelopes to various state and local officials and politicians. Her garden club had abandoned their non-controversial status and was opposing the planned development of the only two remaining undeveloped islands on Florida's central west coast. Both islands lay directly across the bay from Nancy's home, a distance of nearly two miles. As a result of numerous lengthy debates, a committee drew up a position paper that the entire club endorsed. The members debated whether to take a public stand, not what their position would be. Once completed, the position paper lacked only the mechanical task of addressing and stuffing envelopes. The club, along with other organizations, hoped to persuade politicians and citizens alike to limit development to only a portion of one of the islands. The club recommended that the state buy the other island for a state park that would be accessible only by boat. In this manner the club and other supporters hoped to preserve the wildlife and natural environment on at least one island.

Nancy heard her old Buick clang into the drive. Greeting Tracy at the back door, she said, "Good morning, dear."

"Good morning, Mother," Tracy uttered tersely.

The manner in which Tracy spoke and her quick deliberate steps as she walked passed her and into the den where she plopped down in her father's old chair, gave Nancy the impression that Tracy had something important on her mind. Nancy cocked her head and said to herself, "Well." She followed Tracy into the family room and asked, "Would you like some coffee, dear?"

"Not now, Mother, I have some things to say first. Then we can have coffee if you like." Tracy still spoke with a stern tone.

"Well then, just what is it that you have to tell me? You certainly have sufficiently aroused my curiosity," Nancy said as she sat on the sofa and folded her hands in her lap.

"I've decided to leave Alec," Tracy said in the same resolute voice Nancy recalled her using when she insisted she be allowed to date Alec exactly seven years earlier.

"I see," she answered, giving Tracy time to continue. Nancy realized that Tracy had carefully rehearsed her speech, and Nancy decided not to interrupt until Tracy had finished delivering it.

"He hasn't changed one iota since returning from Africa. Do you know what he did the very next night after I poured my heart out to him? He went to a ball game with Jack Winslow leaving me home alone with Richard. If Cynthia hadn't come over, I might have left that very night. I gave him a chance. I told him how I felt. And what did he do? He went to a stupid ball game! Oh, he later paid lip service and made token gestures to pacify me. All along, he has been quietly planning and saving for next year's trip he's so sure we'll be taking. He has regressed into his normal teaching routine and isn't even looking for a better position. We're doomed to our current status forever. It's just as though I never said anything! The situation we were in six months ago and two years before that still exists."

During her speech, Tracy had risen from her chair and paced back in forth in front of the sofa where Nancy sat.

"Have you told Alec?" Nancy asked.

"No, and I'm not going to until after I make my move. James suggested I avoid the confrontation and endless hours of haggling, yelling, and pleading much less many tears that a premature announcement would surely bring," Tracy responded.

"James?" Nancy's eyebrows rose ever so slightly.

"Yes. The reason I've waited to tell you is that our plans weren't complete," Tracy continued without realizing, for the moment, she hadn't told Nancy of her conversations with James.

"Our plans? It sounds like James is assuming a greater role than just an attorney." Her words were subtle, but her tone wasn't.

"Mother, James has been an immense help. He's made me understand that I don't have to please everyone. I only have to please myself. If I'm not happy with myself, I can't make anyone else happy. I'm not happily married, at least not anymore. I've decided that continuing the marriage wouldn't be in Alec's, mine, or Richard's best interest," Tracy responded resolutely.

Nancy sat quietly, watching as Tracy continued to pace in front of her. After a few moments of concentrated thought, Tracy returned to her prepared speech, "You were so right. I truly love Richard, but I made a mistake in marrying Alec. He thought of me as a beauty queen—innocent, pretty, young, and energetic. I became his 'oh, how wonderful' girl. He impressed me with his attention, his education, his knowledge, his worldliness, and the sense of importance and maturity I felt as a result of dating an older man. Everything he said or did or planned, I thought, 'Oh, how wonderful' whether I actually said the words or not, the message came through.

"I've since discovered that his first wife wasn't so impressed. She told him what she thought and refused to follow him to Florida because she realized, as I have, that he thinks first and foremost of himself despite his lip service to the contrary. Aside from the physical attributes he found attractive in me, he loved the adoration I so innocently gave. More importantly, he likes the fact that I don't challenge or threaten his male ego. On the contrary, I reinforced it, something his first wife either didn't do or at least stopped doing." Tracy then chided herself, "What an innocent dupe I've been."

"It sounds like you have given both Alec's and your motivations a great deal of thought since we last spoke of your difficulties. You seem more confident than you were this summer. I will, of course, do whatever you ask, but I'm curious as to the source of this strengthened resolve. Does it have anything to do with James?" Nancy inquired, seeking an explanation as much as a confirmation.

"Yes. James and I have grown closer than we ever were in school. I never told you, I didn't want you to worry, but the night of James's party when you kept Richard overnight, my car wouldn't start. I was the last to leave and the hour was late or very early depending on how you look at it. The battery was dead, as I had left the parking lights on. James offered to drive me home and have the battery charged in the morning and return the car to me. I accepted. He stayed at the house that night later than perhaps he should have. We talked for hours and we've talked more since. He has become something more than just an old friend or attorney. I think he really cares." Tracy glanced toward Nancy for her reaction.

"I don't know why you couldn't have told me earlier, I might have been concerned, but I don't believe I would've worried. I also believe that you should tell Alec soon of your feelings and intentions. I'm bothered by the secrecy. It seems hypocritical. However, I think it's best that you not say anything to Alec about your 'talks' with James." Nancy thought her last statement redundant, but she wanted to make it anyway.

"It's too close to Christmas for an emotional confrontation. I'm not in the right frame of mind yet," Tracy replied.

"You could have fooled me," Nancy retorted.

Tracy undaunted by her mother's remark continued, "Besides, it will not take James long to prepare he papers. I'd rather wait until then. It shouldn't be long after New Year's."

"Don't worry about the confrontation. I'm sure that among the three of us, we can handle the situation. You will, however, eventually have to face Alec. It's something you owe him. I remain bothered by the secrecy however short. However, I'll do whatever you wish as your marriage obviously has already ended. What grounds are you claiming for the divorce?"

"James believes I have a good case for mental cruelty. That's the part that bothers me. I wish Florida allowed divorce by agreement or some other means. It's so demeaning to prove mental or physical cruelty or adultery. Why is it easier to get married than it is to get divorced?" Like Lloyd, Tracy did not appreciate the irony of the law.

"Do you think Alec would agree to a divorce if such a provision existed?" Nancy asked.

"No," Tracy answered flatly.

"Have you thought about how the divorce will affect Alec?"

"Yes, I'm sure he'll be devastated. However, I'm not going to confine Richard or myself to a lifetime of misery just to please Alec. I've done enough of that already. He hasn't shown any willingness to do the same for me," Tracy answered with such resoluteness that convinced Nancy Tracy had rehearsed that line many times.

"At least, do one thing so that I'll feel better," Nancy pleaded.

"What's that?"

"Talk to Alec as soon as possible."

"We will, Mother, we will."

Chapter 14

*A*lec smarted for weeks over Tracy's impassioned reference to Jack Winslow. Attracted to Florida for many of the same reasons as Alec, Jack with wife, Cynthia, two infant children, and a master's degree in educational administration settled in a house immediately behind Alec and Tracy. When they arrived in Clearwater, the school district's existing policy on filling administrative positions consisted of promoting from within. The policy emanated from a belief that internal promotion encouraged loyalty, dependability, and dedication of existing staff and faculty. Jack spent his first three years with the district teaching history and political science. The time served satisfied the district's requirement to qualify as an internal candidate for an administrative post. With student population growing exponentially, the district needed new administrators yearly. Given his educational training and apprenticeship, Jack received an appointment to assistant principal at the high school in the minimum required time. He left no doubt that the position of principal was his ultimate goal.

During his tenure as teacher, he became Alec's best friend. Neither could really explain why for other than migrating from northern climes, they didn't seem to share much in common. Jack's interests lay in administration and school policy, neither of which held any allure for Alec. Jack couldn't sing a note and never played a musical instrument, but did appreciate good music. While Alec walked, Jack played tennis. They did, however, share one important quality—dedication to the goals each set for himself. Alec's unswerving devotion to musical direction and his personal passion, traveling, impressed Jack. Alec, while interested in advancing his profession, displayed no interest in advancing professionally. He did, however, respect Jack for his persistent efforts to attain his goals.

They also shared a similar educational philosophy—one that enjoyed virtual universal support in athletic endeavors but very little support in academic subjects. The athletic vernacular expresses this sentiment by the phrase, "No pain, no gain."

Jack played baseball in college and knew as Alec that physical excellence did not come effortlessly. Exercise, long hours of practice, and a demanding regime were prerequisite for excelling in sports, competitive or otherwise. Neither Alec not Jack could understand the "learning must be fun" philosophy that slowly crept into educational philosophy. They had no objection to learning being fun. Unfortunately, they agreed, it does not always work out that way. Calculus, economics, chemistry, physics, and becoming an accomplished musician were very demanding disciplines that required, for most people, tireless effort to master even for those precious few blessed with innate natural ability. In many instances, they argued, the fun came after having *mastered* the subject and not during the learning process. Alec often quoted the story of a famous musician who after playing particularly well in a concert received lavish praise by patrons and critics alike. One particular patron ended her lengthy litany by stating, "I'd give anything if I could play like you." Unmercifully but candidly, the musician tersely responded, "Madam, would you give eight hours a day, six days a week for thirty years?"

Jack enjoyed quoting the line from the play "Teahouse of the August Moon" when the native house boy says,

Not easy to learn,
sometimes very painful.
But pain makes man think,
thought makes man wise,
And wisdom makes life endurable.

Aside for the calculus teacher, their arguments did not strike a responsive chord. Jack reflected in later years that he and Alec were like two tired Salmon fighting their way upstream, engulfed by an overpowering torrent that flowed in the opposite direction. Despite the overwhelming opposition, neither abandoned their philosophy.

Two days after school resumed following the Christmas break, Jack found himself with an unenviable and unwanted task. He sat in his office, head in hands, elbows on the desk, and stared at the folded legal document before him. The process server stood hands behind his back glancing about the room waiting for the assistant principal to call Alec so that he could serve the papers that Jack agonized over. Jack knew what he must do, but he sat there silently pondering how to do it. Jack knew Alec wouldn't take this news well. He mulled over the papers thinking more about how Alec would react to their lightning bolt contents. He thought perhaps he should tell Alec first. Attempting to give himself sufficient time to think the dilemma through carefully, he told the server that he would wait until Alec's break in half an hour. *Maybe by then*, he thought, *I can think of something to cushion the blow.*

The ringing of the telephone next to his propped left elbow jarred Jack's thoughts. He instinctively answered it and learned, much to his surprise though he later thought he shouldn't have been, the voice belonged to Nancy Ashbury.

"Jack, I'm calling because you're Alec's best friend. You and Cynthia have been such good friends to Alec and Tracy since they've been married. As you may have already learned Tracy has decided to leave Alec and file for divorce."

"Yes, Ma'am. I have the papers before me right now and am about to summon Alec to my office. I must admit this action comes as a total surprise to me, neither Alec nor Tracy ever let on they were having serious problems, I'm speechless," he stated, sounding, as he felt, dumbfounded.

"I, that is, we would like to ask your help. This decision is extremely difficult for Tracy, she's very upset. Even though she considered her decision for some months, she isn't as emotionally prepared as she thought she would be," Nancy explained.

"Where is she now? May I speak with her?" Jack asked.

"That's what I wanted to discuss with you. She's here with me, and so is Richard, and they'll stay here at least until the divorce is final. I know that Alec will want to talk with her also, but I'd like to ask that you relay our wishes that he not make any attempt to contact her for at least a week or ten days. She promises to see him, but just needs a little time to settle down. I'm sure you understand," Nancy said, stating her request more than asking.

It became clear to Jack that Nancy had assumed responsibility for ushering Tracy through at least the first phrase of her separation from Alec. Sheltering Tracy, just as she had when Tracy was a child, she clearly intended to keep Tracy from the grim realities of interpersonal confrontation where feelings, egos, and self-esteem often suffer. She would not be able to spare Tracy all the blows, but she intended to give her a running start and then let the momentum help carry Tracy through the remainder of that gauntlet called divorce proceedings.

"Yes, of course," Jack responded. "Is there anything I can tell him?"

"Just tell him how difficult it is for Tracy to leave, but the decision is irrevocable. A great deal of thought and prayer has gone into the decision, and she intends to stand by it but will honor any reasonable request to visit Richard. As soon as she calms down she will discuss the divorce with him but won't be badgered into changing her mind. Also, tell him that I won't permit him to see Tracy until she and I feel she's ready." Nancy's voice, adamant and stern, gave Jack the clear message that Nancy wanted to leave no doubt in his mind as to her position. She meant no discourtesy to Jack, but she knew that it would be Jack that would have to deal with Alec face to face. She wanted her resoluteness to carry over when Jack spoke with Alec.

Jack also discerned that his involvement in the aftermath of Tracy's decision to leave Alec was no accident. As the conversation with Nancy continued, it became patently obvious to Jack that his role in this drama had been carefully scripted. He would have pounced upon any opportunity to decline his part, but he found himself trapped, as he sincerely liked both Alec and Tracy. Otherwise, he might have resented being drafted without notice into the coming fray.

"Yes, ma'am, I'll tell him and help the best I can. Please tell Tracy that Cynthia and I love her and wish the best for her and are very sorry that she felt compelled to take this difficult step."

As he hung up the receiver he thought, why wait. He called to his secretary, "Mrs. Simpson, please call Alec Driver on the intercom and ask him to come to my office just as soon as he can get here, even," he added, "if he is still in class."

A few minutes later she relayed that his class would be over in ten minutes and he would come immediately afterward.

Alec's face turned ashen as he unfolded and carefully read the papers. Not knowing what to say or how to say it, Jack decided against trying to prepare Alec for the blow. It was a decision he immediately regretted when he saw the anguish spread over Alec's face. Alec became disoriented and confused. Tracy, true to her plan, hadn't given Alec any indication that she was preparing to leave him. He had mistakenly taken the holiday respite from Tracy's discontent as a sign that she had reconciled herself to their present situation. It hadn't occurred to him that the outward respite came as a result of her decision to leave. He felt faint. He sat down, placed his elbows on his knees, and held his head in his hands. His reaction contrasted starkly with his entering remark when he kidded about being called to the assistant principal's office to stay after school for a "pop" by the large wood paddle Jack kept for errant students.

Jack had never seen Alec so disheveled. Alec prided himself for never being nonplused, an attribute he clearly lacked at the moment. Jack had to jostle Alec to sign the papers; an act Alec later could not recall performing. Jack obtained permission from Robert Meadows, John Furst's replacement as principal, for both to leave for the remainder of the day. Jack called Cynthia, told her briefly what happened, and said he was coming home early and bringing Alec with him. Cynthia said she had noticed a truck at Tracy's house that morning but thought they were having some furniture delivered.

Alec sat in Jack and Cynthia's living room, divorce papers in one hand and coffee cup in the other, but not doing much with either. His hands shook so much the coffee bounced around in the cup. Cynthia finally took it from him.

"She accuses me of mental cruelty and demands custody of Richard," Alec said in a disbelieving voice. "Who's this lawyer, James Davies? I've never heard of him."

"I'm not sure," Jack replied, adding, "then I noticed something strange, the divorce petition is filed in Pasco County."

"Why?" Alec whined. "We were married here in Pinellas County."

"Maybe he practices in Pasco County or they didn't want any word of the divorce to leak out until she moved out and felt safer filing it up there," Cynthia offered.

"What made her choose him?" Alec again asked. He then asked for something Jack and Cynthia had rarely heard him request, "Could I have a drink?"

"Wait a minute," Jack exclaimed, "Alec, what's the name of that wealthy friend of Nancy? Isn't it Davies?"

"Yes, yes it is, why?" Alec responded still so disoriented that he could not follow Jack's line of reasoning.

"Do you think they're related?" Jack asked.

"Jack," Cynthia interrupted, "do you remember last summer Tracy mentioned being invited to a party for I believe Mrs. Davies's son who had returned from law school?"

"Yes. Now that you mention it, I do," Jack responded.

In a pathetic sounding voice, Alec said, "Tracy never mentioned anything about a party to me."

After fixing him a very weak Tom Collins, they watched as he sat quietly and sip the drink slowly and deliberately. After a few moments, his glass near empty, Alec announced, "I have to see her."

"No!" Jack shouted then realizing the volume and abruptness of his voice he added in a lower voice, "I mean, I don't think that would be wise right now, Alec."

"Why not?" Alec asked, still sounding confused.

"Her decision was probably very difficult to make and she must be very upset just as you are. Wait a few days or even a week to allow her, and yourself, a chance to calm down. By then she'll have had a chance to think about her decision and might be more willing to talk with you," Jack explained.

"I don't know what to do or why she has done this to me. I love her and Richard so much—" his voice trailed off, choking he desperately tried to hold back the tears forming in his eyes.

"I'm so sorry, Alec. We want you to stay with us tonight and won't take no for an answer," Cynthia offered as she sat down beside him and placed her arm around his shoulders.

As the days turned into weeks and the weeks into months, Jack and Cynthia continued to be supportive of Alec. Jack insisted that Alec ride to and from school with him and used the opportunity to listen to and counsel Alec as best he could. Tracy remained resolute, she refused to return to a life she found so oppressive, so confining, so poor. After the mandatory six-month reconciliation period, Tracy's divorce petition, despite Alec's opposition, quickly worked its way through the legal system. Alec grew to despise the dark, boyish attorney who represented her. There was something in his manner, his attitude that bothered Alec; he didn't know what it was. Maybe, he thought, it was the fervor with which he presented Tracy's case and attacked Alec's. The case was filed in the adjoining county where the attorney worked as an assistant district attorney. The court docket, less crowded in Pasco County, allowed Tracy to receive her final divorce decree in seven months after she moved out.

Alec soon learned why the young attorney marshaled his client's case so quickly and efficiently through the legal process. Three months following the divorce Tracy announced her engagement to James Davies II. Two months following the announcement they were married in Marie's garden in a simple but well-attended ceremony.

Alec experienced increasing difficulty adjusting to Tracy's absence. Her remarriage ended his hopes for eventually winning back her affections. The irony of the date of the divorce hadn't escaped his attention: it lacked three days of the tenth anniversary of his first divorce. Recalling that his and Tracy's wedding was on the tenth anniversary of his first wedding meant that his second marriage had lasted no longer than his first.

The divorce from Tracy exacted a heavy toll from Alec. An extrovert most of his life, he became reticent, intense, and irritable. It didn't take long for Jack and Cynthia to notice Alec's growing dependence on alcohol, something he had previously eschewed. Alec evinced textbook symptoms of depression: loss of appetite, insomnia, a feeling of unworthiness and listlessness interspersed with sudden bursts of energy, and almost incessant chatter about a variety of unrelated topics. Even before Tracy's remarriage, Alec became despondent over his inability to persuade Tracy to return. Her marriage to James only added to his feeling of depression.

The loss of Richard proved devastating to Alec. For twenty years he dreamed of having a son, and now despite the visiting rights granted by the court, he felt he had lost him. He tried valiantly to retain custody of Richard, but the court at the prodding of Davies would not entertain arguments that a father deserved custody of a child especially a man obviously guilty of mental cruelty. Alec felt fortunate to receive liberal visitation rights. He vowed never to consent to their entreaties for James to adopt Richard. The resulting feud made him bitter toward James, but not toward Tracy; he still loved her despite the ordeal she put him through. She remained the object of his love and disquieted affection.

"Do you know what I think?" Alec said as he stared into space over his raised glass rather than at Jack who sat next to him at the bar.

"No tellin'. I can imagine a thousand things," Jack responded.

"I've come to the conclusion that people in this hick town don't like me and never have. They've never made me feel like one of them," Alec lamented.

Jack recalled a similar comment Alec made the night of the Bomber game a year and a half earlier. Jack decided to take the direct approach and counter Alec's assertion, something he hadn't done when Alec first mentioned it at the game. Jack responded, "What makes you say that? You have a reputation as an outstanding music teacher and choir director. Just look at the awards you've won, just—"

"Awards, accolades, reputation, they don't really amount to a hill of beans. Sure some people have recognized my work, but they do the same for migrant workers and winter tourists. Their contributions are recognized, but people still treat them as outsiders—they accept their work and money, but the people? That's something else. You don't see it as much as I do because you've had more success in being accepted." Alec motioned the bartender for a refill of his drink.

"Look, Alec, I don't necessarily agree with you, but you must admit that you project an air of independence, almost aloofness or even arrogance, with a devil-may-care attitude about what others think. You haven't exactly bent over backward trying to accommodate other people," Jack responded, ignoring his drink and concentrating on his argument.

"Why should I? I'm just as good as anybody else. Am I not entitled to my own beliefs and values, my own life?" Alec asked, his words beginning to slur.

"Of course you are. However, when those beliefs conflict with those of many others in the community, you shouldn't be surprised when they meet with a less than a receptive audience. After all, why should people always accommodate themselves to you? There is a quid pro quo at work here. For example, take your attitude lately. While maybe understandable to Cynthia and me, it could be interpreted as hostile. I've noticed that you snap at people a lot. Your students view it as part of your normal in-class demeanor but to others like the bartender you chided when she got our drinks mixed up, you come across as…well, as a pain in the ass. People don't have to put up with it and usually won't," Jack said as he shoved the remainder of his drink away.

"People haven't liked me from the time I first set foot in this jerkwater town whether I was polite or an asshole." Alec's pronunciation of asshole came out more like "acehole."

"Dating one of your students twenty years younger and punching out another in a moment of anger six months after you arrived didn't exactly endear yourself to anyone. People accepted you enough to allow you to keep your job when some others would have liked to ride you out of town on a rail. I'd say the people in this town passed a basic litmus test when they allowed you keep your job and give you another chance," Jack stated resolutely. "You should be thankful," he added.

"If Shirley Strickland, Arthur Oaks, and a number of others had their way, that rail would have been shoved where the sun don't shine. You know it's been over seven years and Arthur still won't speak to me and neither will any of the puritans that signed that stupid petition to fire me. Do you realize that petition is still in my personnel file as is Shirley Strickland's letters?" Alec paused between each sentence to take a breath, think, and continue.

"But so is Reid Collins's letter and the memo by Walter Goss as well as letters and certificates of commendation," Jack pleaded with a broad sweeping gesture of his arm.

"None of that means tea-waddly-squat. The only time I really felt a part of this town was when I went anywhere or did anything with Tracy. Now even she's left me for that scumbag ambulance chaser. Do you realize that son of a bitch screwed Tracy while I was in Africa?" Alec had finally turned and looked Jack in the eyes as he spoke. He ordered another refill.

"That's the four gin and tonics talking, Alec. You don't know that and I don't believe it for a minute. Keep your voice down, people are staring," Jack said in a low voice.

"What the heck do I care who stares?" Alec shouted. "What difference does it make? That snotty nose pillar of the community screwed my wife while I was away—right under Nancy's nose. At least they had the decency to leave Richard at Nancy's that night, assuming that was the only time which it probably wasn't. That snake seduced Tracy when she was vulnerable and then to relieve her guilt over the affair he encouraged her to leave me and marry him. He can give her everything I can't including money, prestige, and a marriage of two established families. No, the clever bastard convinced her I was the outsider trying to make her into something she didn't want to be and that she didn't have to please anybody but herself. What he really meant was please him.

"I'd kill the S-O-B, but that would just make Tracy hate me more. No, I'll figure out something that'll show 'em and the rest of this parochial paradise exactly what I think about 'em. Just you wait and see," Alec warned, finishing his fourth drink.

"You don't mean that. After all, Alec, James and Tracy are the same age and virtually grew up together. That does give them something in common. And you were intransigent. You expected Tracy to do what you wanted; you gave her very little choice. It's getting late. Let's go home. I don't know why I let you talk me into stopping here every day after school. It always ends up the same, you get drunk and depressed, or vice versa, and I have to drag you home. Let's go. Cynthia is expecting us for supper."

"I'm not hungry. You go home. Tell Cynthia I'm 'dining out' tonight," Alec smirked.

"Okay then, give me your keys," Jack demanded, his hand extended.

"What for?" Alec asked without turning his head toward Jack.

"You're driving today, remember? I'm not about to leave you here with car keys in your pocket. I don't mind coming back to pick you up, but I'll be damned if I'm going to go the hospital or funeral home. Now give me your keys, damn it!" Jack said in a raised voice.

Jack left Alec at the motel lounge as he had done on numerous other occasions. Having finally grown tired of returning late each time to help Alec home and into bed, he arranged for the manager to call a cab for Alec when he became too drunk to resist being taken home. Jack hoped that the depression that consumed Alec would soon pass and allow them a measure of rest.

No matter how much he drank the night before, no matter how despondent he felt, he didn't let his music and choir reflect his deep, distraught feelings. He remained organized, dedicated, and determined. Jack described him to Cynthia as Dr. Jekyll and Mr. Hyde. He would behave one way at school and another afterward. His sudden leaps from one state of mind to another fascinated Jack. He had never seen anyone behave in two such completely different ways. It seemed as though he was seeing two people, but he knew that one was only an act. Jack found Alec's ability, when sober, to disguise his feelings in public amazing.

Almost as abruptly as it began, Alec's demeanor changed eight months following the divorce. He seemed to relax, recover his sense of humor, and rebound from his depression—he became one person again. Only his drinking remained as the last visible vestige of that horrible year.

Jack relaxed for the first time in the fifteen months since Tracy left Alec. He felt particular relief one Sunday in late March when Alec, all excited, came running into Jack's house, his hands full of brochures, charts, maps, and a long list of places he intended to visit in Mexico that summer. Jack felt pleased, for Alec's depression had kept him home the previous summer, the first hiatus from a summer vacation since he mustered out of the Air Force in 1945. Alec described in detail all the places he planned to visit. Many were places that he had been unable to see on his first trek through Mexico over eight years earlier, the Christmas after he met Tracy. As he ended his presentation to Jack and Cynthia, he smiled and said, "How about a drink?"

*****

March 1961

"It's Martha, Reid," the voice called from the outer office.

Myrtis Logan had worked as Pop's full-time secretary for six years since graduating from high school and part-time for the preceding year as a cooperative education student. Myrtis, neat in appearance and efficient, served as Pop's right hand. In his absence, Pop knew the office remained in competent, albeit youthful, hands. Like Tracy, Myrtis married a promising young attorney whom she knew for most of her life.

"Reid," came Mother's voice, "I'm worried about Laddie."

"What's the matter? Is he still not back?" Pop asked.

"He returned shortly after you left for work this morning. He plopped himself down by his water dish as usual when he returns. Soon afterward a noisy truck came roaring by and he sprang up and chased it. Halfway through the chase he stopped abruptly, took a few more steps, and fell over on his side. He laid there for a few minutes, then got up and virtually dragged himself to Dean's tree, lay back down, and hasn't moved since. Reid, I'm afraid—" She did not complete her thought.

"How long has it been?" Pop's voice evinced growing concern.

"That's what worries me, he hasn't moved in almost an hour."

"Maybe he's just asleep," Pop suggested.

"I don't know. Maybe you should come home and check on him," Mother suggested, which was more a plea than a suggestion.

"I'll be there in ten minutes," he responded quickly.

Pop hung up the receiver and called to Myrtis that he had to run home and would return in a little while explaining that Mother was worried about Laddie who just returned after an absence of three days.

As he drove the short distance home, he thought of another phone call he received a few months earlier. The caller was the caretaker of the Roebling estate, a large waterfront estate built fifty years earlier by the man who gained fame and fortune as the builder of the Brooklyn Bridge. His grandson, Donald, was the designer and inventor of the amphibious landing vehicle used by the marines in beach assaults during the war.

Pop thought it strange to receive a call from the estate's caretaker, but learned that the caretaker obtained our name from the local veterinarian through the number on Laddie's dog tag. The caretaker said that he heard a dog barking from the bottom of the sea wall at the back of the estate. The wall rose ten feet above the mud flats when they were exposed at low tide and five feet above the high tide mark. At first, the caretaker didn't pay much attention, but when the barking became persistent and more frantic, he walked over to the wall and looked down to find Laddie trapped by the tide with no way to escape its rising waters. The caretaker quickly obtained a long ladder from the tool shed, lowered it down the wall until it stuck in the muddy bottom, climbed down, and picked up the grateful dog standing in belly deep water, and carried the eighty-pound animal up the ladder.

Pop, startled by the story, wondered how Laddie managed to get himself in that predicament because the estate lay on the other side of town from our house. It was the only time that anyone ever had to go after Laddie. We often worried when Laddie was away, for the community was no longer the sleepy village it had once been. Snowbirds, as the locals called them, found Pinellas County an ideal spot for retirement as well as a harbor from harsh northern winter snow and ice. The city's population continued to swell as the growing number of northern migrants became a tide that engulfed the once small community of pioneer descendants.

Births contributed only modestly to the number of new citizens. The entire county became a census rarity: it's one of the few places in the United States where the death rate consistently exceeds the birth rate. Natives gave way to northern retirees, strangers became the norm, and longevity was measured from the time since retirement. Senior citizen communities, condominiums, funeral homes, nursing homes, florist shops, and restaurants replaced dairy farms, fishing fleets, and citrus groves as the county's economic base. Firms such as General Electric, Sperry, and Honeywell (taking advantage of the large concentration of skilled, retired workers) located small electronic and aerospace manufacturing plants around the county. The Clearwater area gave birth to such national firms as Eckerd Drugs, U. S. Homes, Morgan Boats, Klondike Bars, Home Shopping Network and, ultimately, Hooters. A new community emerged.

As Pop pulled into the drive, he could see Laddie's figure beneath the tall Australian Pine that my friends and I rooted and planted in the side yard eight years earlier. The tree had grown rapidly. I took great pride in my efforts and cared for the tree constantly when still in high school. By the time I left for college the tree had grown strong enough to survive on its own. Laddie used the tree as a refuge to lie and sleep under ever since I entered Georgia Tech. Laddie never seemed to understand my long absences and short periodic returns. I wish I could have explained them to him. He and I both delighted in my visits home. Laddie seemed to take great comfort in lying under the tree he had watched me plant and nurtured so carefully.

Pop got out of his car, never taking his eyes off Laddie and looking for Laddie's customary loud greeting of family members. Pop walked slowly the fifty feet to where Laddie lay. He called Laddie's name once, then twice with no response. He stopped short of the body when he realized Laddie was dead. Falling to his knees, he wept. Rivers of tears flowed down his cheeks and dampened his shirt. Mother watched silently from the window. Pop eventually pulled himself up and walked slowly up the street to Jimmy's house. He asked if Jimmy would help bury Laddie where he loved to lay, under the tree we had rooted. Father and friend buried the only dog and best companion I had ever known.

Neither Pop nor Mother mentioned Laddie in any of their letters to me that winter, reserving the hard news for my spring break. Tears welled up in my eyes when they broke the news to me. I didn't cry then. However, I've cried many times since. To me, Laddie was much more than a dog.

The loss of Laddie marked the end of one phase of my life. Another phase had already begun. I fell in love with a cute little gal from Tennessee whom I had the pleasure of meeting a year earlier. Little then did I realize that a Phi Beta Kappa from Emory would become my wife. But then you're already intimately familiar with that story. Laddie died the year before we graduated, married, and moved to Clearwater, I as an engineer for the telephone company and you an urban planner for the County.

Remember because of construction delays we couldn't move into the Mandalay Shores until Christmas? For six long months instead of enjoying a beautiful expanse of the Gulf we had to endure that small, cramped, unairconditioned apartment immediately behind the Carib Theater only a short block from the old junior and senior highs. Do you recall how, at the end of each evening's feature, patrons would leave through the rear exit and walk within five feet of our bedroom window and disturb some of our more interesting nocturnal activities?

One particular hot and humid Saturday night in mid-August 1962 neither the temperature nor the humidity dropped below eighty and consequently I slept fitfully. I rose early the next morning leaving you asleep in bed. I went into the only other room on the apartment's east side where the morning sun made the temperature even higher. Dressed only in my Jockey shorts, I opened the front door just enough to retrieve the Sunday *St. Petersburg Times.* I stepped out to grab the paper only to glance up and greet the disapproving eye of our middle-aged landlady sitting in a lawn chair in the shade of the only tree on the property. I quickly retreated inside the apartment where I turned on the fan, poured a glass of orange juice, and sat down.

Being the organized person I am, I started with the front section reading all the earth-shaking world and national news. All the events of the first section were blurred by the headline on the second or local section of the paper. As I scanned the front page of that section I suddenly stopped and my mouth gaped open as I read the headline and the accompanying story.

*****

Earlier that same week, Jack and Cynthia Winslow spotted Alec on Tuesday morning as he returned home from his Mexican vacation laden, as usual, with backpack, camera, and other assorted items he acquired in his travels. He spent the better part of two months traveling and visiting all the places he planned, including hiking along the old El Camino Real. Busily unloading his car Alec only waved as they left for work. Cynthia had secured a position with the school board after her children reached school age. The board's offices sat next to the high school allowing them to carpool during the school year. As an administrator, Jack had reported to school two weeks before Alec and the other teachers. Jack and Cynthia were surprised when during the next three days Alec failed to call or come over to talk about his latest trip. They knew he was still home for his car remained in the carport parked just the way it had been when they saw him unloading it. That the car had not been moved in three days would have been meaningless two years earlier for Alec walked most places he went. Since his divorce, he drove more and walked less. Jack speculated that Alec's age, the heat and humidity, and the increasing distances between travel destinations caused him to rely more on mechanized transportation. Thus, the undisturbed car became an increasing cause for concern for both Jack and Cynthia. On Friday evening after work, Jack deliberately drove by Alec's house and saw the car in the same place. He quickly rounded the block and pulled into his own drive. He told Cynthia that he was going to check on Alec and would be right back.

Four days earlier, Alec returned with a feeling of satisfaction and a sense of relief. He had enjoyed his vacation as much as any he had taken. He scheduled his return at the time when he knew Denise and family would be vacationing out of town. He gave up trying to see Tracy and resigned himself that Richard wouldn't be raised as his son. The only people who saw Alec after he returned were Jack and Cynthia. Things were coming together just as Alec had planned earlier that spring.

On Alec's first day back, he sorted all his new souvenirs and arranged them neatly in drawers, a habit that carried over from his service days. He returned with a different souvenir in this batch, however. Compact and heavy, it brandished a polished chrome finish that clearly reflected images of him and articles in the room as he handled it and turned it over in his hands before finally setting it on the nightstand next to his bed. Alec removed his clothes and placed them in the laundry hamper with the remainder of the dirty items from his trip. He showered to remove the dust, dirt, sweat, and grime that accumulated on his skin whenever he traveled. Without bothering to dry himself he walked slowly and deliberately back into the bedroom and sat down on the edge of the bed. For a moment he paused and sat quietly, his hands gripping the edge of the mattress. Water dripped off his slightly bowed head and formed a small puddle on the terrazzo floor. He removed a slip of paper and the heavy souvenir from the nightstand where he placed them and looked at his reflection in the polished finish. Clutching the paper in one hand he turned the object over and grabbed its black handle with his other hand. With his thumb, he pulled back the short metal protrusion until he heard a click and felt it snap into place. He raised it to his temple and felt its cool touch. He positioned his forefinger firmly and slowly squeezed.

*****

The headline read, NOTED EDUCATOR DEAD FROM APPARENT SUICIDE.

Teacher dies on ninth anniversary of residence.

Epilogue

"I remember you waking me that morning and reading the story in the paper, but that's been more than twenty-five years ago, long before we moved to Texas," Julie remarked after listening silently and attentively for the duration of the story. She removed and cleaned the accumulated salt and sand from her sunglasses.

The bright afternoon sun, shining through a cloudless blue sky and reflecting off both sand and water, made the darken glasses a necessity. Many visitors unfamiliar with the power of Florida's reflected sun find themselves the victim of harsh burns despite taking the precaution of lying under the cover of beach umbrellas. Julie deciding that the increased risk of skin cancer was not worth any additional tan, she rummaged in the beach bag for a cover-up. Finding one of my old Georgia Tech T-shirts she kept for just such an occasion, she squeezed the clasps of the bag together until she heard and felt them snap into place. She pulled the straps of her bathing suit back over her shoulders and wrestled the T-shirt over her head. She placed her straw hat on her head and turned to me for a reply.

"Yes, it's been a long time, but I remember everything so clearly. The Christmas following Alec's death, while you were in Nashville visiting your mother, I ran into Jack Winslow. Remember he and Cynthia sponsored and boarded Anita Weinberg, who I earlier mentioned. Our conversation soon turned to Alec, and between the two of us we pieced together nearly everything that happened from the time Alec first came to town until his death nine years later. Jack and Cynthia learned much of the story from Alec and then later from Tracy and Nancy." I rose, stretched, and glanced at my watch. I didn't realize how late it was. Stiff from sitting and dried out from the sun, I, too, slipped into a T-shirt and continued stretching.

"Did anyone ever find out why he killed himself? Wasn't there a slip of paper, was it a note?" Julie asked, sensing the story had not yet ended.

"Who knows for sure? The note, according to Jack, contained no hint why he killed himself, only instructions for the disposal of his remains. I find that somewhat surprising," I stated as I popped open the last can of Coke.

"Why? Did you expect some explanation or a last love message to Tracy or Richard?" Julie pursued.

"No, nothing like that. Given Alec's state of mind, I expected him to be cryptic, if for no other reason than to frustrate people further. The remarkable part is the instructions he left—no local funeral or memorial services and that he be interred in Providence," I explained.

"Is that so unusual, to be buried in your hometown? I don't care where I'm buried, but I think you and many others would want to be buried in their hometown," she proposed.

Thinking for a moment, I answered, "If we were talking about anyone else, I just might agree with you. However, I believe in Alec's case it was symbolic. He was no sentimentalist. I believe he couldn't have cared less where he was buried."

"Then what is—" Julie began.

"He was too organized, too planned, and too methodical to let sentiment influence his decision. I believe that his request constituted one final act of defiance. He realized he had been at odds with the community from the very beginning.

"Do you mean at odds with people other than Tracy?" Julie asked, sounding puzzled by my statement. "After all Tracy did defy her parents, at least her mother, and marry him," she added.

"Well, let's say by those people whose values from the very beginning differed markedly from Alec's. I believe Alec's suicide constituted an admission that, in the final analysis, even Tracy, her family, and friends rejected him. That is, the attitudes and values he so bluntly displayed. Her family and friends were his last hope. He already felt rejected by everyone else. His refusal to have any services or be interred in Florida showed her and everyone else that he didn't accept them or their values either. It was the ultimate snub."

"Whoa. Back up a minute. Are you saying that Alec interpreted the divorce by Tracy and the loss of custody of his son as a defeat in his nine-year struggle for acceptance?" Julie asked.

"Yes. I believe that when he won her, he felt he succeeded in overcoming the objections to him expressed by many in the community. When she left him and took Richard, Alec finally realized he had ultimately failed to gain the acceptance that he sought, and thought that he had achieved. It took him awhile to come to that realization and he found a certain peace of mind when he accepted the failure, but it was a state of mind he simply couldn't live with, so he decided to end this, the last chapter in his life. In a mystifying way, Alec's suicide plans appear to follow the first stanza of Schiller's *Ode to Joy* that Beethoven set to music in his Ninth Symphony. Alec's suicide represents a passage from a world where he felt the pain of estrangement into a world where he would feel the joy of brotherhood, if I'm not sounding too ecumenical."

"I've never read the poem," Julie admitted.

"I've thought of little else for the past two days," I answered. "The music and words keep playing over and over in my head. It's been more than forty years since I sang those verses, but they still echo in my mind as if all the rehearsals and the concert were yesterday."

"Why would Alec make that decision then?" Julie asked, adding, "Weren't the old ways giving way to new ones even at that time. It seems to me that a new, less parochial community was forming and growing stronger. Surely he could see that."

"Even if he did see it, it simply didn't matter," I suggested. "Look at it this way, Alec realized that he never fit in except in the company of Tracy, her family, and friends. When he lost their support and comfort, he felt he had lost everything, even the will to live. Who can say why someone takes their life? Notes left to explain suicide actions often prove inadequate. Perhaps the answer is that they don't truly understand the reasons themselves. We can't say with any confidence

THE NINTH PASSAGE

that they decide that death is better than life, perhaps they just can't think of any better alternative."

"Hmm, maybe. How did Tracy react to Alec's suicide?" Julie queried, not sounding totally convinced.

"That I don't know," I answered, feeling disappointed with my ignorance.

"Do you know whatever happened to Tracy and Richard?" Julie asked.

"Alec's death removed the only obstacle to Richard's adoption by James. James was the only father that Richard ever knew. What happened to Tracy is ironic. By taking control of her life and leaving Alec and marrying James, she thought she made the transition from servant to companion."

"What's ironic about that?" Julie asked.

"The irony is that after she left Alec for a younger man, twenty-five years later that man left her for a younger woman."

Reflecting for a moment, Julie answered. "I feel sorry for her. It seems that both men in her life loved her for the wrong reason," Julie offered.

"Which is?"

"Her beauty, they both became infatuated with her looks—what's on the surface. Alec wanted an ideal beauty—innocent and naive—that would never really challenge him. He never considered her feelings, her goals, her needs, or her wishes. The attorney, James, also fell in love with a pretty face and just as soon as it began to fade, he dumped her for another. I don't know what it is about men that make them think they never grow old or ugly. Maybe chasing younger women is their way of fighting old age. Some men can be such cads."

"I think I agree with you at least in this instance," I replied with an audible sigh.

"Wait a minute. How do you know James left Tracy for a younger woman? That's something that you just learned recently," Julie's voice rose in pitch as she spoke.

"I asked a mutual friend who owns one of the food services along the beach when I happened to drop by yesterday," I answered, trying to sound innocent.

"When you just *happened* to drop by? You sound like someone with intent. Do you still have a crush on Tracy?"

"Of course not!"

As we strolled the two-mile trek back to the hotel, the sun slowly dipped into the horizon and for a brief moment, unnoticed by most, a brilliant green flash raced across the horizon and for the first time in a great while, I felt comforted.

> *I've looked at life from both sides now*
> *From win and lose and still somehow*
> *It's life's illusions I recall*
> *I really don't know life at all.*

> —Joni Mitchell, *Both Sides Now*, 1967

About the Author

*C*urrently Professor Emeritus at the University of Houston-Clear Lake, Dale O. Cloninger served in numerous capacities including Dean of the School of Business. Along with forty research papers published in scholarly journals Dr. Cloninger authored (with Kim Hill) *Death on Demand*, a murder mystery that weaves economic analysis into its humorous plot and a textbook, *The Economics of Crime and Law Enforcement*. He and his wife reside in Texas. A native of Clearwater, Dale graduated from Clearwater High School in 1958.

CPSIA information can be obtained
at www.ICGtesting.com
Printed in the USA
JSHW022008101121
20313JS00001BA/5

9 781645 311577